DANIEL

Craig Simpson

ALSVITH BOOKS

DANIEL

ISBN: 978-0-9931155-0-9

Published by ALSVITH BOOKS

This edition published 2015

1 3 5 7 9 10 8 6 4 2

A CIP catalogue record for this book is available
from the British Library

*Printed and bound in Great Britain by
CPI Books (UK), Croydon CR0 4YY*

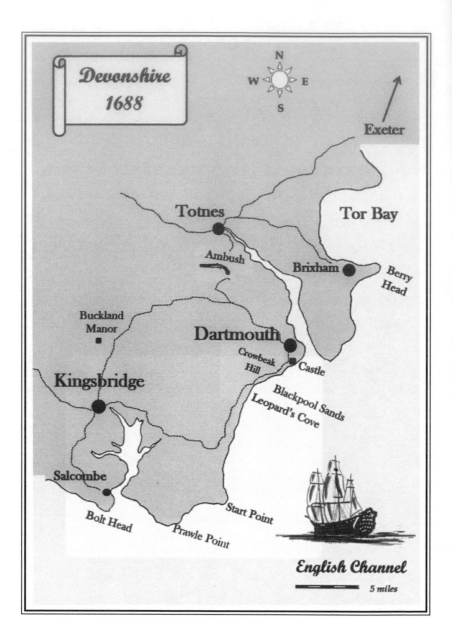

Devonshire
1688

N
W · E
S

Exeter

Tor Bay

Totnes

Ambush

Brixham

Berry
Head

Buckland
Manor

Dartmouth

Crowbeak
Hill

Castle

Kingsbridge

Blackpool Sands
Leopard's Cove

Salcombe

Bolt Head

Start Point

Prawle Point

English Channel

5 miles

1688

They came for her in the night. They said she'd hang. I knew nothing of my mother's secret life. Had she confided in me, I might have known what to do when the nightmare began. But she hid it all from me until it was too late.

Of course, I had to try to save her from the gallows on Crowbeak Hill.

My name is Daniel Drake and I started a revolution.

Chapter One

The Shipwreck tavern, Dartmouth, England. June 1688

NO way could I have done it. Risked everything, that is. Captain Somerville and Lieutenant Thackery held each other's stares, neither daring to blink first, neither daring to hint at weakness. It was the ultimate wager. On the turn of a single playing card rested their entire and considerable wealth – winner takes all.

Moving swiftly, I set about refilling tankards with ale from heavy pitchers. I endured this back-breaking toil at the tavern for just a shilling a week. Even the money I pocketed for mending sails and setting out Old Crabber John's lobster pots at Leopard's Cove didn't stretch far. I was the breadwinner in our house and we were amongst the poorest in town. Occasionally Mother got work scrubbing floors at the fine houses of the gentry but she called it toil fit only for slaves. When our cupboards were bare and the rent was overdue, I'd tell her to start packing as we'd soon be turfed out into the street with nowhere to go. Unless, of course, my best friend Cornelius and I did what we always had to – a little thieving. We called it *filching*, as that didn't sound as bad as thieving, but thieving was what it was. My God, the things we did just to keep a roof over our heads and avoid starving ourselves into an early grave.

Although I knew Captain Somerville by reputation, I'd not seen him before. A tall, lean man in his late forties, he had an educated appearance, a rare sight in this neck of the woods. Standing on tiptoe I could just make out their table.

Thackery, on the other hand; well, all in town knew that rascal. The lieutenant had ruined many a good man through the wickedness of blackmail and extortion. In charge of Dartmouth's garrison and a hundred muskets and cannon, he walked the streets with a swagger and a short temper, and lined his pockets through dastardly schemes that would result in the hanging of most men like him. His uniform and authority offered him protection, as did the rumours that he had friends in high places. In return for their turning the other cheek it was said that he and his gang of thugs did their dirty work for them, collecting debts, hunting down poachers, slitting the throats of their enemies and disposing of their bodies by feeding them to wild dogs.

Here, tonight, Captain Somerville's crew from his ship, the *Sophia*, stood protecting his back while Thackery's men had gathered behind his equally broad shoulders.

Somerville leaned back in his chair and gestured open hands in invitation to his opponent. 'I shall have no man accuse me of poor manners, Lieutenant,' he said. 'So kindly pick a card.'

He spoke without betraying any sign of desperation. Yet even I knew that to wager a ship was a gamble reserved for a captain at his wits' end.

People around here are always willing to gossip in delight at another's misfortune. That's how I knew his story. Captain Somerville had arrived back at Dartmouth this very morning, mooring his ship offshore and beyond the gaze of men who'd recognise her. It was six months to the day since he had last set sail from our shores, running as fast then as he could to escape a long queue of debtors. In the dead of night he had weighed anchor and set his mainsail. By dawn he'd slipped below the horizon, leaving behind men waiting to be paid, men cursing his wretched soul. It had been the talk of the town and I thought him a mighty big fool to have returned.

Lieutenant Thackery placed a hand on the deck of cards, spread them out and chose one. I craned my neck to see. The jack of clubs. The odds in a fair game now leaned in his favour. 'Beat that, Captain!' he roared.

The faintest of smiles formed on Somerville's lips. I thought it an odd expression for someone who might be about to lose everything. Then I realised what the captain was about – a scam. The deck of cards was his and was well worn, each card possessing creases, bent corners and roughened edges. Even in the orange glow of lanterns and flicker of candles fashioned from stinking whale grease, each card could be distinguished from the other if you knew the deck well enough. Such a deception would need a keen eye and I reckoned Somerville had such an eye. The captain was cheating and, as far as I could see, Thackery had no inkling. Cracking each knuckle in turn, Somerville reached forward, seized a card and shielded it with his hand.

Despite the con, I wanted Captain Somerville to win.

'Well?' growled Thackery impatiently. 'Let me see your card, Captain. Or, do you believe you've lost already?'

Somerville shook his head. 'I think my crew are about to get paid, Lieutenant.'

Gobbing a thick lump of chewed tobacco to his left, Thackery drew the back of his right hand slowly across his mouth and replied, 'I've never lost a wager. Isn't that right, men?' A chorus of *Ayes* rang out behind him and Thackery snapped irritably, 'Bring me more ale.'

Time to become invisible. About to crouch down I realised it was too late to hide. Thackery's eyes had settled on me.

'Well, don't just stand there, boy. More ale. Now!'

Grabbing a full pitcher, I willed my hand to stop shaking as I approached their table. The lieutenant studied me with a look of disdain. 'Why, if it isn't that thieving little vermin, Daniel Drake.' He reached out, grabbed my ear and twisted it. 'And where's your partner in crime, Cornelius Trotter, Master Daniel?'

'Ouch! Cornelius is at home, sir.'

'He'd better be, and not out stealing or frightening folk with that ugly face of his. Tell me, Master Daniel, how old are you now?'

'Fourteen, sir.'

The lieutenant's face sharpened. 'Not too young to hang, then?'

'No, sir.'

'Then you'd better pour that ale before I have you flung into Dartmouth's gaol.'

'Yes, sir.' Tightening my grip on the pitcher, even as I spoke I felt the tremble of my hand extend along my arm and then down my right side. Thackery knew well enough what Cornelius and I often got up to but had never managed to catch us doing it. If he did, we would undoubtedly hang for it. That was the law, and Thackery relished the fact. You could hang on Crowbeak Hill for filching just about anything, however big or small.

'Hurry up and don't spill any or I'll have the very dregs of life thrashed from you.'

'Let him be, Lieutenant,' shouted the landlord, Tobias Hawks.

'Aye,' added Somerville. 'Enough idle distraction.'

Steadying my hand, I quickly finished filling the lieutenant's tankard, although I'd rather have tipped the ale over his head. Stepping backwards, I retreated into the throng.

After wallowing in Thackery's impatience a moment longer, Captain Somerville flipped over his card, slumped back, clapped his hands and yelled joyfully, 'The king of spades. Thackery, you old dogfish, you have been well and truly filleted!'

Murmurs of discontent filled the room.

The lieutenant momentarily looked stunned. He stared blankly at the table and then swallowed his misfortune hard. A look of regret settled upon his face and I couldn't help sniggering. That'll teach you.

Captain Somerville turned to acknowledge the whoops of delight from his crew. Cries for more ale rang out. Fearing what was to come, I remained in the shadows. Lieutenant Thackery was a bad loser and had a side to him as black and sticky as tar. The brute's sore temper, when lost, could lead to destruction as fierce as any winter tempest that hammered the Devonshire coast.

'You're a scoundrel and a cheat,' Thackery spat. 'Make haste your departure before I whip you until your back bleeds freely enough to feed a thousand leeches.'

Somerville's eyes narrowed. 'Reneging on a gentlemen's wager, Lieutenant, a wager witnessed by so many others, could prove fateful.'

'But neither of us are gentlemen,' Thackery snarled.

Pounding a clenched fist onto the table, Somerville shouted, 'Don't you dare back out unless you want your guts pulled from your body with fish-hooks!'

The captain's choice of words were, I suspected, ill-advised and this was proven to be the case barely a second later when, with one swift movement, Lieutenant Thackery swept away all that lay on the table and rose abruptly to his feet, sending his chair crashing to the flagstones. From beneath his tunic he drew a pistol and thrust it to within six inches of Somerville's forehead, his hand steady, his arm arrow-straight. He held the flintlock like the experienced soldier he undoubtedly was, a man well accustomed to killing.

Somerville's crew reached for their weapons and Thackery's men matched them. They sized each other up. Having witnessed many drunken brawls, I knew most just involved fists and bloody noses with the occasional clash of cutlass. This was different. Crouching low, I felt certain of only one thing.

Men were about to die.

Chapter Two

THE door to the tavern suddenly swept open and a dozen men filed in led by an exceptionally tall man of dark skin. He was dressed in black britches with a blue tunic embroidered and buttoned in gleaming gold, and his boots, of the finest polished leather, reflected the candlelight like a mirror. He looked about the room and his lips, larger and thicker than I'd ever seen on any other man, gave him a broad smile even in this most deadly moment.

He snapped his fingers and his men quickly took up position either side of him. They drew and cocked their pistols, aiming their weapons at the crowd. Placing his hat on the nearest table, he turned and nodded towards the landlord. 'Tobias! Call this a welcome? Ale for my men and some soup and bread.' Then he approached the table over which Thackery was still leaning, his pistol still inches from Somerville's head.

I'd never seen anyone like him. Did this stranger have no fear? He was dressed in finery that warranted possession of a fortune, and yet he had the ebony skin of a slave. Looking to Tobias, I hoped I might receive an explanation. Tobias, however, merely waved at me frantically. 'More ale, if you please, Danny,' he shouted.

'What foolishness is this?' the tall stranger asked. He cast his eyes to the floor and pressed a boot amongst the scattered cards. 'Aha! I see. Two men equally keen on losing the shirts off their backs.' He roared with laughter, throwing his head back and displaying a cavernous mouth full of unblemished white teeth. He then swivelled on his heels a full circle and, while turning, drew both his pistols, aiming them at Thackery and Somerville. Despite the many guns held in readiness, no one in the crowd dared to challenge him. He spoke quickly. 'It seems you are in luck. I arrived in the nick of time. I can offer you two choices. You can all place down your weapons and we'll bid you goodnight or you can all be sent to hell in the blink of an eye. I care not which, but suggest you not delay in your deliberation as my arms grow weary and my fingers itch to pull the triggers. May I suggest a count of three?' He counted without pause for breath. 'One . . . two . . .'

Thackery let his pistol slip from his grip. It dropped heavily onto the table. 'Have it your way, Dutchman.'

I gasped. John Garret, alias the Dutchman. I'd heard such stories about him – a privateer and pirate all men should fear unless they would choose a watery grave. They say he stole the finest Dutch warship ever built, hence the nickname. Until now, I'd doubted his existence, or at least reckoned his exploits had been embellished for dramatic effect in drunken storytelling. But, seeing him in the flesh, the sheer size and power of the man, I knew they must be true.

'It will not end here,' hissed Thackery defiantly.

'And now your men,' the Dutchman barked.

Both Thackery and Somerville nodded to their henchmen. The room echoed with the clatter of weapons.

Only then did the Dutchman lower his flintlocks. 'The landlord will place your pistols and cutlasses in the street at dawn and you may reclaim them then. Now, be on your way.' His voice rang with impatience as he gestured with one pistol towards the door.

The Shipwreck emptied and the Dutchman signalled for his crew to be at ease.

'Drink up quickly, men, as I fear Thackery will waste little time returning with soldiers from the garrison.' He made towards Tobias and shook his hand firmly, and then warmly embraced Tobias's wife, Elsbeth.

I wondered how it was that Tobias, Elsbeth and the Dutchman knew each other. Tobias had never spoken of him to me. Yet they talked like old friends, occasionally turning to whispers. Naturally, I desperately wanted to listen in. I tried loitering close by but overheard nothing I could make sense of. Their gaze followed me round the tavern and I had the oddest feeling inside which wouldn't go away.

The Dutchman and his men soon departed the Shipwreck and, sure enough, within half an hour Thackery returned with soldiers from the garrison. Not wanting trouble, Tobias was full of apologies, offering Thackery his weapons back and his men free ale. There was a price on the Dutchman's head and I could see that Lieutenant Thackery's anger was more about missing the opportunity to collect the reward than it was about the evening's earlier debacle with Somerville.

Empty-handed, Thackery staggered out of the Shipwreck just after midnight. Tobias bolted the tavern's door, leaned against it and breathed a huge sigh of relief. I was full of questions and now was my chance.

'Tobias, how come you know the Dutchman? Where did you meet? Why was he here? Are all the stories true?'

'Not tonight, Daniel. It's late. We'll talk tomorrow. All I can say for now is that this is just the beginning, the start of something that will change this country for ever.' Tobias gripped me firmly by the shoulder and smiled. It was unlike him to speak of such things, and displays of affection were even rarer. There was also something in his face, a mix of excitement and fear that he appeared keen to conceal from me.

'Now, be off home,' said Elsbeth, gathering up the last of the empty tankards.

About a mile separated the Shipwreck from home, two small rented rooms above a tailor's shop in Cotton Lane, each no more than ten paces square, and sparsely furnished: lumpy mattresses, a couple of old storage trunks, a wooden bench, a rickety three-legged table and Mother's rocking chair. I needed to keep my wits about me. At this late hour, those still out on the cobbled streets staggered rather than walked, and many would end up making do with a doorway for a bed. Ignoring their groans and threats, I hurried past. Reaching into my tunic pocket I grasped the whistle I always carried. Should evil souls dare pounce on me, I'd blow it so hard it would wake the whole town.

Reaching Cotton Lane I saw the flicker of candlelight from our rooms above the shop. My mother, Mary, was still up. That was unusual. Normally she'd be asleep, a sleep so deep it was often difficult to wake her – a sleep often full of nightmares during which she spoke out loud in a foreign tongue. Wrapped in her shawl, she was gently swaying to and fro in her rocking chair. A single candle burned on the mantelpiece. It lit her face with a soft warm glow. 'You're home late, Danny.'

I explained what had happened at the Shipwreck. All the while she just rocked to and fro. Even when I mentioned the Dutchman, she said nothing, just kept rocking. I expected her to share my astonishment, but she didn't – it was almost as if she already knew. 'He really exists, Mother. Never seen the likes of him,' I said, ending my story.

Mother stopped rocking. 'Quite a tale. Are you working at the Shipwreck tomorrow night?'

'Yes.'

'Good.'

'But I thought you didn't like me working there.'

'I don't. Place is full of ne'er-do-wells. Listen, Daniel, I have something very important to ask of you.'

Mother had long given up asking me to do anything, never questioned what I got up to with Cornelius, and certainly never questioned where all the filched food came from. Her manner was making me feel uneasy. 'Ask what?'

'I shall be entertaining a visitor tomorrow evening.' The strike of a nearby church bell interrupted her. It was one o'clock. She corrected herself. 'This evening, that is. And I don't want you here. It's a private matter. Please do not come home before midnight and stay away from Cotton Lane the entire evening.'

It was the oddest request she'd ever uttered. 'Why? Who's this visitor? Why can't I be here?'

'No questions, Daniel. Just do as I say, please. Soon enough I shall be in a position to explain, and then I shall explain everything. But for now you must simply do as I ask. Promise?'

'Yes, but—'

'No buts, Daniel. Now it's time for bed.' She leaned forward and blew out the candle.

I scratched around in the dark to feel my way to the small mattress of straw with its musty blanket so rough even the thought of it made me itch. Lying in the darkness, I wondered who on earth this visitor could be. Unable to rid my head of the burning mystery, I made up my mind. I'd ask Tobias if I could slip home to collect something. It wouldn't take long. I'd loiter in Cotton Lane and try to glimpse the identity of this visitor.

Mother need never know.

Chapter Three

CORNELIUS Trotter often sat beside me while I went about mending sails on the quayside. I was grateful for his company and the distraction from the laborious task of stitching ragged tears with needle and thread in never-ending acres of canvas.

Cornelius was my neighbour in Cotton Lane and my best friend. Though the same age, there the similarity ended. I was short, he was tall. My hair was dark and curly while his was blond and straight. His mother had died giving birth to him and he blamed himself for it; his father died from plague when he was just nine. I'd never known my father. Mother said he had simply left home when I was a babe and not returned – she never spoke of him and always changed the subject when I enquired. Cornelius had an older brother, Edmund, who owned a shop in the nearby town of Kingsbridge, but he rarely visited him.

I was envious of Cornelius because he'd already done what I'd only ever dreamed of doing. He'd been to sea. He'd taken the King's shilling at the age of twelve and served almost a year in the navy, seeing battle off the coast of Spain. Such were his adventures that he'd already accumulated a lifetime's worth of stories. They were tales I never grew tired of.

But my friend had been foolish to accept the job of a powder monkey. Few tasks aboard ship were as dangerous – a warship's gun decks held the greatest risk to life and limb. With even the slightest wayward spark explosions could tear a ship apart. And that very fate beset Cornelius's ship. I looked up from my stitching, stared at my friend, and shuddered. His once handsome face now possessed scars, with eyes that were pearly white and unable to detect night from day.

After the previous evening's goings on at the Shipwreck, for once it was me who possessed a story worth telling.

'Bleedin' heck, Danny. It's good to hear of Thackery meeting his match at last.' Cornelius looked delighted. 'But there must be a good reason for the Dutchman risking coming ashore. The bounty on his head is said to be a hundred guineas. Why has he come? Why now? Why here? What do you reckon, Danny?'

'No idea.'

'The story goes that he was a slave in the Dutch colonies but earned his freedom by saving his master's life.'

'Well, having seen him I have little difficulty in picturing such bravery. Is it true that he never uses his real name?'

My friend nodded and peered out to sea as if he could still make out distant sails. 'Well, if he is here, then where's his ship? Can you see it, Danny?'

Casting canvas and needle aside, I reached for my moleskin bag and, delving a hand deep within, withdrew a spyglass fashioned in brass and polished wood. Extending it, I held it to my right eye and scanned the harbour and deep channels. 'Any idea what she's called?'

'The *Endeavour*. Try looking for one bristling with cannon.'

I was Cornelius's eyes and I described the scene in detail. My spyglass proved invaluable. I'd found it in an old oak trunk Mother kept next to her bed. She kept the trunk locked with a key fastened on a silver chain worn about her neck, but it was a feeble lock that I could easily pick with a bent boot nail.

The trunk contained Mother's life – wads of letters tied with ribbon, drawings she'd done as a girl, a few lace handkerchiefs and fine velvet and silk dresses I'd never seen her wear. I often said that she ought to sell them as I figured they had to be worth a few shillings, but she baulked at the suggestion, telling me in no uncertain terms that the day would come when she'd wear them again and walk the streets with her head held high.

The spyglass and sextant I'd found there, though both well made, were unremarkable except for the engraving – both bore the inscription *Oyster Bay*. At least, that's what Mother told me the inscription said. I'd never been to school and so couldn't read or write. Mother had tried teaching me but I easily got bored and her patience quickly wore thin – I never got beyond drawing a few letters. Eventually, she gave up. The spyglass and sextant were among my most precious possessions, and I carried them with me always, keeping them safe in my moleskin bag.

When Mother first realised I'd taken them I expected a thick ear, but instead she said I could keep them as long as I looked after them properly. She claimed she had found them discarded in a hedge, but I reckon she had filched them, thinking she could sell them at the market for a few shillings. I was just glad I had taken them before she had the chance.

The sea sparkled. Gaff-rigged boats, sloops and a couple of merchant ships lay offshore. I spotted the *Sophia*, Somerville's ship, at anchor. A small naval warship was tied up in port, and on the horizon the square sails of others were just visible in the haze.

15

I described each ship in turn.

'Blast! None sound magnificent enough to be the Dutch-man's ship.'

I agreed, snapped shut my spyglass and returned to my sewing.

'It's market day,' Cornelius said. 'Are we on for filching later?'

'If you like,' I replied hesitantly. Lieutenant Thackery's angry face took over my thoughts and I shivered at what would happen if we got caught. 'But I've got to work at the Shipwreck again tonight. It'll be a long evening too, as Mother told me not to come home before midnight. She says she's entertaining someone.'

Cornelius sniggered loudly.

'What?'

'Don't tell me your ma's got herself a man.'

'Don't be daft.'

'Why else doesn't she want you around then?'

Cornelius had a point. What other explanation could there be? Now I was more determined than ever that I'd sneak back home to find out.

A sudden commotion on the quayside interrupted us. The small naval warship was hurriedly preparing to set sail. We overheard someone call out as they ran past, 'Lookouts on the cliffs have spotted the *Endeavour* less than five leagues from here.'

I watched the sails unfurl on the naval ship, and held my breath as men climbed the rigging and dangled precari-ously as they untied the ropes.

'The fools, Danny. Although the English navy is the finest in the world, they're no match for the Dutchman's ship. I've heard that the *Endeavour* has over one hundred cannon and men skilled in firing them. Wave goodbye to them, Danny, as I doubt those poor sailors will ever see dry land again. They'll be crabmeat before the sun sets.'

Entering the Shipwreck that evening I was intent on speaking with Tobias, desperate to learn how the old tavern keeper had become so well acquainted with the Dutchman, before dashing back home to solve the mystery of Mother's visitor.

The first problem I encountered was that Tobias was nowhere to be seen, and Elsbeth declared he wouldn't be back until late. The Shipwreck was also as busy as ever and, being run off my feet, I soon realised sneaking out for half an hour was going to be impossible.

Late into the evening the rear door to the Shipwreck suddenly burst open and Elsbeth shrieked in horror. Tobias stood in the doorway, his shirt soaked in blood. For a second I didn't recognise him as he wore a disguise of cloak and hat far finer than a mere tavern owner would normally possess.

I ran to him as I could see he was about to collapse, and others came over to help. Together, we guided Tobias to a chair and sat him down. Elsbeth fetched water and cloths and set about tending to him. Tobias groaned deliriously, his face twisted with pain. He had lost a great deal of blood. Removing his cloak, jacket and shirt revealed a deep knife wound to his chest. His breathing was laboured and his lungs gurgled horribly.

Customers demanded to know what had happened, but Tobias couldn't bring himself to speak. Someone announced that he'd run and fetch a local surgeon and left in a hurry while others, believing Tobias close to death, clearly wanted no part in the unfolding horror, and so made their excuses and shuffled quietly away into the night. The Shipwreck emptied, leaving just Tobias, Elsbeth and me.

Elsbeth sobbed, 'Is this really how it is to end? You fool, Tobias. I said it would bring only grief.'

'What would?' I asked, fighting back the tears. Tobias had been the closest thing to a real father I'd ever known. Elsbeth offered no reply.

'Daniel?' Tobias reached out and seized my shoulder.

'Yes, Tobias, I'm here.'

'My jacket pocket. It's in my jacket pocket.'

'What is?'

'My jacket pocket . . .'

I turned and grabbed his jacket and searched the pockets. One contained a letter. 'This? Is this what you want?'

He nodded. 'Your mother wrote it. Take it and guard it with your life.'

I examined the letter. It bore a wax seal and was addressed simply with the number seven. 'What's inside? What does the number seven mean? Guard it from who?'

Tobias clutched my shoulder again and pulled me close. 'Your life is in danger, Daniel. Lieutenant Thackery is intent on arresting you and he will hunt you down. You must go before he comes here. Get as far away as possible. Take that letter with you and keep it safe.'

I was shaking. 'After me? Why? What have I done?'

'That letter is everything, Daniel. Keep it safe.'

'Why is Thackery after me?' I demanded to know.

'One more thing, Daniel . . .' Tobias's voice was fading away and I had to lean close to his lips. 'Do not return home. It's not safe. Thackery may be waiting for you.'

My head was spinning. 'But what about Mother?'

He suddenly opened his eyes and glared at me, a deathly stare. 'She has been arrested, Daniel. And she will hang on Crowbeak Hill for what she's done.' He feebly raised an arm and pointed to the letter in my hand. 'Because of that.'

'This?'

'It proves her guilt, Daniel. Treason!'

'Treason? What do you mean, *treason*? That's ridiculous. Anyway, surely all we need to do is destroy the letter, then. I know, I'll burn it.'

'No. It's too important.' Tobias let his head fall to one side so he could see Elsbeth's face. 'You know what to tell him, Elsbeth. With Mary captured it's up to Daniel now. The boy must deliver the letter safely. The future of England depends on him.' His head fell limp.

I leaped to my feet. Tobias was unconscious and I didn't understand anything. And the fear in Elsbeth's eyes was so bright it bore right into me.

'You had better go, Daniel,' she said firmly. 'Before Thackery arrives at our door.'

'Go where?'

'Head west. Make for the road to Truro and seek out a grand residence called Trelithick Hall. A Lord Blackfoot lives there. Demand to see him in person. Tell him who you are and explain what has happened here tonight. Give him the letter. To him, mind, and to no one else. Understand?'

'No! I don't understand any of this. What did Tobias mean, Mother will hang for treason? What is it that she's done?'

The door thumped open and the local surgeon arrived. He was out of breath and flustered. 'The local garrison's

19

been put on alert. Thackery's men are bound to be on my heels,' he announced, quickly examining Tobias's wound. 'I don't know what's going on, but I fear I've stepped into a hornet's nest of trouble and I want none of it.' He went about his work. 'Say a prayer, Elsbeth, for Tobias will need more than his fair share of luck to recover from this wound. I think I can save him, but we have very little time.'

Elsbeth pulled me to one side, whispering, 'There is no time for explanations now, Daniel. Lord Blackfoot will know what to do. He may even be able to intervene on Mary's behalf and spare her the gallows.' Grabbing my hand, she hurriedly led me to the tavern's back door. 'Go, Daniel. Now!' she implored. 'Before Thackery comes knocking.'

As she pushed me out into the alleyway I realised I had no choice. Racing blindly through the streets, barging aside any who dared get in my way, all I could think was that I was in the midst of a nightmare. I had no idea where I was heading. Out of breath, I dipped into a dark side street, leaned up against a wall and stifled a cry of anguish. I knew I needed to gather my wits and calm the terror eating away inside my belly. And once I'd done so, I needed to forge some sort of plan.

The letter was safely in my pocket. A letter. A simple piece of paper with writing on it. How could such a trivial thing result in Tobias getting stabbed, my mother's arrest, and for me to be hunted down like a wild boar? Nothing made any sense. Was it real? Had Mother really been arrested?

I felt the overwhelming urge to make for Cotton Lane, despite Tobias's warning. I needed to see for myself whether she really had been taken or whether Tobias had been somehow mistaken. Maybe Cornelius had heard something, a disturbance in the street, or her screams as they dragged her away. My mind made up, I headed for home, keeping to the darkest shadows and trying not to make a noise on the cobbles. As I dipped and weaved from one alley to the next, Tobias's words rang in my ears. *The future of England . . .* What on earth did that mean?

Reaching Cotton Lane I hid behind a wooden market barrow. I waited and listened. Certain no one was about I ran to our door, burst inside and scaled the flight of wooden steps three at a time.

The door to our rented rooms was open. I stepped inside. The room had been ransacked, fabrics torn and shredded. My bed's mattress looked as if it had been bayonetted, the straw lying in tufts on the floor. Pots had been smashed, shards crunching beneath my feet. Hesitantly I ventured towards Mother's room and dared myself to look inside.

Empty. Then I noticed a pool of blood on the floor. Sick to my stomach, I clasped a hand about my mouth. I noticed the oak trunk had been taken – Thackery hadn't just taken Mother but also all her personal possessions, and our lodgings had clearly been thoroughly searched. But we owned nothing of value. Or did we? The letter. It had to be about the letter. That's what Thackery was looking for – proof of her guilt. And Tobias must've been here too as he'd escaped with it. I looked at the pool of blood again. Tobias's blood?

Overcome, I slumped to my knees and began to sob.

Footsteps creaked on the stairs outside. Frightened out of my wits, I crawled behind the door, drew a deep breath, held it tightly inside and willed my heart to stop pounding so loud.

'Danny?'

Spoken in little more than a whisper, I knew the voice well. 'Cornelius!' I rushed to greet my friend.

'My God, Danny, what's happened?' His voice trembled. 'I heard . . .'

'Thackery's arrested Mother and attacked Tobias. None of it makes sense.' I pulled at my hair while treading circles about him. 'Tobias said Mother's guilty of treason and will hang.'

'T . . . t . . . treason? Your ma? That's ridiculous.'

'I know, but . . .'

'I heard them, Danny.'

Cornelius's blindness had sharpened his other senses and he'd practised at listening out. He could hear men approach from a great distance, calculate their number, and even discern a man's limp or dragged heel from the sound it made against dirt, cobble or stone.

'I heard Tobias arrive just as the bells struck nine,' he said. 'Later, more men came. I heard them marching. I recognised Thackery's voice. "We've come in the name of King James," he shouted. There was much arguing and then a scream. I heard things being smashed and then someone running away.'

'Then what?'

'Your ma cursed them as they dragged her up Cotton Lane. Then it went all quiet. I wanted to come looking for you and so I rose from my bed. But as I made for the door, I heard more men approach. They spoke in a foreign tongue, like your mother babbles in her sleep. They didn't stay long. What are you going to do, Danny?'

'Good question, Cornelius, and one for which I have no answer. My head's all mixed up. Tobias gave me a letter written by Mother, and said I had to guard it with my life. Said Thackery's after me too. And Elsbeth said I had to make for the road to Truro and deliver the letter in person to a man called Lord Blackfoot.'

'Then that's what you must do, Danny.'

'But I have to save Mother from the gallows.'

'And how are you going to do that?'

I had no idea.

'And if Thackery's after you, Danny, you've got to vanish. He has eyes everywhere. You don't want to end up in Dartmouth gaol as well as your ma – they torture people there, Danny, before they hang them.'

My stomach twisted as I thought of what Mother might endure in the castle's dungeons, and I felt helpless. Then I remembered that Elsbeth had said Lord Blackfoot might be able to save her from the gallows. Cornelius was right: I had to get to Trelithick Hall. It was my only hope.

'I'm coming with you, Danny.'

'No, I'll be quicker alone.'

Cornelius reached out and managed to grab my arm. 'I'm your friend, Danny, and right now you need a friend.'

Cotton Lane was barely a cart's axle-width wide. Together, we headed up the lane while I kept my wits about me. We hadn't gone far when Cornelius suddenly stopped.

'We're not alone,' he whispered. 'Someone's following us.'

I turned and spotted several figures lurking some way back down the lane.

'It's him!' one shouted. 'It's the Drake boy. Stop where you are! You're under arrest.'

'Soldiers, Cornelius. Run!'

'After him, men!'

Four soldiers pursued us up the lane. Brandishing their muskets, the moonlight glinted on razor-sharp bayonets. Running away, I sensed the soldiers gaining on us. I'd been a fool for not heeding the warning to steer clear of Cotton Lane.

I'd been an even bigger fool in allowing Cornelius to come with me. He was slowing me down. They'd arrest him too, although he had no part in all this. And it would all be my fault.

Running hard, I feared capture was moments away. The fizz of sparked powder and the blast of muskets shattered the quiet of the night air and I felt a heavy strike to my left arm just below the shoulder, as if I'd been punched hard. I stumbled. The world began to spin about me.

'Cornelius, I've been shot!'

Cornelius had hold of me and pulled me forwards. 'Keep running, Danny, keep running.'

Chapter Four

OUR escape along Cotton Lane was suddenly blocked by three men who stepped from the shadows with the speed and agility of feral cats. Black capes and hoods drawn about their heads masked them.

'Drop to your knees, Master Daniel. Do it now.' The voice was clear, purposeful and deliberate. It bore no fear yet rang with urgency. I sprawled to the ground, taking Cornelius with me.

A volley of pistol fire flashed from their hands and the groans of soldiers filled the lane, together with the clatter of their muskets falling onto the cobbles.

A large hand and powerful arm helped me to my feet, though I remained unsteady. The ache in my shoulder had turned sharp and the pain seized my breath.

'We must make haste before Thackery's men ruin our evening and steal our freedom. What's the quickest way to the harbour, Master Daniel?'

Barely conscious, let alone able to think straight, I felt as if I was floating, my mind muddied like the water of a swollen river. Who were these men? How come they knew my name?

He repeated his question. I knew the simplest route was back the way we'd come, passing where Thackery's men had begun their pursuit. I pointed. 'This way.' I staggered just a few steps before Cornelius shouted for me to stop.

'No, Danny, I can hear more men coming from Needle

Street. We must cut through Noose Alley and make for the harbour using the storm drains.'

No sooner had we dipped into Noose Alley and, at its end, slipped into the weed-filled drain that snaked downhill, than Cotton Lane filled with soldiers. In single file, we crept forward.

The open drain contained the wash of storms, refuse and excrement flushed from the streets and gutters and I struggled to quell the urge to be sick. I feared making a noise, and prayed we'd not be discovered. My shirt sleeve felt strangely cool and damp against my skin. I thought of Tobias, of all the blood, and suddenly felt twice as sick.

Approaching the harbour we saw the quayside ablaze with soldiers holding burning torches. To proceed without discovery was surely impossible. And our saviours, however valiant and brave, were vastly outnumbered. 'We're done for.'

'Let's not be so hasty in our despair,' said one of the cloaked men. 'Our boat is tied up beneath the pier outside the granary. It is well hidden but cannot be approached from the steps as we'd be seen. There must be another way.'

The granary lay about one hundred yards west of the Shipwreck tavern. Both bordered the quay and both were just yards from the water. These facts had just come into my thinking when Cornelius spoke up.

'The tunnels,' he said. 'We can use the tunnels.'

Beneath the quayside, and reached from the Shipwreck's cellars, stretched a network of tunnels linking houses near the quay to a place where, at the right height of tide, the spoils of smuggling could be sneaked ashore under the unwitting noses of the Customs men. Tobias, I recalled, had taken deliveries of wine and spirits by that very route.

Their existence remained a closely guarded secret, but I supposed that in our hour of need it was one that had to be shared.

'Cornelius is right,' I said. 'We must get to the Shipwreck and pray that Thackery's men have already searched the place and are long gone.'

The back door to the tavern was bolted. Repeated tapping eventually brought a fearful Elsbeth to the threshold. She slid the bolt undone and ushered us all quickly inside.

I slumped down onto a chair and felt myself drifting in and out of consciousness. I captured only snatches of the conversation around me.

'They've arrested Tobias,' Elsbeth wailed. 'With his injuries, he'll not survive time in gaol.'

'*To the cellars. To the tunnels!*' shouted Cornelius with breathless urgency.

'I must speak briefly with Elsbeth,' replied my rescuer.

'The boy is right, we must get going,' said another of the cloaked figures.

'This way,' Cornelius's voice again. 'I can feel my way.'

'Daniel, are you alright?' It was Elsbeth's voice. 'Oh dear God, he's been shot.'

'He'll live. We must take him with us. Our ship's surgeon will tend to his wound.'

Elsbeth again: 'Go, Dutchman, go. Now, before Thackery's men return. Make the horror of tonight count for something.'

The Dutchman. I forced my eyes open. Everything was blurred. I could see a face but not its features. But his skin was as black as coal.

The Dutchman helped me to my feet and we followed

the others down to the cellars. The entrance to the tunnel lay hidden behind a large oak cask which was soon hauled aside. Barely a dozen steps inside, I fell against the wall, knocking the entry wound of the musket ball. I yelped like a dog caught under a cartwheel.

'Lean on me,' said the Dutchman. 'And bite your tongue. Cries like that will reveal us to our enemies.'

Rats scurried about our feet and the air smelled dank. Our boots splashed in puddles that grew deeper with every twist and turn. Soon the water covered our boots, then our knees, and eventually lapped about our waists. 'Not far now,' said Cornelius. He was ahead of me. His words echoed and sounded strangely distant and hollow.

My thoughts drifted and I'd begun to shiver.

Turning another corner revealed the pale glint of moonlight. Cat's-paws, reflections of the water on the arched roof, danced. Cornelius, now some fifteen feet ahead, up to his shoulders in water, declared, 'Perfect.'

We were in luck. Had the tide been any higher it would have filled the entrance and there would have been no way out without swimming beneath the swell with lungs fit to burst. The Dutchman rested me against the wall and swam ahead.

'Our boat is about twenty yards to the left,' he said on his return. 'Now is a good time to set off. But we must make barely a ripple if we are to succeed.'

Swimming in the open was risky. Feeling so weak I knew our lives rested in my hands, but I doubted I could make it. 'You go,' I said. 'Leave me here.' Fearing my time on this world was coming to an end, I pulled out the letter from my pocket. 'Cornelius. Come here and take this. It's Mother's letter. Keep it safe. Remember what I said. It needs delivering to someone called Lord Blackfoot. He lives at Trelithick Hall on the road to Truro. Ask him to do what he can to save her.'

'No,' replied the Dutchman, snatching the letter from me. 'I shall take care of it. You and I are bound by a promise I made to others, and a matter of great importance. There will be no separating us this night. Come, gather your strength and fill your lungs with air.'

Struggling to keep my head above water, I feared that each splash would give us all away. Gasping and swallowing much brine, I fought the need to cough and splutter. The Dutchman's men, aiding Cornelius, made good progress and soon arrived beneath the pier and clambered aboard their rowing boat. I remained barely halfway, but the Dutchman stayed at my side. The agony of each stroke demanded that I cry out, but I bit my tongue to stifle the urge. *I can make it*, I kept telling myself. Not much further. It will soon be over. But the voice of encouragement within me faded as exhaustion took hold. I realised I could no longer feel my legs and the sea no longer felt cold.

Drifting beneath the surface, I felt my collar grasped firmly and in one swift movement found myself hauled from the water and bundled into a boat. As a heavy, damp blanket was thrown over me, I heard the clunk of oars against rowlocks and then felt the boat surge through the water. Sleep drew me into a world of strange and dark dreams of deathly screams and drowning.

Chapter Five

I awoke with a jolt to find myself in unfamiliar surroundings. Unsure whether I was even still alive, I blinked my
sleep away and tried to turn over but quickly received a
painful reminder that the wound to my arm had been no
nightmare. The stab of hurt forced me to lie still until the
worst of it abated.

I realised I was moving – I could feel myself rocking
gently from side to side. The creaking of straining timbers
matched the heaving rhythm of the room, a splendid room.
The walls were oak-panelled and a fine mahogany desk
bore charts, brass dividers and a parallel ruler: all the
paraphernalia of a master navigator. To one side lay a great
chest with leather straps and ornate brass locks that I knew
would take far more than a bent boot nail to pick. Then
there were the many items of silver and pewter – plates,
goblets and candlesticks. Lanterns hung from the low
ceiling and swayed. I must be aboard the *Endeavour*, I
realised. The wave of excitement made me ignore the hurt
and I rose from the bed.

A clean shirt and brown tunic of about my size lay folded
on a chair. My own blood-stained shirt had been removed
and my arm now bore a heavy bandage. The letter. Where
was the letter Tobias gave me? Gripped by anxiety, I looked
frantically about the cabin but saw no sign of it. Then I
remembered. The Dutchman had taken it from me.

A vile smell filled my nostrils and followed me around.

It reminded me of dog pee, but I soon realised that it was me that smelled ripe. Beneath the bandages a poultice had been applied to my wound to stave off infection and pus. Horrible, but I knew it lessened the risk of fever. And that was a good thing, as it was fever that often killed a man. I quickly dressed, carefully pushing my stiff arm into the sleeve of first the shirt and then the tunic, and then went in search of answers.

Once through the cabin's small door, bright sunlight drew me up a flight of steps and out onto the raised deck to the stern of the ship. Blinded by the daylight and with my face buffeted by a stiff and salty breeze, I felt giddy. Gripping a handrail, I steadied myself.

'Ah, Master Daniel, I trust you're feeling better.' The Dutchman stood with two of his men. 'That was a nasty wound. Mr Anstey, our surgeon, cursed on the very grave of his father in his struggle to dig out the bullet. Mr Anstey, you see, is much more skilled at amputation. He can saw off a limb in the time it takes to fill a tankard. He was all for whipping off your arm.'

The *Endeavour* struck me as bigger than I ever could have imagined. Huge sails, taller and broader than any I'd ever mended billowed and snapped from the three masts. The quarterdeck provided a full view of the vessel's main deck. Men went about their work, some adjusting the rigging, others steering a straight course at the ship's wheel. In my imagination I'd always pictured pirate ships laden with ruffians, scoundrels and drunkards, men more interested in brawling than sailing. It wasn't like that at all.

'I run a tight ship,' the Dutchman declared as though having read my thoughts. 'Strict rationing of grog and no man gets fed until the decks are scrubbed clean and ropes are tied. I want no trouble, fever or pestilence aboard this ship.'

Peering up at the masts, they reached so high I thought they could cut the clouds in two. Someone was in the crow's-nest. I gasped. It was Cornelius. 'How did he get up there?'

'He climbed. How else?'

'The fool. Has he lost all sense?' I shook my head in dismay.

'No finer place on such a glorious day,' remarked the Dutchman while gazing upwards. 'On top of the world.'

'Madness,' I replied. 'He can't see anything, anyway.'

'Master Daniel, men do not feel happiness and joy with their eyes but in their minds and hearts. I'm sure Master Cornelius is at this very moment one of the happiest men alive.' The Dutchman pulled a face. 'Provided, of course, he doesn't lose his footing.'

Looking out to sea, I saw that land was but a sliver on the horizon to starboard. 'Where are we?'

'Heading west. For once the wind is with us and we're making fine headway. Eight knots at last measure.'

'Where to?' I held visions of a long voyage to strange lands across vast oceans.

'To Falmouth.'

His words shattered my exotic dream. Falmouth wasn't far west of Dartmouth. It was barely a day's sail away.

'At least, just to the east of Falmouth,' the Dutchman added, as if the clarification was important. 'To Carrick Roads and the deep water estuary. We plan to hold off Nare Head until dusk and then we'll head up the channel and anchor for the night. It is well concealed there by woodland, and few people live in the vicinity. And, more importantly, those that do are sympathetic to our cause.'

'Cause – what cause?' I asked.

'Indeed. I think it is time for us to talk, Master Daniel. Come with me. Come below.'

Chapter Six

THE Dutchman led the way to his cabin – where I'd awoken – and gestured for me to sit down. Stooping, as he was fully a foot taller than the ceiling, he settled behind his desk. 'You must be all of a quandary, Master Daniel.' Grasping a decanter, he poured two glasses of red wine and slid one across his desk.

With my throat as dry as a desert, I gulped it down gratefully. It tasted of currants, blackberries, soil and ripe cheese, and was far finer than anything Tobias served at the Shipwreck tavern. I belched loudly in appreciation. 'Thank you for the shirt and tunic,' I said. 'Can I have my letter back now?'

'It got a little damp during our escape but is intact. Have no fear, for it is safe enough.' The Dutchman shifted uncomfortably. 'Like I said, there are matters we need to discuss. Firstly, I have a question for you. Tell me, Master Daniel, what do you know of King James?'

That's an odd question, I thought, and frowned to show it. James was King of England and Scotland. Even the greatest lackbrain knew that. But then I realised I knew little else. Still, I thought, I was just a boy who served ale, who went filching on market day, who mended sails and dumped lobster pots. So I simply shrugged.

He grinned. 'I suspected as much. Let me ask it differently. I suppose the Shipwreck tavern must be full of gossip. Men's chatter must turn to king and country. Tell me, what do they say?'

I had indeed heard King James's name uttered amid many slurred conversations at the tavern, and frequently it was associated with curses so colourful that women blushed. 'Many say James is a dangerous fool.'

'That doesn't surprise me. Though such men risk arrest for their slack tongues, as uttering such opinions is treason.'

'Is that what Mother wrote in her letter? That James is a fool?'

The Dutchman laughed and shook his head. 'No, Master Daniel.' He paused, stared down at his glass and then glanced up at me. 'But do you know why so many think him so?'

'No,' I replied, although immediately after having done so several reasons sprang to mind. 'Except . . .' I began.

The Dutchman leaned forward. 'Go on.'

'Well, only that everyone knows King James is friendly with King Louis of France. Tobias once said to me that it was a friendship that would only bring trouble to our shores.'

The Dutchman sat back and nodded. 'Tobias is a wise man. King Louis has in mind the control of many lands, near and far. Even now he is eyeing up the conquest of the Low Countries, including Holland. He is happy to go to war to meet his aims, but wars are expensive. Alliances can offer equally satisfactory solutions. However, one between a largely Protestant England and Catholic France was unthinkable until James declared his Catholic faith. That, and the birth this very month of a son and heir to the throne of England, are seen as the last straws by the Protestant majority. There is no doubt that the baby prince shall be brought up a Catholic. And I don't need to remind you that the two churches stand divided and their differences breed contempt and distrust, do I?'

'No, sir, you don't. Not that I've ever really understood why. I rarely go to church on a Sunday on account of having to put out Old Crabber John's lobster pots in Leopard's Cove.'

'As for myself, I am neither Protestant nor Catholic but I know that a man's faith is a powerful thing. Many will willingly lay down their lives to defend it. If, as many fear, an alliance is forged between James and Louis, then this land will be split down the middle like an axe driven through a log.'

'But that's stupid,' I said.

'Is it? History is littered with wars arising from the clash of churches. Sadly God has seen fit to divide men in this way although, personally, I believe it is men who divide themselves. In truth, Master Daniel, what many English-men fear the most is that such a change in the wind will disrupt their freedom and undermine Parliament. James has already taken steps in this direction, and when Parlia-ment voiced its unease, he suspended it. Those are grave matters indeed.'

I frowned. These were strange words from the mouth of a pirate. 'All this talk's making my head hurt,' I said. 'And why are you telling me all this?'

He refilled our glasses. 'It's important. I promised Tobias that should anything happen to him, or Mary, I would take you under my wing. And my word is my bond. Of that you should be in no doubt.'

'How come you know Tobias? Or my mother?' I picked up my glass, held it in front of my face, and pretended to study the way the sun's rays from the cabin's window sparkled through it as though I held a giant ruby. In truth, I didn't wish the Dutchman to see the tears welling up. They were the tears that returned whenever I thought of the horrors Mother and Tobias might be enduring at the hands of Thackery.

'Tobias and I go back a long way.' He reached forward and grasped my good arm tightly. 'Fear not, we shall do all we can to free him and your mother.'

'What does Thackery want with them, anyway? What did Mother do that was so terrible?'

He stared down at his desk. In a voice turned secretive, he whispered, 'Mary has played a vital role in our plan, Master Daniel.'

'What plan?'

'Our plan to save England. Before it is too late!'

Chapter Seven

BEFORE the Dutchman could explain what he meant, there was a brisk knock on the cabin's door. A man entered, stood to attention, and then spoke quickly and pointed to the steps leading up to the quarterdeck.

'Forgive me, Master Daniel,' said the Dutchman, 'but I am needed on deck for a small matter of administering justice. I shall not be long. We will talk again later. Meanwhile, I suggest you rest. You will need all your energy and fitness.'

I sat, confused, questions circling above my head like seagulls about a fishing boat. Saving England? God, my head throbbed. Rubbing my brow, I sighed and allowed my thoughts to turn to Cornelius. I wondered if he was still flying in the crow's-nest. I went to look.

The *Endeavour*'s crew had assembled on the main deck in a semi-circle below the quarterdeck. In the centre I saw a young man of about my age. Without a shirt and with his hands tightly bound behind his back, he had been forced to his knees. He possessed a look of absolute terror.

Spotting Cornelius by a sail locker, legs folded and hands clasped in his lap, I forged through the crowd to join him. 'What's happening?'

'*Shush!* The boy was caught filching, Danny,' he whispered. 'Reckon he's going to get more than a tweak of the nose for his crime.'

The man who'd come knocking for the Dutchman

proceeded to read out the charges from a scroll he carefully unravelled before him – two counts of theft: one of five shillings and one of three pricks of tobacco. Raising his voice so all could hear, he bellowed, 'I can see no reason for your accusers, Misters Catchpole and Weeks, to make up such accusations. So, how do you plead, Master Loodvelt?'

The boy looked up, shaking from head to toe. 'Not guilty, sir.' He shut his eyes tightly and dipped his head.

'Very well,' said the Dutchman brusquely. He turned and consulted with two others standing beside him. It didn't take them long in reaching an agreement of some sort as within moments all were nodding. The Dutchman turned to address the accused. 'Witnesses say otherwise, Master Loodvelt. Guilty as charged!'

There were murmurings among the crew.

'Looks like no grog for him for a month,' I whispered to Cornelius.

'He'll receive far worse punishment than that, Danny.'

'There will be no thieving on my ship,' thundered the Dutchman. 'We steal from our enemies and no other. Our mission, no, our very lives depend on each of us trusting the man standing beside him. If we cannot do that, we shall all fail.'

The sudden transformation in him shocked me. He had lost any vestige of kindness. His eyes bulged like giant pearls from his dark face and his brow bore the deep creases of rage.

'Master Loodvelt, I sentence you to be keelhauled. If you live, and I seriously doubt it, I trust you will learn from the experience. Mr Jacobsen, carry out the sentence forthwith.'

A long rope was cast overboard at the bow of the ship

and allowed to work along the bottom of the hull until it reached amidships. Despite the boy struggling, men tied the ends of the rope to his hands and feet. Then, under the signal of Jacobsen, others lowered him overboard. He screamed. With several sailors heaving on the rope, they slowly pulled him beneath the hull of the ship.

'Hope he's got a good pair of lungs,' fretted Cornelius.

The boy emerged the other side coughing and spluttering. 'Damn you! I'm innocent! *Innocent!*'

'Again, if you please, Mr Jacobsen,' bellowed the Dutchman.

For a second time they hauled the boy under the ship. He emerged choking, spewing out the sea.

'And again, Mr Jacobsen.'

The third time the boy emerged from the waves, he did so without protest. His whimpering cries filled my ears. 'One more time,' the Dutchman yelled before turning on his heel and heading below.

Men pulled hard on the rope. Others shouted encouragement. I strained on tiptoe to see him rise above the swell.

'Is he still alive?' asked Cornelius.

The body lifted from the sea was limp. Men lay him gently on the deck, untied the bindings and massaged his chest. Brine spilled from his mouth but he lay still. 'Think his soul's gone, Cornelius.'

But then the boy coughed violently and thrashed about. He'd survived. Just.

'Don't think we'll be doing any filching on this ship,' I whispered.

Chapter Eight

'ISN'T she magnificent,' shouted Cornelius. He'd risen to his feet and, clasping a taut rope – one of hundreds making up the rigging – had leaned out precariously over the side of the ship. 'Feel her move, Danny, and the wind in your face.'

Only half listening, my thoughts returned to my conversation with the Dutchman. 'Cornelius, what do you think of King James?'

He shrugged. 'Nowt. I think nowt, because I knows nowt about him,' he replied. 'Why?'

'Do you think England needs saving?'

'What twaddle is this, Danny?' He swung himself carefully back onto the deck and reached out for me to give him a hand. 'Did somebody bash you on your head? Saving from what?'

Exactly, I thought. I remained flummoxed by questions larger than any I'd grappled with before in my whole life. Stuff about kings and countries were a far cry from my usual diet. 'I have a bad feeling about all this, Cornelius.'

'That's hardly a surprise. Tobias and your mother have been arrested, you've been chased by Thackery's men and shot, and here we are aboard a pirate ship. All in the space of a day. Not much to be cheery about. It's called fate, Danny.'

'And where will fate lead us, Cornelius?' I cast my friend a despondent look which I think he sensed.

'To our destiny, of course. Or to our graves. Or both. You always said you wanted adventure, Danny. Well, you got it now, in bucket-loads.'

He was right, but being in the midst of an adventure seemed wholly different from dreaming of one. I realised what the difference was – fear.

Later that afternoon a thin man bearing a scar down his right cheek approached and introduced himself as Edward Anstey, the ship's surgeon. I thought he looked an ugly brute, his skin pocked and as rough as a cauliflower.

'Master Drake, sir, I must change your dressing before dinner is served. I have boiled up another poultice, one less fragrant. I think those sitting at the captain's table will appreciate it if you smelled a little sweeter.' He grinned toothlessly.

The new poultice smelled worse to me than the old one and I held my breath as Anstey slapped it onto my wound. It reminded me of rotten eggs and the stink of dead fish washed ashore.

'You are indeed privileged, young sir,' said Anstey as he went about his work. 'Eating at the captain's table, eh. Sat beside the Dutchman. Now there's something you'll be able to tell your grandchildren when you're old and spent.'

The ship's bell rang to indicate the midpoint of the early evening watch.

'Best keep that jacket on when you eat, my lad,' said Anstey. 'Reeks a little more than I thought.' He ruffled my hair with a grubby hand and laughed.

Going below, we entered a room as equally splendid as the captain's cabin, a room dominated by a long polished teak table. Cornelius and I were shown to chairs close to one end and on opposite sides. The ship's officers gathered and the Dutchman arrived. He set about introducing everyone.

'These are my officers, Master Daniel. You know Mr Anstey already and presumably saw Mr Jacobsen on deck earlier. This here is Mr De Veer, my First Officer.' He pointed to a rugged man of considerable ballast who wore a grey moustache so large I figured it must've taken a lifetime to grow. De Veer nodded politely.

'And that is Mr Delaney, the *Endeavour*'s bosun. If you need anything, please ask him.'

Delaney was a figure so slight amid the company of much larger men that I thought he looked like a lost ferret. In his thirties, Delaney spoke a greeting in a thick and lyrical Dublin accent. I decided he was the sort likely to be full of tales and tall stories, the sort worth seeking out for an evening's entertainment.

'And, finally, Master Daniel, this is Miss Lucy Deveraux.'

Miss Lucy wore no frilly gown or summer dress, rather dark britches and blue tunic, her head topped by a hat equal to the other ship's officers. I studied her face and the pair of eyes firmly fixed on my own and was struck by her rosy complexion. Her eyelashes were long, her eyes hazel. That I had not realised she was a girl before rather unsettled me, as close up she so obviously was one. And one that made me stammer and stutter a greeting when she held out her hand.

'Nice to make your acquaintance, Daniel Drake.'

As we settled down to eat my eyes remained fixed on Miss Lucy because I'd never heard of a girl becoming an officer on any ship, let alone one as large as the *Endeavour*. She removed her hat and shook her head. It sent a cascade of flowing blond locks about her shoulders.

I judged Miss Lucy to be four or five years older than me. She possessed a refinement that spoke of a good education and wealth and I doubted she had ever been near grubby places like Cotton Lane, let alone put a stocking-clad foot in establishments as rough about the edges as the Shipwreck tavern.

'Does your wound hurt much?' she enquired as we tucked into fish soup.

'No,' I lied. In dismissing being shot as a mere trifle, I hoped I would impress her.

Anstey reached into his pocket and then held out a clenched fist across the table. Releasing his grip, a flattened musket ball fell from his hand and struck the table. 'A souvenir!'

Picking up the small lump of lead, I thought it rather tiny and could hardly credit that such a thing had caused so much pain.

Cornelius had not touched his soup.

'Is the boy coming down with a fever?' enquired Jacobsen. His query drew concern from all seated at the table.

I guessed otherwise. My friend could not see his bowl or lump of bread, nor the spoon or glass of wine. And the noise about him would have told him that others ate with manners. That was not his way. When Cornelius ate, he did so with gusto and without refinement, sometimes like a pig at a trough, sometimes like a fox inside a chicken coop, grabbing, ripping, and tearing. Supposing he feared embarrassment, I reached across the table and placed the bread into his left hand and spoon into his right. I then manoeuvred the spoon until it tapped gently against the side of the bowl. He ate slowly and deliberately as if for the first time.

After salted beef and stinking cheese served with biscuits, all washed down with wine, clay pipes were lit and everyone sat back in their chairs. Conversation turned to the mission to be carried out that night.

'We'll row ashore once the *Endeavour* has anchored up Carrick Roads,' said the Dutchman. 'The innkeeper at Tolverne can always be relied on to provide us with swift horses, and he will be expecting us. We should make good time to the road to Truro and reach Trelithick Hall by midnight.' He turned to me. 'Master Daniel, our mission is to deliver your letter.'

'You're certain that Lord Blackfoot will be there?' asked Delaney.

The Dutchman nodded.

'How will he react when we arrive without Mary?'

Startled at hearing Mother's name, I looked questioningly at first Delaney and then the Dutchman. 'Mother was meant to deliver it herself?'

The Dutchman nodded. 'She was meant to accompany us.'

'Master Daniel understands what all this is about, doesn't he?' asked Delaney.

The Dutchman held up a hand to calm his anxiety. 'He knows a little of what we are about. Fear not, all will sort itself.' Reaching into his tunic pocket, he drew out the letter and held it aloft. 'And Lord Blackfoot won't care whose hand delivers this letter, just so long as it is done so in secrecy.'

'Tublas gave that to me and told me to guard it with my life,' I said. I held out my hand, but the Dutchman ignored the gesture.

'We shall make sure it reaches its proper destination and does not fall into the hands of rogues,' he replied.

Before he could return it to his pocket I leaped to my feet and snatched it from him. De Veer rose from his chair and moved as if to grab me by the collar. 'Stand fast, Mr De Veer,' the Dutchman bellowed.

'This is mine and I shall be the one to deliver it,' I shouted.

'Don't be stupid,' Delaney replied. 'You're in no fit state to ride to Trelithick Hall.'

'I insist,' I responded, glaring at Delaney. He seemed surprised at my determination.

The Dutchman sighed. 'Very well, you shall accompany us tonight.'

Delaney shook his head. 'Is that wise? Lord Blackfoot will be troubled by a new face, especially at such a critical time in our plan.'

The Dutchman thought a moment. 'He'll accept our word as to the boy's identity.' He rose sharply to his feet and raised his glass. 'Now, a toast is in order, lady and gentlemen. Let us pray that this letter contains everything Lord Blackfoot was hoping for.'

As they drank their toast, all I could figure out for certain was that I still had much to discover. My thoughts shifted to even more important questions burning holes in my head. Questions like, what exactly Mother had been up to, and why I had no knowledge of her secret double life. Then there was the trifling matter of the contents of the letter. Most important of all was the question whether Lord Blackfoot could really prevent Mother or Tobias from swinging from the gallows on Crowbeak Hill and, if not, what on earth I could do to save them.

Chapter Nine

IT was nightfall by the time the *Endeavour* anchored up Carrick Roads, a deep navigable channel so narrow that woodland on either shore seemed close enough to touch simply by reaching out from the ship's deck.

Jacobsen was first to climb down the rope ladder to where a rowing boat had been readied. Miss Lucy followed. It was then my turn, and I'd been dreading it because my sore arm felt weak. Delaney assisted my descent. The Dutchman completed the party and we rowed the short distance ashore to a spot where a single glowing lantern swayed in the night air.

Stepping onto dry land, the Dutchman greeted a wizened old man who held the guiding light. Despite a limp, the stooping figure clad in a brown hooded cape led us along a track and into the woods. The path wound left, then right, and then steeply upwards. Amid twisted boughs and heavy foliage, the outline of two buildings emerged in the light of the half moon. I thought it a place where dark spirits dwelled, a place where man was unwelcome once the sun had set. The old man led us to the door of a barn. Inside, horses were saddled in readiness The Dutchman thanked him and pressed a leather purse into his palm. The man emptied it into his other hand and set about counting the gold coins.

Having never ridden, close up the beasts seemed frighteningly large and, once given a leg up into the saddle of my mount, I felt my elevated position precarious. I said nothing, but guessed my lack of skill would make itself plain to all once we broke into a trot.

The Dutchman led us slowly away from the barn in single file. Though fearful, I felt gripped by the excitement of adventure. And each time my nerve seemed to be failing, I reminded myself that Miss Lucy was but twelve feet in front of me and appeared not the slightest bit scared. No way, I thought, was a girl going to show me up.

When the wood opened out to scrub and heath, the Dutchman paused to take stock. Jacobsen peered through his spyglass into the night and Delaney listened out, his left hand cupped about his ear. 'All clear,' the Dutchman declared. Kicking his heels hard into the flesh of his mount, his horse flew off at a gallop. We followed. Clutching the reins, I bounced and bobbed in the saddle, then my feet slipped from the stirrups and, despite trying to grip with my knees, I felt myself slide. I fell, landing heavily. Rolling head over heels twice, I let out cries with each tumble and saw stars before my eyes.

Delaney caught up with my runaway mount and gathered its reins before hurriedly returning to where I lay. 'No time for a nap,' he called out. 'Quick, get up before we get left behind. Remember to grip with your knees and hold the reins lightly. Feel the beast's rhythm and go with it. Do not fight it or else you will gather more bruises.'

For almost an hour we rode, often at full gallop. Reaching a deeply rutted road, the Dutchman drew his steed to a halt.

'Truro's that way by my reckoning,' declared Delaney.

The Dutchman pointed to faint lights in the distance.

'Aye, and there is Trelithick Hall. Come, we should waste no time.'

We entered through a great stone gateway. Dismounting and tethering our horses we made for the main entrance. It was a grand manor house of three stories and more windows than I could count, constructed of soft grey stone and with many carved features – I guessed it had to be owned by a man of unbelievable wealth.

A firm knock brought a servant to the door and we were quickly beckoned into a large, galleried entrance hall. Black and white chequered tiles covered the floor and an oak staircase wide enough for three men to ascend it shoulder to shoulder led to a gallery. Plastered walls were adorned with larger than life paintings of heroic men posing in fine clothes and armour.

A door opened, and through it emerged a man in green britches and brown tunic. Lace frills protruded from broad cuffs and flamboyant collar. He wore a powdered wig and his face struck me as sickly pale, a hue that was all the fashion amongst the gentry.

'Lord Blackfoot.' The Dutchman greeted the man warmly.

'I hope your journey was without incident,' Lord Blackfoot replied. He peered over the Dutchman's shoulder and smiled. 'Miss Lucy. I trust your father is well.'

'Yes, my lord. He sends his regards.'

Lord Blackfoot frowned. 'Is Mary not with you?'

'No. She's been arrested and languishes in Dartmouth's gaol,' the Dutchman responded. 'Tobias too.'

'Dear God!' Lord Blackfoot gestured to a door. 'Please, come into the drawing room and tell me everything.'

A roaring log fire in a vast stone hearth sent a flicker about the room. Mirrors played tricks with the firelight.

Chairs and sofas upholstered in glowing crimson and gold littered the room amid the finest tables that carpenters could fashion.

Lord Blackfoot settled onto a chair. 'Now, tell me about Mary Drake.'

'. . . And so Master Daniel was entrusted by Tobias to deliver Mary's letter to you,' said the Dutchman, completing his report.

Lord Blackfoot studied me. 'I'm sorry about Mary, Master Daniel.'

'Elsbeth Hawks told me that you might be able to free her, sir,' I replied.

'I see.' He got up and embarked on a protracted wander about the room, his hands clasped behind his back. 'It all depends.'

'On what?'

'Thackery may simply have orders to get her to confess. If he is successful, I fear Mary will be of no further use to them and will be sent directly to the gallows. King James may, however, have issued orders to have her sent to Exeter to stand trial in order to make an example of her. Crimes too serious to be handled by the local magistrate are tried in front of judges who travel around the country, Master Daniel. We call them the assizes, and in cities like Exeter they take place only a few times a year. It is several months until the next one is due to take place. That will buy us some time and I might be able to exert a little influence. But I can make no promises. These are dangerous times and there are many who do not share our vision.'

I said the first thing that came into my head. 'Sir, I have no idea why she was arrested. I have no idea how anyone could accuse her of treason. I have no idea how you all appear to know her. The events of the past day have been little short of a nightmare.'

'Is this true?'

'Indeed, my lord. It seems that for the boy's safety Mary revealed little of her work,' said the Dutchman.

'I see.' Lord Blackfoot turned to address me. 'Tobias and your mother are both loyal to our cause, Master Daniel. Mary has proven invaluable. You see, for our grand scheme to succeed, we need to know the precise location of England's navy and details of any plans to disperse the fleet about England's shores. As you may know, the Earl of Dartmouth is in charge of the navy. Your mother has on occasions entertained a servant of the earl in a manner most profitable to us. By showing him a little kindness, she's been able to gain his trust and, over time, his confidence. Slowly she has managed to get him to reveal what he's read and overheard his master speak of regarding the fleet.'

It dawned on me. Mother was a spy! Her occasional work scrubbing floors at the houses of the gentry had just been a means to an end, a way to get her close to the earl.

'Mary risked much to aid us,' Lord Blackfoot added. 'You should feel proud of her—'

The Dutchman interrupted. 'I'm still troubled as to how the authorities discovered Mary's work. Worse, that Thackery turned up at her door last night. Just when I was due to meet with her and Tobias. Surely it is more than a coincidence. We may have a traitor in our midst.'

'Or perhaps the servant Mary befriended became suspicious,' Miss Lucy offered. 'Maybe Mary asked one question too many at just the wrong time.'

'Let us hope that is it and nothing more sinister,' Lord

Blackfoot replied. 'Now, I assume you have brought the letter Mary promised us.'

The Dutchman turned to me. 'Please give him your mother's letter.'

I pulled it from my pocket and handed it to Lord Blackfoot, who broke the wax seal, inspected its contents at some length, and then waved it triumphantly in the air. 'Excellent! This is just what we need. The Seven and Prince William will be delighted. Now we are in a position to act. The invitation to the prince can now be despatched.'

I settled on a stool next to Miss Lucy. 'Is he talking about Holland's Prince William, the Dutch prince?' I whispered.

'Yes. William is head of one of the main aristocratic families in the Dutch Republic. He has strong links to England as he's married to King James's daughter. But he has no fondness for James.'

'Who are these "Seven"?'

Miss Lucy ignored me, instead directing a question to Lord Blackfoot. 'May I enquire as to the precise nature of this invitation?'

'Simply that we should be glad of his visit to England's shores.'

'And will it be signed by all seven?' she added.

'Indeed. Naturally, on such a delicate matter it would be unwise for them to sign it conventionally, as should the plan fail it would be like signing their own execution warrants. So they will all sign the letter in code. But the prince will be expecting that.'

'Who are these "Seven"?' I asked again, loudly so that all heard me this time.

'Men of great standing, Master Daniel,' Lord Blackfoot replied. 'I cannot reveal more as their identities must remain secret, at least for now. Only once our scheme has succeeded will their identities become plain for all to know.'

I was puzzled. 'What's so special or secret about a simple invitation to visit England?'

Lord Blackfoot smiled. 'It is no ordinary invitation. The prince will not come to these shores alone or ill-prepared. He will arrive with a massive fleet and a great army comprising many thousands of men.'

I swallowed hard. As the others conversed at length, the meaning of all their talk suddenly became clear to me. They had in mind the invasion of England, of war! My head filled with visions of great battles on land and sea, of many thousands of men being cut down by lines of musket fire, of rivers of blood.

Conversation was interrupted by the clatter and thump of hooves on the gravel outside, heralding the arrival of uninvited guests. The commotion painted alarm on the faces of everyone in the room.

'Quick!' said Lord Blackfoot. 'You must all leave by the back way. Follow me.'

A fist hammered loudly on the front door. 'Open up in the name of King James.'

I recognised the voice – Lieutenant Thackery.

Lord Blackfoot led us to a little used storeroom at the back of the house. 'I must return,' he said breathlessly. 'Make haste your departure and keep your wits about you. Thackery must leave here empty-handed, I cannot be caught in possession of Mary's letter.' He gave Mother's letter back to the Dutchman. 'Bring it to the crossroads at Carnon Downs tomorrow. I, or one of the Seven, shall be there at midday. Without the letter, Thackery will not dare to arrest me as I have diplomatic protection. Now go!'

The Dutchman drew his pistols and Delaney and Jacobsen did likewise. Miss Lucy also carried two pistols. From the way she held them I concluded it was not the first time she had done so in action. 'Here, Daniel, have one of mine,' she offered.

I took it without question.

The Dutchman squinted through a small window. 'I don't like it when I cannot see or count the opposition. We have little choice but to make a dash to our horses and then ride at breakneck speed to the *Endeavour*.' Easing open the window, he listened out and then climbed through.

Keeping to the moon shadows and hugging a boundary wall six feet tall, we edged cautiously round the perimeter of the grounds. But Thackery was no fool and had posted guards beside the gate; there seemed no way to get to our horses without discovery. The Dutchman signalled to Delaney and Jacobsen. They replaced their pistols in their belts and drew knives, then crept up on the guards with stealth, clasped hands about their mouths and slit their throats, silently dragging their bodies into the undergrowth.

Untethering our horses, I sensed all was not well. About to rise into the saddle, my left boot firmly in its stirrup, I heard Thackery shout, 'Stop!'

The lieutenant's sword was drawn, and to either side of him were men with raised muskets. The Dutchman, Delaney and Jacobsen were already mounted and I expected them to take flight, praying that the soldiers' aim would prove wayward. Instead, they charged Thackery's men, their pistols discharging a volley of shot. Thackery managed to dodge their fire. Hauling myself into the saddle I gathered the reins in one hand.

Lucy, her horse having been startled by the shots, had

not fully mounted and was in difficulty, her horse skittish, turning circles about her. A soldier emerged from the shadows, his musket aimed towards her. She'd not seen him.

I shouted a warning, pointed my pistol and pulled the trigger. The pistol sparked and then exploded, causing my arm to recoil, jarring my sore wound. The bullet struck the man's hand and his musket fell from his grasp. Lucy gathered her reins and her wits, glanced round and flashed me a look of considerable gratitude.

'Best be on our way,' shouted the Dutchman. He turned his horse and set off through the entrance at a fierce gallop, followed closely by Delaney and Jacobsen. Lucy and I wasted no time in digging in our heels, leaning forward in our saddles so as to make ourselves the smallest of targets. And I was glad of the advice Delaney had imparted to me earlier – grip with your knees, hold the reins lightly, sense the rhythm of the beast. Now was not the time to slip from the saddle.

Chapter Ten

A hard hour's ride returned us to Tolverne. We arrived exhausted to find no sign of the *Endeavour*, and it led to visible panic on the faces of the others.

The Dutchman tied his horse firmly to the branch of a silver birch and crept to the edge of the woods, crouching beside some brambles while staring out across the narrow stretch of deep water. 'In a few hours it will be dawn and our cover of darkness will be lost. Where the hell is my ship?'

Delaney joined him and they whispered together.

Miss Lucy placed a hand on my shoulder. 'I owe you my life.'

I offered back the pistol she'd lent me, but she refused to take it. Instead, she handed me a spare pouch of powder and a small bag of shot. She didn't speak but I understood her well enough. Although we'd ridden many miles, we'd not necessarily reached safety. I thanked her and set about figuring out how to reload it.

I studied the Dutchmen and his followers and knew I faced a dilemma. Should I embrace their cause? I understood little of whatever was really behind their plotting. And yet Mother and Tobias had risked everything to assist them. Why? I couldn't fathom it. Mother was a kindly soul. She'd never get mixed up in something like this without good reason. Why hadn't she told me? Tobias had never hinted at any of this, either. Or Elsbeth. Along with Lord

Blackfoot, what they schemed was treason and war. I was an Englishman and proud to be so. Was their cause worth risking my life for too? Did I have any choice?

A branch cracked in the undergrowth behind me. Startled, I rose quickly to my feet and pointed my pistol blindly into the blackness of the wood. I saw something move. I willed it to be a deer, a fox or a badger but then another branch snapped and I thought I heard the heavy footsteps of a man. My pistol shook in my hand.

'Come out with your hands raised. I can see you. I am armed and not afraid,' I lied.

A bush rustled not more than twenty feet from me. I took aim and pulled the trigger. The blast shattered the night, startling rooks in the tree tops and causing the others to rush back from the shore.

I must've missed as I heard no cries of agony. And I now understood the merits of carrying two pistols. Fumbling desperately with the bag of shot while keeping my eyes on the shadows, I heard the bush rustle again, and then from the midst of its thick foliage a figure broke through.

He was huge. I thought the giant, fully two yards in height and with the girth of a great oak, must be Herne the legendary wild huntsman about whom many stories were told. A menacing apparition to be feared, Herne lacked flesh and blood and tales spoke of him being accompanied by a pack of hounds of considerable bloodlust. They too were spectres and filled men with dread. Shaking violently, I dropped my pistol.

'There you are, Mr McLeish,' roared the Dutchman. 'Where have you been? And where's my ship?'

The ox of a man stood, hands on hips, glaring at me, his eyes wild and indignant. His long, matted red hair and beard, dishevelled and sticking out like the flames of a fire, gave him the look of a beast. He snarled at me, 'Och, ye wee tyke,' his Scottish accent thick on a rolling tongue. 'I'm minded to snap you across my knee. Fancy shooting me, did you? Well, it'd take more lead than you have in your purse to stop Hamish McLeish!' He strode forward and raised an arm as if to strike me down but Delaney stepped between us.

'Halt yourself and gather your senses, Mr McLeish, you big fat clodpoll,' barked Jacobsen.

The Scotsman swore and backed away.

'I'll ask you once again. Where's the *Endeavour*?' said the Dutchman.

McLeish tugged at his beard. 'Well, you see, Captain, it were not long after you set off that word came of soldiers riding this way. Mr De Veer spoke of not wanting to risk the ship and so weighed anchor. Reckoned it was safer to stay offshore long enough to let them go about their business, so he'll not be back until the afternoon tide. He'll pick us up off Nare Head. And he left me here so I could explain it all to you.'

'And the soldiers?' asked Delaney.

'Just a patrol. Three men. Came along the coast road.'

'Where are they now?' asked Jacobsen.

'I dealt with them like I always do.' McLeish inspected his hands and I realised they were his weapons, as they were huge and attached to arms whose strength probably knew no equal.

The Dutchman deliberated on our course of action. 'The shelter of the barn is preferable to the woods. All we can do is await the *Endeavour*'s return. Back to the barn, everyone. Mr Jacobsen, you can take the first watch.'

Settling amid bales of straw, Miss Lucy sat down a few feet from me and took to humming. She removed her hat and combed down her hair with her fingers, freeing her curls of knots that had tied themselves during the long day.

'How come you're involved in all this?' I asked.

She looked at me but didn't reply.

'I mean, finding you in the company of pirates came as quite a shock,' I added.

'The Dutchman and his men are more than just pirates.'

'I've worked that out already for myself! Lord Blackfoot knew who you were too.'

She nodded. 'He has done much business in the past with my father. Lord Blackfoot's family have a rich Dutch and English ancestry that are intertwined. He currently lives in England although he has extensive property abroad. He and my father are well acquainted, although they've not seen much of one another in recent years as my father's business in Amsterdam has expanded greatly and Lord Blackfoot's work as a diplomat on behalf of Prince William occupies much of his time.'

'Have you ever met the Dutch prince?'

She patted some straw and settled down onto her back. 'Many times. Now, enough questions, Daniel. Get some rest.' She pressed her eyes firmly shut.

I couldn't sleep. Until yesterday the most important people I'd ever met were sea captains and innkeepers. Now I was acquainted with lords, and with those who brushed shoulders with royalty, and with the Dutchman, the most feared pirate sailing the oceans. I wish Tobias could see me now, I thought. Wish Tobias had seen me defend Miss Lucy.

Delaney slept lightly while the chest of McLeish heaved like an ocean's swell, his snoring like distant thunder. The

Dutchman, sitting with his back against a beam, had drawn his knees up against his chest and, with folded arms, cradled his chin. Quietly I got up and moved nearer.

'Cannot sleep either, Master Daniel?' he whispered.

I nodded and settled cross-legged beside him. 'What happens now?'

'That depends on the Dutch prince. Once he's received the invitation he will no doubt make final preparations to come to this country. He is determined to protect England's Parliament, and to do so will mean having to seize the crown.'

It had dawned on me that by keeping Mother's letter safe and delivering it, I was responsible. Unwittingly, I had helped start a revolution. I wondered why I hadn't just destroyed the letter by burning it back at the tavern, just as I'd suggested to Tobias and Elsbeth. I now began to wish I had. 'So there will be war.'

'Yes, but hopefully not a bloody one. A peaceful, glorious revolution is what we all wish for in our prayers. If our intelligence is right, there will be little resistance from James's men.'

Unable to picture England's army and navy simply laying down their weapons without some sort of fight, I frowned in disbelief. 'Lord Blackfoot said the invitation to Prince William will be signed by seven great men. Do you know them?' I asked.

He nodded. 'One day, when our history is written down, our story will either speak of them as famous men or infamous devils, depending on how it all turns out. But I suppose, either way their deeds will make them immortal in the minds of others.'

'The Immortal Seven,' I said, thinking aloud.

He reached for a small flask resting beside him. He held it aloft intent on making a toast. 'Aye, Master Daniel, here's to the Immortal Seven's glorious revolution!'

'Can I ask you something else?'

'Just one more question. Then you really must try to sleep.'

'How did Thackery know we were at Trelithick Hall?'

The Dutchman cast me a glance and then returned his gaze to the floor.

'You see, I can think of only one explanation. Either Mother or Tobias must've told them. They must've been tortured. Thackery must've broken their will to resist, and forced them to confess all.' My words began to crack before even leaving my mouth.

Still he said nothing, but he didn't need to. I knew he was thinking the same thing.

Chapter Eleven

DAWN delivered a stiff breeze and heavy grey clouds on the horizon. I awoke to find that the others had already risen and that McLeish and Delaney had gone off in search of food. Jacobsen was saddling the horses and the Dutchman was standing in conversation with Miss Lucy some distance from the barn.

Delaney returned clutching a bag full of bread and some oatmeal biscuits, while McLeish lugged a pitcher of weak ale in one hand and held two skinned rabbits in the other. A small fire was lit behind the barn and the rabbits cooked on spits made from slender branches.

'We shall divide ourselves,' announced the Dutchman. 'Mr Delaney and Mr McLeish will escort Master Daniel to Nare Head and shall signal the *Endeavour* this afternoon as she passes.' He addressed me directly. 'Mr De Veer will send a boat to pick you up from the beach.' Abruptly he turned away. 'Now, Miss Lucy, Mr Jacobsen and I have other business to attend to. We must deliver Mary's letter safely to the crossroads at Carnon Downs. After last night's incident, let us hope we don't encounter further trouble. Mr Delaney knows where and when to pick us up and shall pass my instructions to Mr De Veer.'

I didn't like the sound of the Dutchman's orders. While in his presence I felt relatively safe and I liked Miss Lucy's company. Although Delaney was a likeable sort, McLeish I rather distrusted. Ever since firing my pistol at him, I'd felt a vengeful eye following me around. I regretted that I'd missed.

By late afternoon, threatening black clouds heading in from the west foretold of a storm brewing. Stood on Nare Head, fifty feet up from a sweep of golden beach, the stiffening breeze whipped up the sand. My eyes stinging, I was forced to shield my face. There was no sign of our ship.

McLeish huffed and cursed between swigs at a flask of whisky. It brought a glow to his cheeks. 'That boy will bring doom on us all, Mr Delaney,' he snapped while glaring at me. 'You mark my words.'

Gripping my pistol, I swallowed my fear.

Delaney took no notice of McLeish's rantings, instead keeping a watchful eye on the growing swell.

I smelled rain in the air and then it arrived, just a smattering of spots at first. In the heat of the afternoon, the splashes of droplets on my face felt refreshing. But it quickly turned into a torrent, with arrows of water lashing the ground, flattening the sand and grass and soaking us to the skin. Worse, it brought with it a strange light, not quite dusk but close.

Delaney gazed out to sea. 'This storm is bad news. Even if the ship makes headway, I can see no way of signalling her.'

We sat on the wet ground and shielded our heads with our capes. 'Have you known the Dutchman long?'

'Since last summer.' Delaney appeared to predict my next question, continuing, 'I was on the run and managed to gain passage from Dublin to London. Within half a year I found myself in the West Indies. One night I stumbled on a brawl between several of the Dutchman's men and some

Spanish sailors. Being well acquainted with the finer points of swordsmanship, I saw an opportunity for practice and merely had to choose sides. I believe I chose wisely. My reward was to be offered employment, if you can call it that.'

'What about McLeish? I fear to ask the man myself.'

'I don't know his story. But Mr McLeish is the sort you always want on your side. He is worth a dozen men, maybe more. I've seen him throw men from their saddles by grappling their horses to the ground, and observed him raise great sails with his own strength alone.'

With the wind howling and driving the rain so hard that droplets danced on the ground, Delaney pulled his cape tightly about his face. We sat for almost an hour.

'Why are you all involved in this?' I asked. 'Until a few days ago, all I'd ever heard about the Dutchman painted a picture of piracy. Yet I've seen no pirating. This mission you are undertaking is under the instructions and orders of the Dutch prince.'

'Be in no doubt, Master Daniel, that the Dutchman deserves his reputation and renown, although strictly speaking he's more a privateer, as much of what he does these days is at the behest of the Dutch prince. And there will be reward enough should we succeed.'

I looked at him questioningly. 'What reward?'

'The Dutchman only ever speaks of having struck an important bargain with the prince. He has never explained the details to us. But if you ask me, assisting the prince will win the Dutchman great favour and the possibility of being awarded land and property.'

'Do you know my mother?'

He shook his head. 'Naturally I've heard much about

Mary Drake from the Dutchman. I sense he knows her well. He always speaks fondly of her.'

Yes. How could that be? I wondered. Then again, I thought, until I saw Tobias speaking to the Dutchman like an old friend, I'd no knowledge of their acquaintance either.

'Ahoy!' yelled McLeish. He waved his arms frantically and jumped up and down. The storm had begun to abate and three hundred yards offshore the ghost-like outline of the *Endeavour* slipped into view. Ten minutes later, a rowing boat set out for the beach.

Once back on board ship I sought out Cornelius, desperate to share with him the previous night's adventure and how I'd saved Miss Lucy's life. Seeing he wasn't on deck, up the rigging or in the crow's-nest, I headed below.

The cramped existence of the crew struck me as awful; I thought it no better than an overcrowded prison. And the stench of sick was overwhelming – the storm had unsettled the stomachs of many. The worst affected stayed confined to their hammocks on the gun decks, row upon row of them groaning pitifully while clutching their bellies. I saw no sign of Cornelius among them as I crept ever deeper into the ship. It was as if he was no longer on board, but that was surely impossible. Returning to the quarterdeck, I spotted De Veer and set about questioning him. What I heard drained the blood from my face.

'Threw the boy into the brig, Master Daniel. Caught thieving, he was. Lad gave me no choice. Rules are rules. Charges will be heard by the captain in front of the crew, and the captain shall decide the boy's fate. That's how it is on this ship. Now I'll speak no more of the matter, so you run along now, before I have you locked up too.'

Rushing below again, I ran to the stern of the ship, to a deck below the waterline. There, in one of the cages in the brig sat Cornelius, his hands bound. 'Cornelius!'

'Danny? Thank God.'

'What happened?'

'Two men accused me of filching. Said I stole a silver pocket watch. I didn't, as God's my witness, Danny.' His voice trembled. 'Mr De Veer said I had to be locked up until tonight. Said justice would be served on the Dutchman's return. And we already know what that means. I can't hold my breath, Danny, not longer than a count to ten.'

Not for one second did I doubt his innocence as I knew such a trinket would hold no appeal. And, believing it unlikely my friend would survive being drawn beneath the hull, I frantically tried to think of a way to prove his innocence. 'Who are your accusers?'

'Dunno, Danny. Anyway, what would a blind man do with a pocket watch? I don't want to die, Danny. Not here. Not on this ship.'

Reaching through the bars and resting a hand on his shoulder, I tried to comfort him. Surely, I thought, De Veer would listen to reason.

Chapter Twelve

DE Veer shrugged off all attempts at petitioning him and grew surly and dismissive when pressed. 'His accusers, Misters Catchpole and Weeks, are relatively new to this ship but are known to Mr Delaney, who speaks highly of them. I have no reason to doubt their word. Now, like I said, the captain shall sort the matter out on his return.'

Hunting down Delaney, my pleading with him brought little joy. He refused to listen to me and said that such matters were none of his concern.

Cursing their deafness to reason, I stormed off to the Dutchman's cabin and threw myself on his bed. Staring at the ceiling, I tried to arrive at a plan to free Cornelius. Reaching for the pistol Miss Lucy had given me, I practised at aiming about the room, at lanterns, at the desk, anything and everything. It grew heavy as my arm tired but my dogged determination kept my aim still and straight. Just as I felt confident I could strike between the eyes of any man at twenty paces, I despaired. What use was one pistol against several hundred men? If I wasn't careful, I might be joining Cornelius and barnacles beneath the ship.

I howled in frustration. It was no good. I couldn't just stand by and watch my friend die, as he was sure to if found guilty. If I could free Cornelius from the brig I could get him ashore in one of the ship's tenders. It was a long way to row and my arm was sore, but I was a skilled oarsman, having rowed to Leopard's Cove in all weathers to set out Old Crabber John's lobster pots. Hurriedly I set about searching the cabin for a knife to cut Cornelius's bindings. In a small cupboard I found a blade I judged sharp enough to cut hemp, and in a drawer I found another pistol. I needed one additional item for my plan to succeed – something suitable for picking the lock of the door to the cage in the brig. All I could find was a long needle. I would make do.

'Danny, is that you?'

'Quiet, Cornelius,' I whispered. 'Place your hands against the bars.'

With perseverance I gradually sliced through the rope.

'And now what?' my friend asked. He rubbed his wrists made sore from the rope's chafing.

There was a noise behind me. Someone else was entering the brig. 'Shush, Cornelius.' I held one of my pistols aloft and aimed into the darkness. 'Who's there?'

A boy's face appeared.

I frowned. 'You're the one who was keelhauled, weren't you? Accused of filching like Cornelius.'

The boy drew closer. 'Yes. I'm Peter Loodvelt, and I'm no guiltier than your friend. Our accusers are the same and they seem intent on trouble. I saw you and guessed you might be planning to escape. I want to help. I want to go with you.'

'What's your plan, Danny?' asked Cornelius.

'We take our leave of this ship before it claims our lives. Peter, hold my pistols while I try to get Cornelius out of this cage.'

I began work on the lock. It proved stubborn and the needle needed much bending and twisting before, finally, a clunk heralded my friend's release. I retrieved my pistols from Peter's grasp. 'Follow me and stay close to my back. Our lives depend on it.'

Finding a way back on deck while avoiding being spotted proved tricky. With so many men crammed aboard, some activity or other occupied every nook and cranny. Our every movement needed perfect timing and stealth to avoid attracting an eye and I dreaded that Cornelius's blindness was one burden too many. Yet, darting from one hatchway to the next, from behind one barrel to another, we seemed invisible. Peter knew the ship far better than I did, and so I let him lead the way.

Slowly we climbed from deck to deck, but just as the reek of the ship gave way to fresh air it appeared my plan was foiled. Blocking the hatchway were two men and they talked noisily together. I turned to whisper of our predicament but saw written on Cornelius's face a mix of hatred and loathing.

'They're the ones,' he hissed. 'I recognise their voices, Danny. I'd bet my soul on it.'

'Aye, that's Catchpole and Weeks alright,' Peter whispered. 'If they see us, they'll waste no time raising the alarm.'

I sank a shoulder against the bulkhead and groaned. Not only was our escape blocked, but before us stood Cornelius's accusers. And, from what I could see of them, they appeared men of great strength and little charm. Oddly, they struck me as familiar as if I'd seen their faces and heard their voices before. However hard I racked my brain though, I couldn't place them.

There was no going back and no going forward, and where we stood would only bring our eventual discovery.

Drastic action was needed. Gripping both my pistols tightly, I whispered, 'On the count of three we charge them and hope that surprise buys us the upper hand. Try knocking them off balance, Peter. If that doesn't work, I'll blast a path through.' I paused and took a deep breath. 'Ready?'

Peter swallowed hard and nodded.

'One . . . two . . . three.'

Barging between Catchpole and Weeks we leaped through the hatchway and emerged on deck. We guided Cornelius towards where we could climb down into the ship's tender tethered amidships, the same rowing boat that an hour earlier had brought me from the beach below Nare Head.

Catchpole and Weeks quickly gathered their wits and set off after us. Only the barrels of my pistols pointing at them forced them to keep their distance.

'I've got them covered, Peter,' I hissed. 'Help Cornelius over the side and down into the boat.'

It was still raining hard, drumming down on the deck amid quite a squall, gusts of wind arriving on every compass bearing and making the ship heave and roll. I found it hard to keep my balance.

'Hold it right there!'

The voice, loud and determined, came from above. Instinctively I looked up and saw the face of De Veer glaring down at me over the railings of the quarterdeck. Men bearing muskets stood at his side.

'Drop those pistols now, Master Daniel. Drop them!'

'What is it, Danny? Are we scuppered?' fretted Cornelius.

We'd so nearly succeeded. To put down my pistols would mean defeat and that I'd failed my friend. Peter was sure to suffer as a consequence too. Yet to keep them raised appeared a short cut to the grave. Or was it? Would De Veer really invite the wrath of the Dutchman by shooting me?

'We're leaving this ship, Mr De Veer,' I shouted. 'I'll not let my friend die as a result of trumped up charges.' Despite the risk, I stood firm and kept my pistols aloft. Sailors crowded on deck and surrounded us. Our actions became their entertainment. They taunted us, calling for us to be hanged from the yardarm. The loudest cries of all came from Cornelius's accusers.

'I stole nowt,' Cornelius remonstrated, fighting off their jeers. 'They're lying.' He pointed towards the voices of Catchpole and Weeks. 'They were friendly enough at first. Gave me ale and let me laugh at their jokes. Then I became their fun. They jabbed me with fingers and knives and roared heartily when I could not fend them off.' He lifted his shirt to reveal a dozen cuts.

'Aye,' shouted Peter angrily. 'Exactly what happened to me!'

His accusers wore innocent masks, denying everything.

I saw McLeish emerge through a hatch and my heart sank further. Our predicament had surely just taken a turn for the worse. But then a remarkable thing occurred. Grabbing Cornelius's accusers by the scruff of their necks, he snarled, 'Now, Misters Catchpole and Weeks, does Master Cornelius Trotter speak the truth? Was Master Loodvelt falsely accused too?'

When they failed to reply, McLeish bashed their heads together in a manner that made me wince. It rendered them desperate to confess that their accusations were indeed a pack of lies.

I dropped my pistols to the deck. 'It's alright, Cornelius. We're safe.'

Peter Loodvelt stood tall next to me. 'We demand justice,' he shouted.

De Veer nodded. 'Indeed, and you shall have it. Take Misters Catchpole and Weeks below and lock them in the brig. Post armed guards outside. We don't want them escaping as well. The Dutchman will decide their fate on his return.'

Peter gripped my hand and shook it. 'Thank you, Danny, for letting me in on your scheme. I'd begun to fear I had no friends on this ship, and no one who'd believe me. On a ship like this such misfortune usually costs a man his life. If you ever need my help, just ask, and I'll happily repay the debt.'

McLeish stomped purposefully across the deck and I took a fearful step back.

'Well now, you three may be nothing more than wee young men but you've more guts than whales, lads.' He slapped me so hard on my back it drove the air from my lungs. 'You're a fine schemer, Master Daniel. And not afraid to stand firm and defend your friends in front of fifty men who'd happily fillet you all with their knives. Glad I could be of assistance.'

Chapter Thirteen

THE Dutchman returned just after dusk. At dinner De Veer spoke at length of the antics of Catchpole and Weeks. The Dutchman groaned heavily as though it were all one problem too many. 'They appear to be men intent on causing trouble. Have them flogged, Mr De Veer. Forty lashes each. Then cast them ashore without a penny to their name. And make it clear that should I set eyes upon them again, they shall perish.'

Bowls of mutton stew steamed in front of us, but only Anstey's appetite seemed hearty. I drew pictures in the broth with my spoon and divided my glances between Cornelius and Delaney. 'Mr De Veer told me that you know Catchpole and Weeks,' I said to Delaney.

'Mere acquaintances. What of it?'

I shrugged. 'Nothing. Just that their faces seem familiar to me too.'

Unease crept across his face like a shadow. 'Your paths have crossed?'

I shook my head. 'Not exactly. I can't place them. But I know I've seen them somewhere before.'

'I have come to a decision.' The Dutchman placed his napkin on the table and rocked back in his chair. 'I have decided that the *Endeavour* is no place for you, Master Cornelius. A warship has enough practical dangers and a man with no sight is destined to encounter trouble at every turn.' He glanced in the direction of De Veer who nodded in agreement. 'Tomorrow, we shall return you to Dartmouth.'

My friend said nothing. I knew him well enough to understand his silence. On the one hand he'd be glad to leave the ship, especially after the day's events. Yet on the other, he loved being at sea.

'I wish to accompany him ashore,' I said.

'Dartmouth's not safe for you at present,' replied Jacobsen.

'Perhaps, but I must call on Elsbeth Hawks at the tavern. These are difficult times for her too, and I owe her much. In many ways Tobias and she have been like parents to me. And I must collect some personal things from there.'

'Very well, Master Daniel. You shall accompany Cornelius,' said the Dutchman, stifling any further discussion on the matter. He rose from his chair and signalled to Jacobsen and Delaney. 'Please excuse us, but we have business to discuss in my cabin. Perhaps Miss Lucy could entertain you all with a song.'

In need of fresh air, I headed for the steps up to the quarterdeck but hesitated outside the door to the Dutchman's cabin as voices from within filtered out into the corridor. Leaning against the bulkhead, I eavesdropped.

'All is set here for our glorious revolution and so we must return to Holland and prepare ourselves,' said the Dutchman.

'Any trouble today?' asked Delaney. 'Any sign of Thackery's men?'

'Thankfully, no. Today's particular rendezvous remained a secret as intended. Mary Drake's letter is now in the hands of the Seven and so we can breathe easy. However, that Thackery turned up at Trelithick Hall last evening suggests the worst regarding Tobias's and Mary's plight.'

Knowing what he meant, I swallowed hard.

'And what of the boy?' enquired Delaney.

I held my breath.

'There is little to keep Master Daniel in England, and anyway he's not safe here,' said the Dutchman. 'After his visit ashore he shall sail with us to Amsterdam and will stay at the house of Miss Deveraux. Should he so wish, I will happily bring him back to England aboard the *Endeavour* with the invasion fleet.'

The Dutchman had mapped out my life for me and, although the prospect of spending the rest of the summer in Lucy's company was alright, I'd miss England, Cornelius, Elsbeth and the Shipwreck, and then there was the small matter of trying to get Tobias and Mother out of gaol – I didn't want to go anywhere until they were free. I'd heard enough and so climbed the steps and sat on the deck. Peter was high up in the rigging. He called down and waved.

The rain had stopped and the sky had cleared. The breeze, a shadow of the blow of the storm, did little more than ruffle my hair. I gazed up at a night full of stars and constellations, their positions vital aids to the navigator. Towards the bow of the ship I spotted several men lugging barrels. All appeared to struggle except for the bulk of McLeish.

I had been all for hating the Scotsman, for wishing he were dead. How wrong. If it weren't for his assistance the day might have ended tragically for Cornelius, Peter and me. We owed him our lives.

I then thought of Delaney, recalling the moment in the

corridor below, the moment I'd asked for his assistance in pleading Cornelius's case. Delaney had been deaf to reason. He had an odd choice of acquaintances too, I reckoned, recalling the faces of Catchpole and Weeks. Then it struck me. I'd seen them at the Shipwreck tavern. Just once or twice, faces among the crowd. And then something else hit me like a bolt of lightning. They'd been among Thackery's mob of hangers on, men he paid to carry out his devious schemes and dirty work. Or were they? Perhaps I was mistaken. So many faces came and went at the tavern. Perhaps they'd just been there on the same evenings as Thackery. I couldn't be sure.

Feeling the chill and unable to resist a shiver, I returned below.

With the Dutchman's cabin occupied, I slept on a sack of grain beside Cornelius in a storeroom beneath the raised forecastle deck. We were woken by Jacobsen at dawn and instructed to ready ourselves to go ashore. My plan, such as it was, was to give the others the slip and head out of town. I'd make for Cornelius's brother's shop in Kingsbridge. He was sure to offer me sanctuary. From there I'd try to figure out a way to free Mother and Tobias.

We sailed in close to shore and the coastline was familiar. Passing Leopard's Cove made me think of Old Crabber John and his lobster pots. Bet Old Crabber won't be best pleased that I've failed to turn up for work, I thought. He'll reckon my excuse of being taken aboard a pirate ship to be a pack of lies, little more than the fanciful imaginings of a lazy boy. I supposed I could expect a thick ear next time I saw him.

Jacobsen and McLeish received orders to accompany us. And with the Scotsman at the oars, it didn't take long to row on the tide towards the glistening curve of Blackpool Sands. I knew the sheltered horseshoe-shaped beach well. Surrounded by hills, it lay a few miles to the west of Dartmouth. Landing there presented a stiff walk into town, climbing up past Crowbeak Hill before a steep descent towards the harbour.

Approaching the beach, Jacobsen checked that his pistols were loaded and that the powder charges remained dry. He instructed me to do the same. 'Should we come across soldiers we shall need our wits. We must avoid capture at all costs. And I mean all costs!' He looked at me sternly.

And then we were ashore.

McLeish, though strong, was poorly built for climbing. Wheezing and sweating, he took barely twenty steps up the hill without a pause to catch his breath and to slap dead the many insects intent on biting his neck. 'Keep up, Hamish, you sack of spuds,' cursed Jacobsen.

Half an hour's walk brought us to Crowbeak Hill. Jacobsen had taken the lead, striding some thirty yards ahead. I guided Cornelius and spoke encouraging words to the floundering McLeish.

Crowbeak Hill was a horrid place on account of the gibbets. Some criminals were executed there by hanging. Others, already executed by other means, had their bodies strung up in full public view as a deterrent to wickedness; while many dangled on ropes, others were slumped in iron cages. Left to sway for months at a time, they slowly decayed, providing food for circling crows. Gradually their flesh rotted, their eyeballs got pecked from their sockets and their clothes tore and flapped in the wind. Worst of all, though, was Crowbeak Hill at night, when even the lightest breeze set the bones of skeletons rattling. Out of respect, and to avoid the worst hideousness of the place, the tradition was to pass the gibbets with head bowed, focusing only on the dirt of the road.

Approaching the brow, I noticed Jacobsen had turned on his heels and was rushing back towards us. 'Oh, for the love of God, Master Daniel, do not look up,' he implored.

About to explain that I'd seen many dozen poor wretches strung up on the hill, I suddenly realised the full horror behind his plea. Pushing past him, I ran blindly to the brow from where the gibbets could be seen fully. There I sank to my knees as if struck down by an arrow.

'No!' I cried, but the word barely left my lips.

Chapter Fourteen

TOBIAS dangled by a noose about his neck, his dead eyes staring out to sea. His flesh looked the colour of talc and his clothes were streaked crimson with dried blood.

Cornelius, guided by Jacobsen and having had the horror whispered into his ear, dropped down beside me and grasped me tightly about the shoulder.

'Come, Mr McLeish, we must cut Tobias down and provide him with a respectful burial,' said Jacobsen. 'None was truer to our cause and I'll not leave him there.' He removed his tunic and rolled up his sleeves.

In the hour it took McLeish to cut Tobias down and for us to dig a shallow grave amid the heather and buzzing insects close to the cliff top, I said very little as I was wondering what had happened to Mother.

My head was filled with a thousand sickening possibilities. Why wasn't she here too? Was she still alive? Was she heading for Exeter to stand trial at the forthcoming assizes? Sitting next to Tobias's body, I said my goodbyes, but I desperately wanted answers to so many questions.

We carried Tobias's body with the care of those not wishing to spill a drop of water from a bucket filled to the brim. We laid him down gently and filled in the grave, setting on top a pile of stones. Jacobsen then put his tunic back on and, with grubby hands clasped and eyes pressed shut, offered prayers.

'Come, Daniel,' said Jacobsen finally, 'it's not safe for us here. We can return to the ship if you like. Mr McLeish can guide Cornelius into town.'

I shook my head. I wanted to see Elsbeth more than ever now. We could grieve a moment together. I looked one last time on Tobias's grave and then towards each man about me in turn. My despair had turned to rage and consumed me to the point I struggled to restrain myself from shaking violently. 'As God is my witness,' I hissed, 'I swear that Thackery shall pay for this.'

Cornelius nodded. 'Danny, I don't know how much help a blind man can be, but I hear your oath and I too swear that I'll assist you with every ounce of my strength.' He grasped me tightly and with that simple gesture our bond was sealed.

At first I thought the Shipwreck tavern was closed, and Elsbeth nowhere to be seen. But my patience and repeated drumming of fist on the door was eventually rewarded. Shocked at the state of the woman who peered out at me, I reckoned Elsbeth hadn't bathed, eaten or slept since I last saw her. McLeish kept watch outside.

The air inside the tavern reeked of stale beer and neither the floor nor tables had been swept. I hugged her tightly as soon as the door was shut and bolted. She wept into my shoulder. 'After you led the Dutchman to the tunnels, Thackery came back and searched the place a second time,' she explained. 'He found nothing, of course. Arresting Tobias wasn't enough and so he arrested me too. I think it was out of desperation. Until last night I languished in a dark cell in the castle's dungeons.' She grasped my hands in hers. 'The gaoler interrogated Tobias, but he held out until his last breath. Lieutenant

Thackery ordered that his body be strung up on Crowbeak Hill as a warning to others.'

'I know. We've just come from there. We cut him down and buried him on the cliff top.'

'Thank you, Daniel.' The wretchedness of it all rang in her voice as she hugged me again. 'Mary's letter – what happened to it?'

'Don't worry. It was safely delivered to Lord Blackfoot and the Seven. What about Mother? Is she still alive?'

'Yes. They questioned her, but she's confessed nothing. I think Thackery would relish seeing her strung up on Crowbeak Hill as well, but he has orders to keep her alive and fit enough to stand trial.'

'Lord Blackfoot mentioned the Exeter assizes. They're some months away, aren't they?'

'Yes, Daniel. So time is on our side.'

'The other thing in Mother's favour is that without her letter to the Seven the prosecution's case must boil down to her word against that of the Earl of Dartmouth's servant. Surely that's enough to save her from the gallows.'

'In just times that might be so, but I expect Judge Jeffreys will preside over the case.'

I swallowed hard. Judge Jeffreys was Chief Justice of the King's Bench and was notorious for his brutal sentencing up and down the land. 'Lord Blackfoot may be able to intervene. He said he'd do what he could.' I tried to sound positive but knew I was clutching at straws.

'Pray that he will, Daniel. I'm so sorry you're caught up in all this. You know what it is all about now, don't you?'

'Yes. The invasion of England.'

'Shush, not so loud.'

'Tell me, Elsbeth, how it is that we're all mixed up in this?

It's a nightmare and I can't fathom it. Mother kept everything from me.'

'It's a long story, Daniel. Many years ago, before you were born, things were different for your ma. She was a beautiful young woman who turned heads dressed in all her finery. Your father and she were happy. But then it all changed. It would take hours to explain how we got to where we are today and it isn't safe for you to remain here that long. In any event, I do not know everything. You'd be better off talking to the Dutchman.' She looked a little unsteady on her feet.

'Did they torture you, Elsbeth?'

'A little, but I'd rather go to my grave in silence than tell Thackery anything!' she spat.

I tried not to show it but I was struck by a worrying thought. If Elsbeth spoke the truth and none of them had confessed, then who had revealed to Thackery that we'd be heading to Trelithick Hall? It pointed to the Dutchman having a traitor in his midst, after all. I thought of Catchpole and Weeks. Were they spies? Had Thackery sent them on a spying mission to infiltrate the Dutchman's crew? Then again, was Elsbeth speaking the truth? How come she'd walked free? Had she made some sort of deal with Thackery?

'What will you do now?' I asked.

She gazed about the tavern and the thousand memories soaked into every wood panel and flagstone. 'I shall leave here.'

'Where will you go?'

'I have a niece at St Ives. I shall pay her an extended visit and seek a small cottage to rent.'

I'd never heard either Elsbeth or Tobias speak of any niece or mention St Ives. My misgivings grew and I wondered if my visit to town had been wise after all. Perhaps soldiers were lying in wait for me outside. I moved to a window and peered out towards the quay but saw nothing suspicious.

Observing my caution, Elsbeth said, 'You can trust me, Daniel – you do know that, don't you?'

'Yes,' I replied, doubting that I sounded convincing.

'You're probably wondering why Thackery let me go.'

I nodded.

'I had to bribe him, Daniel. It cost me everything.'

'What do you mean?'

'He owns the Shipwreck now. He forced me to sign the deeds over to him. That was the price of my freedom. And he wants me gone from here. And I shall be gone soon too, as I don't want to risk him arresting me again.'

'I'm sorry,' I said, angry that I'd doubted her. 'St Ives. I'll definitely come and visit. Now, it's best I go. One of the Dutchman's men is keeping watch outside and I need to give him the slip. The Dutchman wants me to sail with him to Holland. He says it's too dangerous for me here. But I'm going to head to Kingsbridge and lie low. I've got to find a way of freeing Mother myself in case Lord Blackfoot fails to secure her release.'

'No, you must go to Holland where it's safe. There's no way you can get Mary out of that prison. It's too heavily defended. You'd need an army.'

I wasn't listening and Elsbeth knew me well enough to see it in my face. 'Your mother would never forgive herself if you suffered at the hands of Thackery,' she said urgently. 'Listen to me, Daniel . . . listen! If the invasion succeeds, your mother will be spared. Go to Holland and pray that it all unfolds in time. It's her only hope.'

She made me promise, although I had little intention of

keeping it. I collected my small moleskin bag left behind several nights before, the bag containing my precious spyglass and sextant, and after a long embrace bid Elsbeth farewell.

McLeish loitered outside. Leaning against a doorway, he whistled tunelessly while keeping watch. He spotted I was carrying my bag. 'Have you got everything you came here for?'

'Yes, thank you, Mr McLeish.' I turned and looked back towards the tavern. 'Elsbeth had to give Thackery the deeds to the Shipwreck. That was the price of her freedom.'

McLeish grimaced. 'Well, one day such wrongs will be righted, Master Daniel. You'll have realised by now that things are going to change. And when they do, it'll be the likes of Thackery who'll be begging for mercy.'

'Indeed he will, but I have no intention of showing him any. Where are Mr Jacobsen and Cornelius?'

'Master Cornelius spoke of a brother. Said he lives in Kingsbridge. Said he'd be safer there. Mr Jacobsen has gone to seek passage for him by boat.'

'I know the way to the boatyards.' I set off before he could complain.

He hurried to catch me up. 'Have it your way. Just don't blame me if we get caught and arrested.'

At the boatyard Cornelius and Jacobsen possessed bad news.

'We couldn't find anyone intent on sailing to Kingsbridge today,' said Jacobsen glumly, adding, 'I could not press the matter without raising suspicion.'

McLeish spat at the ground. 'I don't like the way today's turning out, Mr Jacobsen. First Tobias, and now this.'

I glanced about the yard, seeking inspiration. Despite my promise to Elsbeth, I still felt the urge to make a break for it, to run from McLeish and Jacobsen, to chance my arm. And yet I felt torn. Yes, I wanted revenge, but Thackery could not be easily defeated, and the gaol was a formidable place to free Mother from. I'd need a plan that was as cunning as it was devious. I'd need to catch Thackery off guard, unsuspecting, and in some sort of surprise attack. The guards at the gaol would have to be bribed or dealt with as well. Such a plan would take time to perfect. I'd need help too. And, anyway, could I really escape Jacobsen and McLeish?

Jacobsen cursed. 'Well, we can't hang around here all day.'

I spotted Old Crabber John's boat and briefly entertained the idea of borrowing it. It was moored in its usual place at the end of one of the jetties. Provided it was rowed in the safe waters close to shore it was well suited for the trip. About to propose such a scheme, I saw the ruggedness that was Old Crabber John himself, ambling through the yard clutching two mended lobster pots.

'Daniel!' He dropped the pots and lumbered towards me. 'How are you, lad? I heard about poor Mary. I'm so sorry. I dared not believe it when first I heard.' He arrived and grabbed my hand. 'Why? That's what we're all asking ourselves. Mary accused of treason! If it wasn't so serious we'd have laughed.' He glanced at Jacobsen and then his gaze settled on the bulk of McLeish. He frowned. 'I suppose you're alright. Not in any trouble, are you?' His frown turned to a look of suspicion.

'This is Mr Jacobsen and Mr McLeish. They're friends.'

Old Crabber John nodded an acknowledgement but I

could see he thought my companions rather dubious.

'Cornelius urgently needs transport by sea to Kingsbridge but none seem willing to make the journey,' I said quickly, before he had the chance to put two and two together and realise there might be truth in the rumours about Mother after all. 'I had thought about borrowing your boat.'

He mulled over the matter. 'If it weren't for my pots needing seeing to, I should be happy to take him myself.'

I looked to Jacobsen. 'Perhaps we could offer payment.'

'What price for a trip on the morning tide?' Jacobsen asked.

Crabber John scratched at the long grey stubble on his chin. 'Five shillings would make it good.'

Jacobsen reached for his leather purse and counted out five silver shillings into Crabber John's outstretched hand. Then he counted out five more. 'And there's five shillings more in payment for your forgetfulness.'

Crabber John tugged at the peak of his cap. 'Thank you kindly, sir. Be assured that no sooner do I depart Kingsbridge, then I will have fully forgotten why I went there in the first place.'

'Good,' said Jacobsen. 'Then we understand one another perfectly.'

'Indeed we do. Right, Master Cornelius, give me a minute and we'll be away.'

It was time to make my mind up. Was I going to make a run for it, or was I going to go to Holland? Cornelius struck me as looking as bewildered as I felt. I knew I could rely on him to help me, but there was no one else. Thackery and his mob had that effect on people – few would entertain confronting him even for the best or noblest of causes. It was hopeless and I knew it. I'd made up my mind.

I took Cornelius to one side, beyond earshot of the others. 'Listen carefully. We shall have our revenge but not today or tomorrow. I have to go to Holland with the Dutchman. I shall be staying with Miss Lucy.'

'Holland!'

'Yes, but I shall return soon, and then we shall have our day. Remain in Kingsbridge and await my return. Do nothing rash or that will reveal your whereabouts to Thackery.'

'Don't leave me here, Danny,' he begged. 'I need your eyes. I rely upon them.' Tears welled up.

I seized my friend's shoulder. 'Have no fear. You were right the other day when you said it was time for us to meet our destinies. And I think our fate will be tied to great happenings, of great days that will be talked of for generations to come. We shall both be part of it.'

My words offered little consolation. From my pocket I took out my whistle and pressed it into his hand. 'Take this, Cornelius. You know it's one of my most precious possessions. Look after it for me. I shall want it back, and soon.'

Crabber John stood in his boat and waved to indicate his readiness to depart.

'You must go now,' I said. 'Think of me every day and remember our oath. I shall use my time away to devise the perfect plan. And I'm sure Peter Loodvelt will help us. I shall try and recruit more of the crew too. If I can get McLeish on our side, then I'm sure we'll succeed. He's worth a dozen men.'

I stood and watched him depart, waving until my arm

ached, despite knowing he could not see it. And I felt a coward for not making a run for it, for instead choosing a journey to safe shores.

Jacobsen grew anxious. 'Come,' he said. 'We must return to the ship.'

Chapter Fifteen

TO the west, a burning sunset glowed red and orange. The *Endeavour* made good headway eastwards through the English Channel, touching ten knots under full sail. Stood beyond the forecastle, I rode the bow like it was a galloping horse, not caring that I got soaked. A fury boiled inside me like the froth of the waves crashing against the hull.

I thought of Thackery and spat into the wind. I thought of Mother and tears welled up. I realised I barely knew her. Why had she kept so many secrets? Why had she got involved in such a nightmare? Was it for money? Like the Dutchman, would the Dutch prince reward her for her loyalty? Only one thing was certain. I was alone now. Totally alone.

With nightfall came a drift of songs from below deck. The sky was black and studded with stars. The Dutchman approached from behind and startled me when he spoke. 'I'm so sorry about Tobias, Master Daniel. It's a terrible business and one that a lad should not have to witness. I shall say a prayer for the safe passage of his soul.' He grasped the rigging tightly as if in great pain. 'May I sit with you a while?'

I nodded and made room.

'Thackery wasted no time, damn him.' He clenched a fist in anguish. 'Tobias was a good man. The best.'

'How come you knew him?'

'That's a long story, Master Daniel. It'll save for another time.'

'Well, anyway, Thackery will pay for his deeds.'

'Aye. Mr Jacobsen informed me of your oath upon Tobias's grave.'

I said nothing but simply stared out to sea.

'Mr McLeish remarked to me that he would be proud to stand at your shoulder or protect your back in any confrontation with Thackery. And then there's your good friend, Cornelius.'

'Then with their help I shall succeed. I shall devise the perfect plan.'

The Dutchman nodded thoughtfully. 'Of course, should you prevail, you might hang for it.'

I shrugged. 'Only if we get caught.'

'True.' After a short pause, he continued, 'Listen, Master Daniel, it does no man any good to harbour bitterness of that kind. It can twist a man inside. It can change him, and not for the good, either. I know this because I have experienced it. It is better to rely on the law to deliver justice in such matters. And once Prince William arrives on England's shores, the likes of Thackery will be held to account. He will stand trial for his actions. You shall witness it, and you should be content with that.'

No way, I thought. I wanted to serve revenge myself. I wanted to look Thackery in the eye when the moment came.

'Do you understand? Foolish actions are to be avoided.'

I didn't reply; instead, I asked simply, 'When shall we return to England?'

'Some months, I fear. All depends on the Dutch fleet's readiness.'

'Months! But if Lord Blackfoot can't free Mother, it'll be up to me to rescue her. How can I do that if I'm in Holland?'

The Dutchman looked away and heaved a sigh.

'I do not want to be idle during the wait,' I said. 'I wish

to learn how to handle a pistol and to fight with a sword as good as any soldier.'

The Dutchman slowly shook his head. 'Have you been listening to a word I've said?'

I turned and glared at him. 'Have *you*?'

He stiffened. 'Very well, if you insist. I'll see what can be arranged. I trust you have no objection to residing with Miss Lucy's family in Amsterdam. They shall treat you well.'

I nodded. The Dutchman was about to get up when I added, 'Mother didn't confess, you know.'

'I'm sure she didn't, Master Daniel.'

'No, really. Elsbeth Hawks told me. Despite what they did to her, Mother revealed nothing. Neither did Tobias. Or Elsbeth.'

'That's good to hear.'

'But don't you see?' I said.

'What, Master Daniel?'

'If they didn't reveal our meeting with Lord Blackfoot, then who did?'

The Dutchman frowned. 'It points to a traitor.'

'Yes, and there's something else. It's about those two men who accused Cornelius of thieving. At dinner last night I said to Mr Delaney that their faces were familiar. Well, I've remembered. I've seen Catchpole and Weeks at the Ship-wreck tavern.'

'I see.'

'No, I don't think you do. The more I think about it, the more I'm sure they were among Thackery's men. Not soldiers from the garrison, but among the crowd Thackery employs for all his dirty work.'

The Dutchman thought a moment. 'It's a good job we

had them flogged and then put ashore. They'll do us no more harm. I'm grateful for you telling me this, and I shall have words with Mr Delaney about being more careful regarding the sort of company he keeps.'

The *Endeavour* rocked gently as she cut through the swell. I looked up at the night sky and the millions of stars reminded me of something I'd been meaning to ask. 'Will you or Mr De Veer teach me navigation? I know it's possible to find your way by the stars and position of the sun but I've never learned how.'

'That I am happy to do, although our passage to Holland is short, barely enough for a rudimentary glance at a chart.'

'I have my own sextant,' I declared proudly. I reached down for my bag and took out the brass instrument.

'May I see?'

I handed it to him and he inspected it. 'A fine example. And this is really yours?'

'Yes.'

Repeatedly turning it in his hands, he noticed the engraving and peered at it closely. 'Oyster Bay,' he read aloud and then frowned. 'Tell me, Master Daniel, how is it that you have your father's sextant?'

I had no idea that it was Father's, but now realised that must have been why Mother had kept it safely in her trunk. She hadn't just found it lying in a hedge, or filched it, after all. What puzzled me was how the Dutchman knew it belonged to Father. I pulled the spyglass from my bag and pointed. 'Then this must have been his too, as it also has "Oyster Bay" written on it.' As the Dutchman seized it from me, I added, 'Do you know what the Oyster Bay refers to?'

'Indeed I do. Tell me, what do you know about your father?'

'Not much, just that he left while I was still in my crib. Mother never speaks of him, and when I ask questions she always changes the subject. I suppose he's made a new life somewhere, remarried and probably has a dozen children by now.'

The Dutchman muttered, 'No. That isn't true.'

'What do you mean?'

He got to his feet. 'I know your father well. He and I go back a long way. Come with me and I shall tell you his story. I'm sure one day Mary would have shared it with you, and she won't mind that I do so now instead. And, believe me, it is quite a tale, Master Daniel.'

Chapter Sixteen

THE Dutchman's account of my father, Benjamin Drake, came as quite a shock. I discovered he had been a master mariner and captained his own ship – I supposed that was why I'd always dreamed of going to sea; I had salt running through my veins too. My eyes widened as the Dutchman explained that Father had accumulated substantial wealth in just a handful of years, wealth which he used wisely, turning himself into a respected merchant in Amsterdam, trading cotton, porcelain and tobacco.

'Eventually your father did what many such men have done, investing in a sugar plantation in the Caribbean. That plantation was called Oyster Bay. It was there I first made his acquaintance.'

'So that's how you know the sextant and spyglass were his.'

'Yes. And it was from that moment on that our lives have been intertwined. With Tobias's too. He worked for your father, seeing to the day-to-day running of the plantation. I don't know how much you know of life on the sugar plantations, Master Daniel, but suffice it to say I was once a man with no rights. I was a slave. In the eyes of most white men not really a man at all. Dogs were more highly prized. And better fed!' He stared into his glass of rum as if reliving terrible times. 'From dawn to dusk we toiled in the cane fields. If we dared to look our masters in the eye, or rested for even a moment, we were severely beaten. Let me show you, so you are in no doubt I speak the truth.' He paused to raise his shirt to reveal the many deep scars across his back.

'Father did that to you?'

'No. And neither did Tobias.' He settled back down and continued. 'When your father took over the plantation it was as if an eternal night of horror ended. Tobias and Benjamin no longer beat us, you see. Not unless it was fully justified. They said such ways were barbaric. Instead, they gave us better food and allowed us to build proper shelters. Benjamin even let us rest on the Sabbath, unheard of on other plantations. Unlike our previous masters, they were both good men. You are a fair likeness to Benjamin,' he added, briefly inspecting my face.

'What happened to him?'

'The other plantation owners did not take kindly to his good treatment of us. They said it would breed discontent and lead to trouble amongst their own slaves. Your father took no notice, and their bitterness grew. He should have seen trouble coming. Maybe he did and reckoned he could handle it. If so, he was mistaken. It was late one summer's night that we saw the burning torches on the horizon. White men from the neighbouring plantations came in force and set among us with guns and swords. They spared no one, no matter what colour their skin. They butchered hundreds of us without remorse or compassion. Men, women and children. I witnessed my two younger brothers, my mother, my father, and all whom I knew as friends get either shot or cut down before me. Of course, we fought as best we could, but our bare hands and the few machetes we could muster were no match for them.'

'Why didn't my father stop them?'

'Oh, he tried. He and Tobias and a few others remonstrated until it was clear to them that their words fell on deaf ears. They could have run. Perhaps they should have. But they didn't. Instead, to their credit they tried to defend us. They fought beside us and they fought well.'

'And?' I was now on the very edge of my seat, fearing that the Dutchman was but a few sentences from describing the moment my father met his death.

The Dutchman spoke slowly now, as if taking great care to recall every detail just as it had happened. 'Eventually they cornered Benjamin. By that time all the buildings and cane fields had been set alight, and screams filled the air together with dense smoke and the hiss and crack of flames. Benjamin had run out of shot, his pistols spent, and so turned to using his sword, slashing and cutting with courage and defiance. In the end they overwhelmed him.'

'So that's it? They killed him too?'

He shook his head. 'No. It was just as they wounded him I managed to reach his side. I had seized an axe and I put it to good use.'

Picturing the horror, I gulped.

He leaned back in his chair and twisted his glass in circles on his desk. 'Having done so, I dragged your father to a ditch. It provided cover. We hid there until well after dawn and the white men had left. I tended his wound as best I could but he was bleeding badly – I knew we could not stay there long. To cut a long adventure short, those few of us left, including Tobias, eventually made it to the harbour and set sail in your father's ship. We were short of deckhands and of supplies and the weather proved far from kind, but by the grace of God we made it to Holland. It was on our arrival and your father's full recovery that he made me a free man. That was my reward for being loyal. And freedom is the greatest of gifts.'

Recalling the story told by Cornelius, not in my wildest dreams could I have ever imagined that the man of whom Cornelius spoke, the man who granted the Dutchman his freedom, was none other than my father. 'What happened once you arrived back in Holland?'

'We went our separate ways. Of course, I was naive. I supposed that as a free man all would look upon me as an equal. But I was forgetting the colour of my skin. I remained a slave in the eyes of white men, and I again came to know desperate times. It was that predicament that led me to steal the *Endeavour* and, well, the rest is history.'

'She's the finest ship I've ever seen.'

'She's the best in the Dutch fleet, Master Daniel.'

'And that's how you earned the name the Dutchman.'

He nodded. 'That's how most know me now. It's been quite a while since anyone's uttered the name John Garret.'

'Have you been back to the Caribbean to seek revenge?'

He shook his head. 'No. That day has yet to come.'

'Could my father have given you work? After all, you said he was a successful merchant.'

'Indeed, if he could have, I'm certain he would. But losing the plantation and sailing without profitable cargo meant he reached Amsterdam a ruined man. Great debts led to the seizure of his property. He too became desperate and was but one step away from the debtors' prison when he fled to England with Mary. There they started over, renting rooms in Dartmouth. Tobias followed a month or two later.'

'Mother and Tobias never mentioned any of this to me.'

'They probably thought it for the best. They were difficult

times. Anyway, soon after you were born, Benjamin returned to Holland, hoping he might be able to salvage a little of his fortune. It was not his best move. Men owed money always have the sharpest of memories and they caught up with your father within a month of his return. Unable to make good his debts, he was arrested and languished in gaol for a considerable time.'

Piecing together Father's life story, I mapped it out like positions on a great chart and committed it to memory.

The Dutchman continued, 'He might still be there now if it were not for the prince intervening. He knew your parents well and rightly supposed they could be trusted. He offered Benjamin a bargain of sorts – his freedom in return for working as an emissary, a go-between and a spy. Keen to assist, I have made my own bargain with the prince in return for my support. Our work has taken us far and wide, although rarely together, and I believe we have been of great service to Prince William. Until a few months ago, your mother had no knowledge of these matters. However, that all changed when it was clear Mary was best placed to gain access to the Earl of Dartmouth's staff, and so could spy for us. As an old and loyal friend, Tobias was roped in to assist Mary in any way he could, and to offer her protection if the need arose. That had been my idea and, given the outcome, it is a regret I shall carry to my grave.'

I shook my head slowly. 'I still don't understand why Mother never uttered a word of any of this to me.'

'I don't know for certain, but she probably thought it best you knew nothing. That way no slip of the tongue could compromise them.'

I slowly let it all sink in. My whole life felt like a lie. Nothing I'd known had been as I'd imagined it. And then it struck me hard like a punch to my stomach. Father had not died that night on the plantation or while languishing in Amsterdam's debtors' prison. He was still alive.

As if anticipating my next question, the Dutchman said softly, 'Last I heard, Benjamin was heading for Paris under an assumed name. But that was many months ago. As to his current whereabouts, I have no idea.'

Suddenly I couldn't wait to get to Holland. Maybe the Dutchman could make enquiries. Locate Father. Reunite us again. I spoke of these things and the Dutchman made vague promises that he would do what he could but, with war looming, such a reunion might have to wait, maybe for months. I didn't care. Just knowing Father was alive was enough.

Later, as I tumbled towards sleep, aided by the gentle sway of the ship, I made myself promise that once this adventure was over, once I had freed Mother, I would return Father's spyglass and sextant to him and we'd be a family again.

I wondered what he was like. Was I like him? Would we get along?

Would he even want to know me?

Chapter Seventeen

STEPPING foot in Amsterdam, I felt overwhelmed. Delaney had said to me on board the *Endeavour*: 'Amsterdam's the greatest port in the world, Master Daniel. More than one hundred thousand dwell there.' But the picture his words painted hardly prepared me. Until that day, Dartmouth had been the largest town I'd ever seen.

Everything looked and sounded unfamiliar. Walking from the docks, my eyes didn't know what to marvel at most. Canals packed with fully laden barges and bordered by cobbled paths carved great ravines between streets of tall buildings four or five stories high. The houses were squeezed together like a crowd pressed shoulder-to-shoulder. Some were built from reddish-brown brick; others had been brightly painted in yellow ochre, the blue of the sky, or a dark crimson wash like that of congealed blood. They were giants with their ornate roofs and gables. And the crowds, the bustle, the noise, and the smell of flowers, and spices, and smoke all made me giddy.

Miss Lucy led us through the throng, explaining to me as she forged a path, 'My family resides at a house on the Herengracht. It is quite the finest address.'

The Deverauxs' house was indeed impressive, enjoying pride of place midway along the street. Outside, dozens of containers were being unloaded from a barge, each bearing the inscription and mark of the Deveraux Import Company. I thought of Father and supposed that once he must have been just like Mr Deveraux. And Mother; she must have known these streets like the back of her hand too.

A servant greeted us at the front door. The Dutchman turned to us. 'I must bid you all a temporary farewell for now. Come, Mr Delaney and Mr Jacobsen, we have important matters to attend to.'

The servant showed me to a small room in the attic. Though cramped, the bed was comfortable and the linen smelled fresh, a far cry from my straw mattress and itchy blanket in Cotton Lane. An empty chest of drawers provided storage for the clothes I didn't possess and a small table bore paper, quill and ink for writing I couldn't really do. A selection of books I didn't know how to read rested on a shelf.

The window was open and I leaned out as far as I dared and looked down. The fine view of the canal and thronging masses below held my gaze. I now knew what men in the crow's-nest witnessed from their lofty position. It was like being on top of the world.

With the house being so narrow, the rooms tended to be long and thin with tall ceilings. The staircases were steep like the cliffs back home and, although I tried, I couldn't count the number of steps that led from my room down to the ground floor – there were simply too many. With several doors to choose from, I knocked briskly on each in turn and waited for a reply. When I finally heard a voice call out, I turned a handle and ventured in.

The room before me contained a clutter of chairs, sofas, desks, books, mirrors, stuffed animals and various strange brass instruments to which I couldn't put a name or use. Not one thing, I considered, matched with any other, yet all, I thought, would keep a curious man content for hours.

Miss Lucy introduced me to a tall man who puffed on a clay pipe while leaning on the marble surround of a splendidly ornate fireplace. The man, it turned out, was Mr Deveraux – not that he bore the remotest resemblance to Lucy. He seemed a rather dull man, a man without humour and whose head was full of figures and contracts. His grey pallor suggested more exercise and fresh air would be beneficial. His greeting to me was polite but gruff and to the point.

Mrs Deveraux, a slight woman perched on a sofa, spoke little but at least managed a limp handshake and a smile from a rather pinched face.

'Master Daniel,' began Mr Deveraux, 'Miss Lucy will show you the ropes and instruct you as to the daily rhythm of this household. You are expected to be punctual for meals and must not run about the house. No shouting or loud laughter either, if you please. Otherwise, there are few rules. I must apologise now if our paths do not cross often. I am a businessman and am often away.'

I nodded, but thought such rules were surely only ever found in a wretched workhouse.

'I was not expecting guests,' he added. 'However, Miss Lucy informs me that she owes you her life. That is enough to make you welcome in this house. We are indebted to you. Miss Lucy shall give you instruction to improve your reading and writing while you are here; with luck and hard work, your time with us shall not be entirely wasted. After all, a man may be measured by his intellect.'

I forced a smile while wondering who on earth would want to waste time indoors bent double over books when there was an incredible city to explore outside.

'In addition, I have been informed that Mr Delaney shall

visit you here on Wednesday and Friday afternoons for the purpose of instruction in the soldierly art of swordsman-ship. I cannot say I approve, but it seems I have no say in the matter, as the Dutchman has apparently organised this for you. Now, if you have no questions I must get back to work.'

'Just one, sir,' I said. 'My family used to own businesses in Amsterdam. I'd quite like to see where they lived.'

'I see. Do you know what the companies were called?'

'No, sir. Only that my father was a merchant and imported cotton, tobacco and sugar. He also once owned a plantation in the Caribbean. Called Oyster Bay, I believe. Our family name is Drake.'

For the first time I gained Mr Deveraux's undivided attention. He just stared at me for what felt like for ever. 'Drake . . . Oyster Bay . . . Hmmm, can't say either rings any bells.'

Mrs Deveraux shot her husband a furtive glance that confirmed to me what I suspected. He was lying. But I didn't press the matter, not for now. I'd find out the truth later.

'Please, show me the city,' I said to Miss Lucy as we left the room.

'Very well,' she replied. 'Just a short walk this afternoon. Tomorrow, we shall explore further. And then I'll begin teaching you how to read and write properly. Does that sound a reasonable bargain?'

I nodded, although I'd never had much need for reading and writing.

That afternoon and the next day we walked the streets beside the canals that formed the heart of the city. I quickly got my bearings and soon the sights and sounds grew familiar. All the while I kept my eyes peeled, seeking out any trace of my family's past, a faded sign perhaps, or a reference to Oyster Bay. Although I couldn't read properly, I knew I'd recognise the words engraved on my spyglass and sextant if I saw them.

I spotted nothing that hinted of our past wealth until late the following afternoon when we approached a warehouse that stored mostly sugar and rum. Miss Lucy initially failed to realise that I'd stopped to study the building, and only when she turned round to say something noticed I was a good twenty yards behind her. 'What is it?' she asked returning to where I stood.

I pointed. 'There. Those sacks.'

'What about them?'

'See what's written on them? That sugar comes from Father's plantation, Oyster Bay.'

Miss Lucy frowned. 'If I know the story right, your father lost his property on returning to Holland. It is owned by others now. Legitimately too.'

'But he lost it through no fault of his own, but by showing his slaves some kindness.'

'Perhaps, but that's not how the law interprets it. Now, Daniel, we mustn't loiter. It's getting dark. We should head back.'

'I want to know who owns it.'

'There is no value in that. Come, or else we'll be late for dinner.'

I turned and followed Miss Lucy back along the street, all the while committing the route and location to memory. I would return alone another day. I would have answers to my questions.

Life at the Deveraux house quickly took on a familiar routine. Mornings were spent in the company of Miss Lucy and musty books of all shapes and sizes, books bound in leather and vellum, pages yellowed from sunlight.

We began my learning with a horn-book, a flat board with a handle, on which a piece of paper bearing the letters of the alphabet had been glued, then covered with a thin layer of horn. She insisted I write out the alphabet again and again until I could form each letter well. Mother had tried to get me to do the same years ago but always grew exasperated when my attention quickly wandered. Miss Lucy proved far more patient, but only once I'd mastered that did we move on to proper books. Reading even a single sentence without stumbling on word or syllable led to gushing praise and warm hugs from Miss Lucy, which was reward enough. But I found the work rather hard and it made my head pound. Miss Lucy was a fine teacher – not that I'd known any others, apart from my mother – and I was happy that I had her company all to myself.

Delaney arrived punctually at one o'clock on every agreed day and I looked forward to his visits. A long back room, once cleared of clutter, was ideal for the instruction of fencing.

'I favour the rapier,' he declared on his first visit. He showed off his long, narrow, two-edged sword with guarded hilt. 'It is to be preferred over the single-edged, curved blade of the cutlass because it is much better suited to killing more men in a short space of time.' He pressed the point gently against my throat, and the rapier was agreed upon.

It was when he demonstrated his art that I realised he possessed great agility and skill. Able to stride back and forth the length of the room with perfect balance, his blade carved wide sweeping slashes and lunging stabs all at astonishing speed.

It looked so simple. How wrong, I soon realised. I felt ungainly, the sword heavy in my hand.

Delaney shouted instructions: 'Leading foot forward . . . Close up your back foot . . . Step to your right . . . Lunge . . . Parry . . .'

Of course, trying to defeat him, even in light practice, was like swimming the width of an ocean. Annoyingly he seemed able to predict my every move and was able to knock aside all my feeble attempts to get near him. Yet from such defensive strokes he conjured attacks so sudden and unexpected his blade came to rest an inch from my tunic before I even recognised an attack was afoot.

'You have to outwit your enemy,' he told me repeatedly. So often, in fact, I could still hear it in my sleep. 'Know what he is thinking and anticipate his every move. Be fleet of foot and remember this, if nothing else, Master Daniel: to beat the best swordsmen you need to strike quicker than the eye can see.' The first time he uttered those words, he lunged forwards and with a deft flick of his wrist cut a button from my tunic. The button had struck the floor before I even realised what was happening.

Every time we practised I felt like giving up. But I knew that proficiency meant the difference between life and death and between success and failure in my quest for avenging Tobias's murder and Mother's imprisonment. So every time my will faltered, I gritted my teeth and redoubled my efforts.

Delaney also taught me how best to handle pistols. Naturally, firing them inside the house was forbidden, but he showed me how to load one within seconds, how to change the flint, and how to keep it clean and in perfect working order.

In the evenings, after dinner in the Deveraux household, and when I was quite certain that I'd exhausted my welcome in their company, I pretended to retire to bed, instead slipping out to explore the city streets. Occasionally I'd get lost, losing count of the number of bridges and canals. Although I heard English spoken amid French, Spanish and Portuguese, most men spoke Dutch, a peculiar tongue, sounding as if whole plums were lodged in their mouths, just like Mother talking in her nightmares. It was a constant reminder that I still had to devise the perfect plan.

Day and night Amsterdam buzzed. And come nightfall rowdiness emerged from dark back streets and alleyways. Where Dartmouth possessed a few dozen taverns, Amsterdam counted them in the hundreds and they provided homes for a rough and wicked crowd. I watched harlots plying their trade amid pickpockets, roisterers, thieves and drunks who staggered about in the murk of gloomy streets. If I were up for a spot of filching, I figured there was sufficient easy prey to make a good living.

As I walked late into the night, I heard splashes and screams and wondered how many bodies were fished from the canals each morning. Amsterdam was a place full of danger *and* opportunity, I decided. And despite having a pistol lodged in my belt beneath my tunic, I wandered the streets filled with caution. Tobias had once given me good advice: 'If you want to avoid trouble,' he had said, 'don't drink yourself legless, don't venture down unfamiliar dark alleyways, and avoid the eyes of evil-doers. Always be prepared to run, be swift of foot and quick of wit.'

I missed the old man.

Most evenings my route took me past the warehouse storing sugar from Oyster Bay. I'd pause on the path on the opposite side of the canal and wonder whether Father had once owned the building. One night I plucked up courage and decided to seek out someone who might be able to provide answers, as Miss Lucy had evaded any further discussion about my family's past in Amsterdam. Entering the warehouse, I looked about and spotted a lantern glowing in an office reached up a flight of steps. I climbed them and knocked on the door. A voice replied in Dutch. I had no idea what the man was saying, but took it to mean I could proceed. I stepped inside.

The clerk, a man in his thirties, looked up from his desk. He frowned.

'Do you speak English?'

He placed down his quill, leaned back in his chair, and folded his arms. 'A little. What do you want? You're not supposed to be in here.'

'I know. Sorry. Did this warehouse once belong to a man called Benjamin Drake?'

My question drew a puzzled look. 'Who wants to know?'

I side-stepped that awkward question by continuing, 'I saw the sacks of sugar and the name Oyster Bay. I know Mr Drake once owned that plantation in the Caribbean, and so I was wondering if—'

The man got up from his chair. 'Who sent you?'

I began to think my visit was a really bad idea. The clerk did not like the questions I was asking.

'I said, who sent you?' he repeated. 'What's your name?'

'No one. I know the Drakes, you see. That's all,' I replied, matching his advance towards me with my retreat towards the door.

He stopped and studied me hard. It was almost as if he saw something familiar in me, as he seemed to relax. 'Not heard the name Drake mentioned in years. You know Benjamin, you say.'

'Yes, but not well. I know all about his woes, of losing his businesses and ship on his return from the Caribbean.'

The clerk nodded. 'A sorry tale indeed. Yes, this warehouse was once owned by him, along with half a dozen others, all the way up to his house on the Herengracht.'

That was where I was staying. 'The Herengracht! Which house did he own?'

The clerk's description matched the Deveraux household perfectly. I was fizzing inside. I was staying at the very house once owned by my parents!

'Have you seen Benjamin recently?'

I shook my head.

'Well, if you do cross paths give him my regards. The name's Karl van Keup. As a boy I worked for Benjamin, you see. In the old days, before he lost everything. He was a good employer too. The best. Mind you, Mr Deveraux gives me no cause for complaint either. Two of Amsterdam's finest merchants. Both honourable men.'

'Thank you,' I said. I held out a hand and he shook it. 'My name's Daniel. Daniel Drake. Benjamin's my father.' I stiffened with pride.

The clerk smiled. 'Thought you looked familiar. Yes, you do bear a likeness. Well, like I say, give my best wishes to Benjamin.'

'I shall.'

When I returned to the Herengracht that night, I felt like

I was arriving home. I sat on the windowsill of my room and wished that one day it might truly be so. It was while dreaming of such wealth I gazed down to the street below and saw the cloaked stranger for the first time.

Chapter Eighteen

HE remained there for an hour, loitering some fifty yards from the house on the other side of the canal. He kept to the shadows and so I couldn't see his face. Had I been followed? Was he watching the house? Was he spying on us? He was there the following night too. Then he appeared no more.

July drifted into August, and with September came a change in the weather. Long hot summer days gave way to the chill of autumn and blustery gales.

The Dutchman paid few visits to the house. He was preoccupied with matters relating to the readying of the fleet. On the rare occasions he did knock on our door, I reminded him not to sail for England without coming to collect me first. He did, however, bring me one piece of good news sent through diplomatic channels from Lord Blackfoot: Mother was still being held in Dartmouth's gaol and a date for her trial had not yet been fixed, although it would be held in Exeter, as we'd suspected. Lord Blackfoot was doing what he could for her, but despite the optimistic tone in the Dutchman's voice I knew Lord Blackfoot could probably do very little.

The more I thought about trying to free Mother from Dartmouth gaol on my return, the more I realised such a plan was doomed to failure. The castle gaol was impregnable and heavily defended. Instead, I began to think that my best hope lay when they transferred Mother to Exeter.

Delaney had suggested it to me some time ago as being the best approach. Soldiers would escort her but not in vast numbers, he reckoned, and they'd be out in the open. Somewhere along the route there had to be the ideal ambush site. With McLeish's help and maybe a few others from among the *Endeavour's* crew, Delaney believed we could succeed.

On the other hand, dreaming up the perfect plan to exact revenge against Thackery was proving harder. I couldn't assume he would accompany Mother on her journey to Exeter. Dealing the final blow wasn't the problem as I'd grown confident in my use of the rapier and handling pistols. My problem was getting Thackery into a situation where such a blow could be delivered. He was no fool and rarely went anywhere alone. If it wasn't soldiers from the garrison at his side, then it was men from his mob, their loyalty paid for through cash and favour. Despite the difficulties, I knew I had to come up with answers, and quickly too, as my return to England grew nearer with every dawn.

Midway through September, Delaney broke the news that he could no longer visit the Deveraux house. 'Preparations of the fleet are well advanced and I am needed aboard the *Endeavour*,' he announced.

By now, the simple slash and cut routines of our practice had been embellished. Tables and chairs were placed about the room, and our swords clashed whilst we ran, jumped, leaped and generally created mayhem until I was left bent double and breathless. My arm had healed, the stiffness had vanished and my strength returned. At times, I even felt that my rapier was an extension of my arm, as it had begun to feel so natural to me. Despite my progress, I was yet to get within a mile of victory against Delaney.

'From now until the *Endeavour* sets sail, the Dutchman has asked that Miss Lucy spar against you in my place,' Delaney added.

I laughed out loud at the thought.

Miss Lucy looked decidedly put out. 'It seems Daniel does not think much of playing a man's sport with a mere girl.' She picked up a sword and strutted about the room, one hand resting on her hip, the other twirling the blade in the air. 'Come, Mr Delaney, let us spar and in doing so make Daniel realise I'm a worthy opponent.'

Delaney grinned. 'As you wish, Miss Lucy.'

Supposing they were intent on an amusing game I settled against the wall of the room in anticipation of a short battle in which he chased her about the room in a manner that would put us all in stitches.

With their swords held in outstretched arms, the tips of the blades touched lightly, almost as if kissing. Such a respectful opening, however, quickly evaporated and I stood aghast at their speed and technique. Back and forth, over tables, across chairs, around pillars, their swords clattered and clashed in a flurry of strokes so quick, deliberate and exacting in their execution I hardly dared breathe. Astonished that Lucy could hold her own, I took considerable delight in observing both perspiration and unease creep over Delaney's face for the first time in months.

With a second wind, however, he set about driving her back on her heels and did not hold back one ounce of ferociousness in his will to succeed, even taking to a two-handed grip in order to win each battering stroke. It seemed he was, as always, intent on victory, although I thought it the closest battle I'd ever witnessed.

Lucy leaped and spun while fending off the heavy blows. But, just as I thought her about to concede defeat, her back to the wall and with strokes raining down on her, she let out a scream of unfettered barbarity, one so loud I was forced to place my hands about my ears. Her sword flashed from side to side so quickly I couldn't see its blade although I heard it fizz as it swished through the air. And then, in a single movement that saw her step forward and bring her sword round and upwards in a wide sweeping arc, a look of horror came across Delaney as his sword was forced from his hand and sent flying upwards. She lunged forward and brought the tip of her weapon to within an inch of his throat.

'Not bad,' he said. She lowered her blade and he bowed, took a handkerchief from his tunic pocket and dabbed the sweat from his brow.

Miss Lucy cast me a wry smile. 'So, Daniel, do you consider me up to the task? Am I worthy to test my metal against your skill?'

'You beat him,' I stammered. 'You actually beat him, fair and square.'

'Indeed I did,' she replied. 'I think that makes us even, doesn't it, Mr Delaney? Five each as I recall.'

'Aye, and I fear it will soon be six–five to you. You are improving all the while. My lack of proper practice is rendering me stale.'

My gaze was fixed on her like a limpet. 'How did you learn to do that?'

'Father is well acquainted with a Mr Guus van der Stolten, the finest swordsman in Holland. My tuition was in payment of a debt. And as it was quite a sizeable debt, I received a great many lessons, starting from an early age.' She smiled. 'I believe you must be aware by now, Daniel, that I am allowed many opportunities not often available to a young woman due to my father's standing and service to the prince. Swordsmanship is but one part of this, and my place on board the *Endeavour* is another.'

'Then why haven't you been the one teaching me?'

'Mother does not approve of me practising in the house. But as the request has come from the Dutchman, I'm sure she'll make an exception on this occasion.'

Delaney gathered up his things. 'Alas, I must take my leave of you both. I am needed on ship.' He turned to me. 'Daniel, make the most of the coming days, for soon we shall be returning to England.'

He bowed with a flourish and then, taking hold of Lucy's right hand, imparted to it a lingering kiss. He exited the room walking backwards and bowing on every third or fourth step. We both laughed at his ridiculous antics, Miss Lucy still red-faced from her exertion. I also saw a look in their eyes, a look that left no doubt Miss Lucy liked Delaney a great deal and that the feeling was mutual. I don't know if it was because I felt a little jealous, or for some other reason, but I just had this sense that it would all end badly for them.

At eight o'clock that evening a carriage arrived outside the house. Leaning as far out of my bedroom window as I could manage without falling, I saw men exit the carriage and enter the house. Minutes later, another carriage arrived and then another. The front door repeatedly thumped open and shut.

Descending the stairs, I was intrigued at the many voices

filtering from the front room and so tried to eavesdrop, but was discovered by the Dutchman and Mr Jacobsen who caught me with my ear pressed to the door on their arrival. To my relief they didn't reprimand me.

'Master Daniel, you're looking well,' said the Dutchman. 'And I must congratulate you. Mr Delaney informs me that you have made substantial progress with the sword.'

'Yes, but I'm still no match for him, or Miss Lucy. Who are all these people?'

'Good question. The Deveraux household is indeed privileged tonight. Prince William has paid them a visit and invited many important people to a meeting. Come,' he said, beckoning towards me with an outstretched arm, 'come and meet him. I am sure he would like to make your acquaintance.'

The Dutchman opened the door and I peered in, observing a room full of great men, some in uniform, others clad in the brightest and most expensive clothes. All stood except one. And this one exception sat on a chair close to the fireplace. In possession of a fine wig of black, shoulder-length curls and a slender moustache curved up at its edges, I judged him to be about forty years old. He wore a dark tunic stitched with gold thread and, although he seemed relaxed, he held an unmistakable air of authority. He looked exactly how I imagined a prince to be. The Dutchman strode in and nodded a greeting to each man in turn. The prince smiled and held out a hand.

Dropping to one knee, the Dutchman bowed his head. He clasped the prince's hand and kissed it lightly. 'Sir, I apologise at my lateness.'

'Yes, yes, stop fussing,' the prince replied brusquely.

The Dutchman introduced me.

'I was sorry to hear of what happened to your mother,' said the prince. 'However, be assured that we remain indebted to her and that, whatever her fate, you must always speak of her with pride as well as affection.'

'Yes, sir, thank you, sir. Do you know the whereabouts of my father, sir?'

He smiled at me, raised a hand and wafted it in the air. 'He's here, there and everywhere. His work for me takes him near and far, and it is work of a most dangerous kind.'

'I know, but where is he right now, sir?'

The prince baulked at the determination in my voice. 'I'm not entirely sure and it is better people don't know. That way they cannot capture him!' He raised an eyebrow and then changed the subject. 'I trust the Deverauxs have welcomed you into their household.'

'Indeed they have, sir, although I believe this house once belonged to my parents.' I shot Mr Deveraux a glance. 'And maybe one day soon it will again.'

The prince laughed. 'You are just like your father, Master Drake, not afraid to speak his mind. This house now belongs to Mr Deveraux and was acquired quite legitimately, I believe.'

'That's enough, Master Daniel,' interrupted the Dutchman. He could see I was fully intent on arguing the point further.

Mr Deveraux scowled at me.

'Indeed it is,' muttered the prince. 'We are all present now so let us not waste any more time.'

A man stepped forward. In possession of a chart, he spread it out on a table and everyone gathered round. I learned that he was the admiral entrusted with leading the Dutch fleet. The chart showed a good portion of the English

Channel and North Sea and the coastline of our two countries. Opinion in the room seemed divided regarding the best place along the English coast at which to land.

'The coast of Northumberland, or maybe Essex,' suggested the admiral. 'Some captains in our fleet favour Bridlington Bay.'

The prince appeared thoughtful. 'And the precise whereabouts of the English fleet?'

'Most at anchor off Gunfleet on the north shore of the Thames estuary, sir,' the admiral replied, pointing to its spot on the chart. 'Only half a dozen warships are patrolling the English Channel. It seems that the intelligence regarding the Earl of Dartmouth's plans has proven accurate.'

I realised they were speaking of what Mother had written in her letter.

'And their strength?' asked the prince.

'About nineteen hundred cannon in total on fifty or so English warships.'

The prince grimaced slightly and set about twiddling the ends of his moustache. 'And we have mustered?' His tone hinted at a fear of asking.

'Just over two thousand cannon, sir. Divided amongst fifty-four warships,' the admiral replied. 'To that, of course, we must add the ships carrying supplies and our army, numbering some forty thousand men. In total, I suppose we must speak of four hundred and fifty boats and ships or thereabouts.'

The prince sighed heavily. 'Clearly our naval warships are closely matched in number and firepower. I wish we possessed better odds. Still, it will have to suffice. And we must pray that our men possess the greater hunger and strength for victory.'

The room echoed with murmurs of agreement.

'Winter is just around the corner,' said the admiral. 'I would prefer going to war in the spring. Already strong and unfavourable winds are blowing and they will impede our progress.'

Agitated, the prince hissed, 'It's now or never. James is no fool. He knows we are readying ourselves. Any more delays and he may be able to muster more men and ships and thereby tilt the scales of war in his favour.' He turned away from the chart and paced the room, his stride slow and deliberate.

The Dutchman spoke up. 'There is one aspect in our favour, sir. We know the French fleet is embroiled in the Mediterranean and Louis also has his army occupied in the Rhineland. So King James cannot rely on the assistance of his friend.'

The prince nodded, but the admiral remained unconvinced and continued trying to persuade him that going to war now was folly.

Mr Deveraux had been standing in the corner of the room. Despite hosting the gathering, he'd played no formal part in the evening's discussion until that moment. He stepped forward and coughed lightly to attract attention. 'If I might say something. None of us should forget what is at stake,' he began. 'Even in the last few weeks, Louis of France has ordered the seizure of our wine fleet. And as his army presses eastwards across Europe, each day brings closer the moment he will step foot in Holland and claim it as his own. In the past we endured and survived the repression of Spanish rule with all its ugliness and destruction, and now France seems intent on repeating our misery. We vowed that never again shall we be ordered to kneel before a foreign king. Never! We have been a free nation for but a few decades and yet, already, our graft and industry has led to a golden age. It is worth the fight.'

The prince applauded his speech and others quickly joined in. 'Well said,' he remarked. 'Once in England, and most importantly in command of its fleet, my supremacy shall dissuade Louis from invading Holland. Of course, should he prove foolish enough to try, then we shall possess the might to defeat him.'

Discussion continued well into the night. Later, as I lay in bed, unable to sleep from the excitement of it all, I mulled over all that I'd heard. No one had uttered a word about dangers to the English Parliament, English Law or the freedom of its people, all those matters about which the Dutchman had spoken. Instead, I'd listened to a plan whose purpose was to enable Prince William to defend Holland against a French invasion. Under his control England and its navy would simply tip the balance in his favour. Was this really what it was all about? Was this what Mother and Tobias had risked their lives for?

Chapter Nineteen

ON the afternoon of the 18th October a messenger arrived at the door bearing instructions that Miss Lucy and me were to be on the quayside at dawn the following morning where a tender would take us to the *Endeavour*. We would sail on the afternoon tide. The invasion was on.

That evening Prince William hosted a celebratory ball at his palace and the Deverauxs were invited; I wasn't, but I didn't mind. I watched them climb into a carriage, all dressed in their finest clothes. Once they set off the house suddenly seemed horribly empty.

I decided to spend my last night in Amsterdam with one final walk about the city. I grabbed my pistol and cape and headed out the door. As I stepped onto one of the canal bridges it began to rain. I pulled my hood down over my face and was about to turn for home when I spotted a familiar figure some way ahead of me.

I couldn't be sure, but it looked like Delaney. I was surprised as I had understood from the Dutchman that unless invited to the prince's celebrations all officers had orders to remain on board their ships. So what on earth was he doing in town? He walked purposefully too, as if late for an important appointment. In case it was indeed him, I ran to catch him up but stopped dead in my tracks when he suddenly paused to greet two men loitering on a corner. I felt a fizz of panic. Not only did

I recognise Delaney, but I also knew the two other men as well – Catchpole and Weeks.

They spoke a moment and then all headed off together. What was going on? Why were Catchpole and Weeks in Amsterdam? I knew they were all acquainted as Delaney had said as much to me on board the *Endeavour*. But did he know that those two rogues were almost certainly in the employ of Lieutenant Thackery? That they might have been spying on us? I assumed the Dutchman had spoken to him about it, but what if he hadn't? If the Dutchman had simply told Delaney that these men were bad company and troublemakers, he might be blind as to their true intentions.

Determined to follow them, I set off, maintaining a good distance between us. A horrid thought then struck me. If Catchpole and Weeks were intent on luring Delaney somewhere dark and deserted to slit his throat, outnumbering him two against one, would I be ready to intervene and shift the odds to an even match? After all my training I felt more than prepared and I reckoned Delaney's skill with the rapier and mine with a pistol would prevail if it came to a showdown. I reached beneath my cape and gripped the handle of my flintlock in readiness. I was strangely unafraid and almost relished the prospect of a fight. Just a few months earlier, working at the Shipwreck tavern, at the first sign of trouble I'd be looking for somewhere to hide, to become invisible.

For an hour they walked briskly towards the harbour, dodging carts and horses, turning left, then right, crossing one canal after another.

Curiously, their route was far from straight. They zigzagged, sometimes doubling back while frequently glancing over their shoulders, as if fearing they were being followed.

Yet I was certain they'd not seen me. With every canal bridge we crossed my trepidation doubled. They appeared secretive. And I was starting to worry that I'd got everything muddled up, because all three looked as thick as thieves.

Eventually, among a series of run-down warehouses in a deserted and grubby part of the city's docks ripe for demolition, they reached a sturdy wooden door, one braced and reinforced with ironwork. The building looked like a fortress and I suspected it had once been used to store goods of enormous value.

Catchpole knocked. Someone answered and all three stepped inside. Once the door closed behind them, I counted to ten and then ran and pressed my ear against it. Although voices were muffled and indistinct, I got the impression of quite a gathering within.

I took a few steps back and surveyed the building. Was there another way in? It struck me as pretty secure with no obvious point of entry other than the front door. The place was a good choice if you were intent on a clandestine meeting – we were in a part of the city in which few would dare to walk alone at night and, if you did dare, you'd probably end up floating face down in the harbour with your pockets emptied of valuables. I tore back the hood of my cape, blinked the rain from my eyes, and looked again. Surely there had to be a way.

The barred windows were high up and there was no easy route to access them. I then spotted a glimmer of hope. To one side was a single-storey building with a pitched roof and cast-iron drainpipes. If I could get on top of it, I reckoned I might be able to reach the guttering and parapet to the warehouse roof. Once there, I might be able to watch the goings on inside as there were shuttered ventilation openings.

The drainpipe was a doddle to climb. It was sturdy with sound fixings. The pitched roof tiles held firm as well, although the rain made them slippery. Lying belly down I pulled myself up to the ridge and then rose to my feet. Balancing precariously, I stretched up to see if I could reach the guttering on the warehouse roof. It was during moments like these I cursed being so short. Just a few inches taller and it would have been easy. As it was, only my fingertips touched the guttering.

I swore under my breath and sought an alternative route. There wasn't one, so I gritted my teeth and reached up again, straining every sinew. I could just about do it, just about get enough grip. I counted to three and lunged, using all my strength to haul myself up, over the guttering and to the relative safety of the brick parapet. Crouching to keep my balance, I stifled a cry of pain – my hands stung from where the sharp edging of the iron guttering had bitten deep into my palms.

So far, so good. I'd done the hard part. I was right too about the ventilation openings. They were the perfect vantage point. Again lying flat on my belly, I slid along the roof, feet wedged against the parapet, until the indistinct voices below grew louder and I could make them out. Hearing them wasn't enough, though. With just a little more effort clambering up the roof, I'd be able to peer down and see what was going on.

Laughter from Catchpole filtered out into the night air. 'I must say, this is an unusual business, Mr Delaney. As an agent of King James, I never expected to find myself colluding with an agent of King Louis of France in matters that will define the shape of Europe for generations to come.'

'Aye, these are indeed strange times. The French throne in bed with the English. Whatever next? Well, I have fulfilled my orders and brought you everything you asked for. Here, gather round the table and I'll show you.'

I shuddered at the revelation that Delaney was spying for the French king. He'd hid his deception well. I recalled saying to the Dutchman that I knew King James was on good terms with King Louis of France, but not for one minute had I suspected that such friendship might extend to their spies joining forces in espionage against the Dutch prince. And I'd only been half right about Catchpole and Weeks. They were indeed the enemy, but were in the employ of King James and not Lieutenant Thackery, at least not directly.

This was worse than I could have imagined, as spies working for the king were likely to be clever, resourceful and quick-witted – far more dangerous than the mere rogues Thackery had working for him. I peered down through the wooden slats and watched as Delaney unfolded a detailed chart of Amsterdam's harbour, spreading it out on a table. I quickly counted the heads below me and realised that as well as Delaney, Catchpole and Weeks there were half a dozen others.

Delaney spoke. 'As you know the harbour is jammed full of the invasion fleet. Therefore, I have marked the precioc positions of the prince's main warships. If you can scupper those, then the invasion will have to be postponed. Prince William will not risk his army without sufficient covering cannon fire.'

I was seething inside. How dare he aid men intent on

destroying our ships in the harbour. Worse, how could he bring himself to betray the Dutchman and all his friends on the *Endeavour*?

Catchpole leaned forward and by lantern light studied the chart at length. 'You have done well, Mr Delaney. My men shall deal with as many of the fleet as we can manage in the hours of darkness available to us. We have plenty of gunpowder and fuses and I anticipate that our small rowing boats will go unnoticed as the harbour is awash with legitimate vessels making their final deliveries. We may not get them all, but hopefully enough to weaken the prince's enthusiasm for invading England.'

Delaney nodded, adding, 'Well, just make certain that the *Endeavour* is at the top of your list, Mr Catchpole. I've waited a long time for this moment. I want to see her burn before she sinks without trace.'

'Don't worry, we're going to deal with that one ourselves,' Weeks interrupted. 'After Mr Catchpole and I each received forty lashes aboard that ship, you can call it a personal vendetta. It's payback time. And as she's no doubt fully loaded with powder and shot, she'll provide us with quite a colourful display.'

'She'll wake up the whole city when she blows. You'll see the flames for miles,' Catchpole added.

Delaney slapped Catchpole on the back. 'I look forward to it. Now I must take my leave. I was invited by Miss Lucy Deveraux to dance with her at the prince's ball tonight and I'm late enough as it is. The Dutchman gave me special permission to remain ashore – although he thankfully remains fully ignorant of my true purpose.'

Weeks roared with laughter. 'And there's Miss Lucy thinking you be the perfect gentleman, Mr Delaney. From the way she looks at you, it's like she's waiting for a proposal of marriage.'

'Indeed she has proven a most useful distraction and her fondness for me certainly made my deception easier. Still, after tonight, my job is done.'

They were going to scupper the *Endeavour* by blowing her up. I knew what I had to do – run and raise the alarm. I'd have to run fast too. Time was against me. Their gathering was over and they were preparing to go about their deadly work. I had maybe an hour, maybe less. That's how long I judged it would take a rowing boat to reach the deep channels where the *Endeavour* was anchored. Placing some charges at or below the ship's waterline would only take a few minutes, and even less time than that for the fuses to burn.

I slid back along the roof to the point where I could drop onto the ridge. I reached the parapet safely and began clambering down. Dangling by my fingertips I tried to feel the ridge beneath the soles of my boots, but in the dark I couldn't locate it. I heard the heavy door to the warehouse open. Then voices. Then footsteps. My sore hands screamed at me to let go. If anyone looked up they'd see me in an instant. My grip was weakening and I could feel my fingers slipping . . .

I was going to fall. I just knew it. They'd hear me. If the fall didn't break my neck, I had little doubt these men would kill me anyway. It was no good. There was nothing I could do. I fell, striking the ridge of the roof. Twisting and tumbling, I dislodged some tiles, scattering them to the ground. I tried to find something to grab hold of but it was no use.

Crying out in horror, I saw wet cobblestones hurtling towards my face.

Chapter Twenty

MY head throbbed and I could taste blood. I'd landed heavily and was winded. I felt dizzy too. Opening my eyes, I saw faces peering down at me.

'Why it's Master Daniel Drake,' said Weeks. 'The vile little rat must've followed us.'

Together with Catchpole, Weeks dragged me to my feet. He then glanced up at the roof, saw the ventilation openings, and figured out that I must've overheard everything. I quickly found his knife at my throat.

Shock filled Delaney's face. He just stared at me. I desperately tried to think of something clever to say. Words failed me. Could I wrestle free and grab the pistol from my belt? No sooner had the thought entered my head than I felt Catchpole relieve me of my weapon. I despaired. Weeks then glanced up and down the street, no doubt fearing I'd not come alone. But I *was* alone, and he quickly realised it.

'Suppose you were going to run and tell, weren't you?' Catchpole spat, twisting my arm roughly behind my back.

'No,' I lied. 'I just saw Mr Delaney and wanted to catch him up.'

'Liar, that doesn't explain why you climbed the roof and spied on us.'

'You'll never get away with it!' I shouted, trying to break free. Their grip was too tight.

'Oh, we'll get away with it alright. And you being here

is just a little bonus. We have a score to settle. If it hadn't been for you meddling, we'd never have been flogged and thrown off the *Endeavour*.'

'You shouldn't have falsely accused Cornelius and Peter,' I replied. 'Anyway, it was a stupid thing to do. If you were intent on spying on us you should've avoided drawing attention to yourselves.'

'All part of our deception. At least, that was the intention. We wanted to cause trouble among the crew. Mr Delaney's idea. There's nothing like discontent on a ship to divert attention. With all eyes focused on us, Mr Delaney could go about his work.'

'I recognised you two. I've seen you in the Shipwreck tavern in Dartmouth and I suspected you were in the employ of that oaf, Lieutenant Thackery.'

'In the employ of Thackery?' Weeks laughed. 'Hah, now there's a joke. It's the other way round. He takes orders from us, and we take ours from King James. Now, enough idle chatter. We're going to make you suffer. I'm going to have Mr Catchpole and the others hold you down while I cut out your tongue and then slit your throat from ear to ear.'

I redoubled my efforts to break free but it was no use. They wrestled me down and pinned me to the ground. I saw the glint of Weeks's blade.

Delaney took my pistol from Catchpole and said, 'Wait! All this nonsense is wasting valuable time. Leave him to me. I'll silence him and dispose of the body. You have far more important matters to attend to. Ships need sinking, and you only have a few hours of darkness to complete your task.'

'He's right,' said Catchpole. 'The boy is a distraction. Leave him be, Mr Weeks.'

His face full of hate, Weeks reluctantly stepped away, but not before cutting my ear with his knife. I felt warm blood trickle down my neck. Delaney bound my hands and dragged me back inside the warehouse. I was helpless as the others headed off to where their rowing boats were moored, boats packed with kegs of gunpowder.

Inside the warehouse, Delaney forced me to sit down on a chair. My ear throbbed.

'You're a fool. You should have minded your own business, Master Daniel.'

'How could you?' I spat angrily. 'How could you betray the Dutchman, Miss Lucy and all those who would call you their friend?'

'They're not friends of mine and I bear no allegiance to those aboard the *Endeavour* or to anyone intent on supporting the Dutch prince's scheme to invade England.'

'How come you're working for King Louis of France? And what do you care about England? It doesn't make sense.'

'My mother was French. I grew up in Normandy, moving to Dublin when I was nine. I have family in England too, and as Catholics they've endured a lifetime of persecution. Not that their suffering motivates me. I have no time for religion of any description, Master Daniel, apart from how a divided country might be profited from. And I care nothing for England, either. Rather, I see it all as merely an opportunity for a man without scruples to get rich. Louis pays me handsomely for my work and, if his alliance with James succeeds, I can look forward to becoming a very wealthy man indeed. I have been promised extensive property and land.'

I remembered the Dutchman telling me that he feared England being divided down the middle like an axe splitting a log, and this was what Delaney had in mind. A burning fury was building inside my sore head. 'What are you going to do? Shoot me? I'm tied up and defenceless, but that's just the sort of cowardly thing you'd do, isn't it? Why don't we fight, rapier against rapier? Why don't we see how well you've taught me? Why not let us determine whether I can wield a sword as well as Miss Lucy? How about it, Mr Delaney? Are you up for it?'

I could see he was tempted. Nothing would give him greater pleasure than to run me through with his blade.

'Well, Mr Delaney, shall we fight a fair fight? Or are you scared you'll lose?'

Musket fire outside made Delaney straighten up in alarm. Something was wrong. He knew it and I knew it.

'Hah, I bet Catchpole and Weeks have run into trouble out there,' I taunted. 'I bet your plan has been uncovered. It's over, Mr Delaney. You've lost.'

More musket fire. Someone screamed. Fearfully he looked towards the door.

'They'll be here soon, Mr Delaney. As a spy you'll hang. Untie me and surrender. It's all over.'

'Not yet it isn't,' he hissed. Clenching a gloved fist he swung it and punched me hard on the jaw. My head reeled and everything went black.

I wasn't unconscious long, but when I did come round Delaney had vanished and the warehouse was crawling with Dutch soldiers. I was still tied up and there was something wedged in my mouth.

Someone bellowed orders and I was hastily untied. The cloth that gagged me was unravelled and left draped around my neck. I felt sick and the world seemed unreal, just like the half-sleep when waking from vivid dreams.

'Can you speak, Daniel?'

Through blurred eyes I saw a hooded figure in front of me. I couldn't see his face but I suspected he was the same man who I'd seen watching the Deveraux house. I nodded. 'I think so.'

'Thankfully we have averted a catastrophe. We knew of their planned meeting and were lying in wait. We've had one of Catchpole's and Weeks's accomplices under surveillance for several days, ever since he arrived in Amsterdam. We were all set to strike when your arrival complicated matters. To avoid you getting hurt in the crossfire, I decided to wait until they were all outside the warehouse. I have no idea what you're doing here, Daniel, but an explanation shall have to wait. I must report our success to the Dutch prince at the palace immediately. One of my men shall look after you and return you to the Deveraux household.' He called one of his men over. 'This is Korporaal Jules van Elber. He speaks good English and will see you safely home.' The hooded figure made for the door.

'Who are you?' I asked. 'How do you know my name?'

He hesitated a moment and then turned round and swept back his hood. 'I'm your father, Daniel.'

Chapter Twenty-One

IT was like looking into a mirror but seeing my face twenty or thirty years from now. I instantly had a thousand things I wanted to say, but as I tried to say them the words tumbled out and tripped over one another, making no sense at all.

'We shall talk soon, lad. Once the invasion is over we can become properly acquainted. And I can explain everything.'

'Mother's going to hang,' I blurted out.

He glared at me.

'She was arrested by Lieutenant Thackery and put into Dartmouth gaol. They will take her to stand trial at the Exeter assizes. I have a plan to free her.'

The blood drained from Father's face. 'Dear God, I didn't know. No word of it has reached me.' He seemed lost in thought for a moment, but then stiffened and placed a comforting hand on my shoulder. 'Are you sailing with John Garret, the Dutchman?'

'Yes.'

'Good. Then I know where to find you. We may need his help.'

'I'm sure we can rely on him, or at least some of his crew.' I thought of McLeish, worth a dozen men.

Father nodded.

Korporaal Jules van Elber helped me to my feet and I leaned on him for support as we headed out of the warehouse. Jules was tall but only a few years older than me.

Outside, Father had already departed, heading off with most of the soldiers. Just a few remained, positioned far down the street, standing over the bodies of the men who'd been intent on destroying the Dutch fleet. Our route took us past them.

'It was a close thing,' Jules said to me. 'They almost managed to get away.'

'Oh hell, some of them did!' I shouted, spotting that there were only six bodies. Although still unsteady, I pushed Jules aside and peered at the face of each corpse in turn. I was looking for Catchpole and Weeks – but they weren't among the dead.

Jules caught hold of me and shouted, 'What are you saying?'

'There were two more of them. They're going to scupper the *Endeavour*.'

We ran to the quayside and jetties behind the warehouses and peered out across the harbour. There were ships everywhere, many displaying lanterns. Despite the wind and rain, it looked like the stars had fallen from the heavens. I searched left and right, trying to make out any small rowing boats.

Jules shook his head. 'I can't see them, can you?'

'No. See if you can spot the *Endeavour*. She's the largest warship and should be displaying two lanterns. She'll be moored in the deeper channels.'

Jules pointed. 'Is that her?'

The ship did indeed have two lanterns lit but I could see from her silhouette that she wasn't the *Endeavour*. 'No. Keep looking.'

He pointed again. 'What about that one?'

It was hard to be certain but I reckoned Jules had indeed

spotted the *Endeavour*. She was moored in deep water a good distance away, making her silhouette hard to make out. But I could see no larger ship among the fleet. 'I think that's her, Korporaal. We've got to signal her. Warn her of the danger.'

Jules called out to one of his fellow soldiers. The man nodded and ran off. 'I just hope he can signal her in time and that on board ship they have watchmen with a keen eye. Come, we have done all we can.'

I had a really bad feeling inside and it wasn't just my sore head. The *Endeavour* and all her crew were in peril and I feared Catchpole and Weeks would succeed. I spotted a rowing boat tethered to a jetty and instantly made up my mind. 'I'm going after them. There's a rowing boat over there. Give me your pistols.'

Jules hesitated. 'I have my orders. I must see you home safely.'

'Yes, but not until I know the *Endeavour*'s safe. Give me your pistols. Quickly!'

Jules thought a moment and then nodded. 'You're right. We must try. I'll accompany you.'

We reached the jetty, jumped down into the rowing boat and cast off. Jules was all for rowing, but I insisted I'd be quicker. 'Just point me in the right direction, Korporaal.'

I took hold of the oars and heaved. The flat-bottomed rowing boat felt heavy beneath me as I hauled on the oars, long powerful strokes, and we gathered speed. I could feel the cuts on my hands from the guttering and they began to bleed, making my grip feel tacky. I forced myself to ignore the hurt and rowed even harder.

Jules was no sailor. Unsteady, he gripped the sides of the boat tightly. 'A little to the left, I think.'

'To port, you mean?'

He nodded and I gave the opposite oar an extra-hard pull. 'Is that enough?'

'I think so.'

We surged ahead, and as we reached deeper water a growing swell rocked the boat. Jules looked terrified.

'Don't worry, I know what I'm doing. I've been rowing for years. Keep your eyes peeled. Catchpole and Weeks are out here somewhere.'

With the invasion fleet at anchor we moved between vessels of all shapes and sizes. Twice we collided with anchor chains, twice I cursed, and twice I altered course. The further I rowed out into the harbour, the more our little boat was exposed. The gale whipped the water into a swirling cauldron of a swell, waves breaking over our bow, the rain lashing against our faces. We were blinded and drenched.

I turned to measure our progress – halfway, maybe a little less, hard to tell. I reset the oars and put my back into each stroke. I could feel my hands blistering and the skin on my palms peeling away around the edges of the cuts. I found myself stifling cries with each pull on the oars. Stroke after stroke I heaved. As my lungs burned and my arms grew heavy, my companion could see me tiring.

'We're nearly there, Master Daniel.'

I took another peek over my shoulder and saw the vastness of a hull looming like a great mountain of wood. It was the *Endeavour*. I ceased rowing and let us drift. I peered all around, trying to locate Catchpole and Weeks. Jules produced a pistol from his belt and raised it into the air. I seized his arm. 'No, don't give our presence away. If Catchpole and Weeks are here, we need the element of surprise. Give me your other pistol.'

He handed it to me and we rocked and bobbed as the tide and swell drew us towards the *Endeavour*'s hull. There was no sign of Catchpole or Weeks. I was unsure whether that was good news or bad. Had we beaten them to it, or had they decided on another target? Had they already set the charges and beat a hasty retreat?

We drifted towards the stern; I could hear voices on deck. I placed my pistol in my lap, picked up the oars once more and gently dipped them into the water. With small strokes I quietly rowed us round the stern so we could see the other side of the ship. With my back to where we were heading I waited to see if Jules spotted anything. And no sooner had we turned beyond the stern than his expression changed, his stare narrowing and hardening.

I turned quickly and saw two men in a boat pressed up against the *Endeavour*'s hull. Jules stood up, pointed his pistol and shouted, 'Ahoy! You there, you're under arrest. Place your hands where I can see them.'

I saw a flash, heard a crack, and felt our boat rock. The air filled with splinters, some pricking my face. They'd fired at us and missed, their bullet catching the hull. Jules returned fire. One of the figures slumped. A large wave struck us. Thrown off balance, Jules let out a cry as he toppled overboard and fell headfirst into the water.

He was flailing about, splashing and shouting for help, and I realised he could barely swim. Ignoring his cries, I turned and aimed my pistol. With the boat so unsteady, the shot was tricky. I pulled the trigger, the flint sparked, my pistol flashed and cracked, and spat its lead from the barrel.

To my horror, I'd missed. I hurriedly set about reloading. With Jules drifting further and further away, I tried to ignore his pleas for help, knowing that if I didn't succeed in shooting the second figure in the other boat, we were all likely to perish.

The commotion had alerted the *Endeavour*'s crew. Faces peered over the side. Voices called out and I heard the gruff voice of De Veer demanding answers.

'Ahoy!' I shouted. 'It's Daniel. You're in danger. Over there! They're trying to scupper the ship.'

Having reloaded, I aimed once more and pulled the trigger. As I did so, I saw my enemy's weapon flash too. A searing pain on the side of my head knocked me off balance and I fell backwards into the bottom of the rowing boat. Dropping my pistol, I landed heavily. My whole body seemed to hurt. Gingerly I grabbed the rowlocks and pulled myself up onto my knees. I'd already lost one oar and could do nothing to stop the other one as it suddenly twisted free when yet another wave struck the boat side on. I scrambled about in the bottom to retrieve my pistol.

A deafening volley of musket fire from the ship's deck made me duck fearfully. I looked towards Catchpole's and Weeks's boat and saw only lifeless shapes draped over the side.

'Help me,' Jules spluttered, his voice sounding horribly distant, his pleading snatched by the wind.

I wiped what I thought was rain from my brow, but to my horror quickly realised was blood. I had no idea how badly I was hurt. I looked out across the harbour. There was no sign of Jules and I panicked. Then I spotted him briefly surface from beneath the swell.

'Help me,' he cried weakly again.

I jumped overboard and swam towards him. The cold water stole my breath, chilled me to the bone, and the salt made my hands and head sting as if I'd tumbled head first into a hedgerow of nettles. When I got to where I'd last seen him, he was nowhere to be found. I dived under, frantically searching one way then the other. I came up for breath and dived again. And again. About to abandon a hopeless cause, I bumped into his lifeless body. I grabbed hold of him and dragged him up to the surface.

I yelled for help and several men jumped from the *Endeavour*. Quickly at my side, they guided us towards the hull of the ship and the rope ladders that would see us safely aboard.

'Here, grab one of those ropes, Master Daniel,' shouted De Veer.

About to do so, and with waves lapping about my shoulders, I spotted something odd, a flickering flame in the water close to the stern of the ship. I blinked. It was still there. Then I realised what it was – a keg of gunpowder floating frighteningly close to the hull, a keg with a burning fuse in it. I shouted the alarm and pointed, fearing Catchpole and Weeks were going to succeed after all.

Chapter Twenty-two

MCLEISH dived overboard from the stern of the *Endeavour*, landing with a whale-like splash. He made for the explosives, seized the floating keg and yanked the fuse from it. Judging by the short remains, he'd succeeded within seconds of a blast that would have holed the ship.

On deck, men set to work on Jules. They pressed on his chest and turned him, allowing brine to spill from his mouth. He'd swallowed much and breathed in enough to kill a man, but the crew worked fast to revive him. His lifeless body suddenly twitched, and then he was coughing and spluttering fitfully in a manner that had the crew cheering and welcoming him back to the land of the living.

De Veer and Jacobsen wanted an explanation from me the moment I'd got my breath back. While Anstey worked on my head wound, stitching a sizeable gash in my matted hair, I told of the night's events. It was only as I was nearing the end of my tale that a watchman knocked on the door to De Veer's cabin and reported that a signal had been received, warning us of the danger. Meanwhile, Anstey inspected my hands, pulled a face, and then went off to fetch some bandages and ointment which, I had little doubt, would smell as bad as any of his poultices.

De Veer sank back in his chair and shook his head. 'Mr Delaney's part in all this is wretched. To think we've had a French spy among our ranks all this time and had no idea. I would've trusted the man with my life.'

'And he's still at large, you're saying, Master Daniel,' said Jacobsen. 'He got away from your father and the Dutch soldiers.'

'Yes. I'm surprised he didn't kill me before he fled. He should've too, because if he'd dealt with me no one would be able to prove he was there at all.'

'True, but if it comes to it, it will be your word against his,' De Veer noted.

'Not quite,' I said. I pulled the knotted cloth from about my neck, the cloth Delaney had used to gag me. 'Recognise this? This neck scarf belongs to Mr Delaney, and he used it to stop me from shouting for help.'

Jacobsen nodded. 'That is indeed his. I've seen him wearing it many times. Give it to me, please. It's evidence of his guilt.'

De Veer cursed. 'The scoundrel. Well, I expect we've seen the last of him. But if our paths do ever cross, he'll regret it. We owe you our thanks, Master Daniel. Now, I suggest you get some rest. No doubt the Dutchman shall want to speak to you once he returns to the ship in the morning. And I'll have Korporaal van Elber take a message to the palace. The prince needs to know what has happened here tonight.'

Jules stood on deck, pale and shivering, a blanket wrapped about his shoulders. 'They're going to row me ashore,' he called out, spotting me emerge from a hatchway. 'Thank you. I thought I was going to drown.'

'So did I. And I must thank you for helping me I couldn't have done it alone.'

He laughed and nodded.

'Are you taking part in the invasion?' I asked him.

'Yes. I'll be on the prince's flagship, the *Leiden*. I'm a member of his personal guard.'

De Veer appeared and handed Jules a letter. 'This is my report. Make sure the prince gets it this very evening. He will no doubt want to issue a warrant for Mr Delaney's arrest without delay.'

I waved Jules off and then spotted McLeish near to the bow of the ship.

'That was a close call,' I said. 'You only just removed the fuse in time.'

'Aye, lad, guess I did. You know, I have a bad feeling in my old bones, Master Daniel. If it weren't for you our grand plan would have failed before it had even begun. And I sense the weather has turned against us. The prince is expecting an easy victory, but I fear he may be in for a rude awakening.'

'I hope not.' I felt the burning urge to share my great news. 'I saw my father this evening. First time I'd seen him since I was too young to remember. In fact, until the Dutchman told me his story, I had no idea where he was or whether he was even still alive. Do you have family, Mr McLeish?'

'I did once. But no more, Master Daniel.' He gazed out across the harbour.

'I'm sorry.'

'Not your fault, lad. Famine and plague saw fit to take them.'

'I told Father about Mother's arrest. He was shocked. I said that I have a plan to rescue her and Father said he'd seek me out so we could work together. I said that maybe the crew would help us. Will you help us?'

'Aye, you can rely on me, Master Daniel. But you say your father didn't know of Mary's plight. That's odd. The prince and many others know of her arrest, so why didn't they tell him?'

'Because the prince knew that Benjamin would abandon whatever mission he was on and return to England to save her,' said Jacobsen, approaching us from behind.

McLeish nodded. 'Makes sense.'

'So, Master Daniel, what sort of rescue did you have in mind?'

'Well, I reckon Dartmouth castle's gaol is impossible to break into. And no doubt the prison they'll hold her in at Exeter will be equally impregnable. So that just leaves the journey from Dartmouth to Exeter. I was thinking of some sort of ambush.'

'Do you know the route?'

I shook my head. I'd never been to Exeter.

'I see,' said Jacobsen. 'Then there is much work still to be done regarding this plan of yours. I shall ask among the crew for anyone who knows the road to Exeter and who might be able to suggest the ideal spot. There are one or two brigands among us who once earned a living holding up stagecoaches and the like. They're the ones we should be keenest to seek out.'

'Thank you.'

'Now, I suggest you get some rest. Your face is beginning to swell up and that bruise on your jaw is enough to frighten crabs out of their shells.'

The following morning the Dutchman and Miss Lucy returned to the ship. Both were in a foul mood. They had learned of Delaney's true colours and the attempt on the ship from De Veer's report delivered to the prince at the palace by Jules. By all accounts it had ruined everyone's evening and brought an early end to the celebrations. Delaney never showed up there and Miss Lucy's initial worry that something may have happened to him turned to embarrassment and fury when she learned that she had been nothing more than an entertaining distraction for him.

'Shouldn't go in there, Master Daniel,' advised Jacobsen when he spotted me heading for Miss Lucy's cabin. 'There's nothing like a woman scorned.'

Ignoring him, I knocked and entered. Miss Lucy was pacing her cabin, busy tearing up letters that I presumed had been sent by Delaney at some time or other, confessing his love for her, and which she now understood to be a pack of lies. 'Go away!' she snapped.

'He fooled all of us, you know.'

'Indeed!' She glared at me, her eyes wide and wild.

'I know you are fond of him.'

'*Was* fond of him, Daniel. Past tense. Let me tell you something else too. If I ever set eyes on that little cockroach again, I'll . . . I'll . . . I'll . . .' She picked up her sword and thrust it towards me. 'I'll slice that grin off his face, chop off his ears, and run him through like a pig on a spit.' She began swinging the blade furiously. 'His face will look ten times worse than yours does, Master Daniel.'

I backed out of her cabin and closed the door. Jacobsen was right; now wasn't a good time.

The *Endeavour* was being readied to set sail on the afternoon's tide. The Dutchman stood on the quarterdeck alongside De Veer, his expression like thunder. He bellowed orders at the crew and all feared what would happen if they failed to carry them out promptly.

'Danny, are you coming?' Peter Loodvelt was all set to climb the rigging. 'I've got to keep lookout from the crow's-nest.'

I gazed up at the tall mast and shook my head. 'No, it's alright. You go ahead.'

'Aw, come on Danny. You can help me keep watch.'

'No, really, I'm fine.' I raised my bandaged hands. 'Still a bit sore.'

He grabbed hold of some ropes and swung on them. 'You've never been up there, have you? Don't tell me you're scared.'

'Me? Scared? Never,' I lied.

'Come on, then.'

I thought of that first morning on the *Endeavour* when Cornelius had climbed the mast, and the Dutchman's remark that being in the crow's-nest was like being on top of the world. What the hell. I swallowed my trepidation, grabbed the rigging and pulled myself up to the rope ladders that stretched towards the sky.

'Follow me, Danny. And watch your footing. The ropes are wet and slippery.'

Peter scrambled up like a monkey, confident and fearless. I followed and tried to be as brave, telling myself not to look down, not to think of what would happen to me if I slipped and fell.

The higher we climbed the more the wind blew, the more the ship seemed to be rocking from side to side.

'It's a bit blowy today,' Peter shouted. 'Reckon a storm's coming.'

Up and up we climbed, passing men strung out among the rigging. Higher still until almost all of the ship lay below us.

'This is the hardest bit,' Peter called out. 'Letting go of the ladder and climbing into the nest. It's best just to get on with it and not think about it too much.'

He did it with ease, but it looked a dangerous manoeuvre. I made the mistake of glancing down to see how far I had to fall. The ship looked tiny beneath me. I pressed my eyes shut and swallowed hard. I gripped the rope ladder fearing I was unable to move up or down.

'Don't freeze on me, Danny, or else other men will have to come up here to get you down, and Mr De Veer will have me flogged for encouraging you.'

With a deep breath, and a guiding hand from Peter, I managed to scramble up.

'There, you see. Easy!' Peter looked all around. 'Never seen the like, Danny. So many ships.'

The view was breath-taking. Although we swayed horribly from side to side, I soon forgot about it as masts stretched almost as far as the eye could see, and beyond was the sprawl that was the city of Amsterdam.

'I heard about what happened to you last night,' said Peter. 'Shot in the head, eh! Everyone's wondering why you ain't dead.' He peered at the bruising and swelling on my jaw and then the stitches in my scalp, and pulled a face. 'You look like you've been trampled by a horse. A bleedin' heavy one too.'

'The bullet just grazed me.'

'And they said Mr Delaney knocked you out with a single punch.'

'He got lucky,' I replied, trying to show some bravado. 'I was tied up at the time.'

'Tied up? Suppose there was nothing you could do, then. What about your ear? Did Mr Delaney do that as well?'

'No, that was Mr Weeks. Mr Catchpole had me pinned to the ground. I was a bit dizzy and unable to defend myself because I'd just fallen off the roof of a warehouse.'

Peter gawped in astonishment. 'What were you doing on the roof?'

'Never mind. It's a long story.'

Peter sniggered. 'A lot seems to happen when you're around, Danny.'

'Aye, and much of it ends up hurting like hell.'

He laughed.

'So how come you ended up on the Dutchman's ship?' I asked.

'I ran away from home.'

'Why?'

'My father beat me once too often. I'd had enough.'

'Why on earth did he beat you?'

Peter shrugged. 'I suppose I just got in his way. After an evening's drinking he beat up anybody who got in his way.' He turned and looked into the distance, hiding his face from me, a face I suspected had tears welling up. 'I had nowhere else to turn. This is home now.'

'Last night I met my father for the first time in years. He spies for Prince William. I don't think he'd ever beat me, not unless I did something really bad.' I thought of all the times Cornelius and I had gone filching, and supposed that if Father had been there and found out, then he probably would have given me a hiding, and I'd have deserved it.

'Any news about your mother?' Peter asked.

'No.'

'Word below deck is that you're going to try and rescue her.'

'That's right. That's why I can't wait to get back to England.'

'You're going to need help.'

I nodded. 'Yes, I expect so.'

147

'Then you can count me in.'

The *Endeavour* weighed anchor at three o'clock. Strung out on the rigging, men unfurled her vast sails.

I stood to the left of De Veer on the quarterdeck and looked on as he issued one order after another. The ship's wheel was spun clockwise and I felt the ship turn. The canvas sails snapped, cracked and billowed as they captured the wind. I felt the *Endeavour* surge beneath me.

'Steady as she goes,' De Veer bellowed. 'We have been instructed to lead the fleet into open water, so we mustn't dawdle.'

With my spyglass I surveyed the harbour full of sails. All had begun to move, jostling to find their correct positions in the fleet, the warships spread to offer maximum protection, smaller vessels keeping as close as they dare. Within the hour we were out in the open sea. A stiff gale caused dark clouds to race across the sky and, as dusk fell, it started to rain again.

With orders to light the ship's deck lanterns, McLeish approached the quarterdeck, stomping heavily on the wet wooden steps. 'It's an ill wind, Master Daniel,' he grumbled. 'A mighty storm's brewing and she will cause us much grief before she blows herself out.'

'Take no notice of him,' shouted De Veer.

'I fear we're all going to perish long before we get to England.'

'You speak drivel,' barked De Veer. 'Once you've lit those lanterns go below and make yourself useful.'

As soon as the Scotsman was out of earshot, De Veer turned to me and sighed. 'I fear old McLeish speaks the truth. I sense a storm heading our way too. If the fleet is to avoid being scattered, we're going to need our luck to hold. Do me a favour, Master Daniel. The Dutchman's in his cabin. Ask him to join me on deck.'

I went below and knocked on the Dutchman's cabin's door.

'Enter . . . Ah, Master Daniel. How are you feeling?'

'Not bad, considering. Mr De Veer asked if you could join him on deck.'

'I see. Very well.' He moved as if to rise from his chair, but then slumped back down and beckoned for me to close the cabin door. 'So, you finally met Benjamin last evening.'

'Yes, only briefly.'

He nodded thoughtfully. 'But long enough for you to tell him of Mary's plight.'

'I was surprised he didn't already know, but Mr Jacobsen reckoned the prince withheld it from Father in case he abandoned his mission and headed back to England to rescue her.'

'Mr Jacobsen was right. When Benjamin came to the palace last night to report to the prince, I'd never seen him so angry. He was like a man who'd been betrayed by those closest to him. The prince tried to explain but Benjamin was understandably deaf to reason. I fear their friendship has been strained to the point of breaking.'

'Maybe Prince William can make rescuing Mother his first priority when we land on England's shores,' I said. 'That might renew Father's trust.'

The Dutchman smiled. 'Indeed it would, but the prince has far more important matters to concern him.'

'Then it will be up to us.'

'I agree. I understand from Mr Jacobsen that you were thinking of an ambush somewhere between Dartmouth and Exeter. There are men on board the *Endeavour* who know the roads well and will provide us with guidance. However, our timing may be critical.'

'What do you mean?'

'As far as we know they've not transported Mary to Exeter yet. If the invasion succeeds quickly, the prince can issue the order for her to be released and the matter will be dealt with. However, if there are delays or we encounter fierce resistance, King James may simply issue an execution warrant rather than send her for trial.'

I swallowed hard. 'If he does that, then all is lost. We'll be too late.'

'Yes.' The Dutchman looked thoughtful.

'There's something else, isn't there? Something you've not told me.'

'It may be nothing, but the prince has not heard from Lord Blackfoot for some days now. Lord Blackfoot sends regular reports through diplomatic channels – that's how we've been kept informed regarding Mary's situation and whereabouts. That his communication has suddenly stopped suggests he may have encountered trouble. Still, let's not get ahead of ourselves, or fear the worst. Not yet, anyway.' He rose from his chair. 'Now I mustn't keep Mr De Veer waiting any longer.'

Passing Miss Lucy's cabin, I decided to see how she was. She looked tired and fed up but forced herself to make polite conversation.

'It looks like the swelling's starting to go down, Master Daniel. Soon your head will be back to its normal shape. I suppose it must still hurt, though.'

'Yes, and I think one of my teeth is about to fall out.'

'How horrid. Still, despite all that, I expect you're excited to be heading home.'

'Sort of. It'll be good to be back in England, but there's much still to do, and although I have a plan, the Dutchman's worried that we may be too late.'

'Keep believing, Daniel. Keep believing that you'll succeed, right to the end if needs be. Hope is a powerful thing, you see. It can keep you going even when all seems lost.'

A cannon blast made me jump. 'Are we under attack?'

'Wait.' Miss Lucy listened out intensely and then relaxed. 'No, we're just sending a signal. It must be the bad weather. The Dutchman will want to keep the fleet together. In poor visibility ships can scatter and that could be dangerous.'

When I next ventured on deck a few hours later, the buffeting wind almost knocked me off my feet. I desperately needed some fresh air as the stench of vomit emerging from the lower decks was making me retch, and even covering my nose with a cloth strongly smelling of tar was unable to conceal it. Opening the hatchway, water rushed over my feet. I headed out, slamming the hatch closed behind me.

The *Endeavour's* bow rose and fell in a sea full of wild white horses and mountainous waves. Walking the corridors below had been challenging enough but now, exposed on deck, I had to grip a handrail tightly to avoid being thrown off my feet. The howling wind was accompanied by the constant roar of the sea, a terrifying noise only interrupted by the thunderous crash of waves breaking over the ship. She creaked as she heaved and rolled. I battled my way to the quarterdeck where the Dutchman stood with De Veer, both shouting to one another despite being less than a shoulder's width apart. I joined them and saw that wild look in the Dutchman's eyes.

'My God, it's a foul night,' he cursed.

Another single cannon shot was followed by De Veer raising his spyglass to his eye. He surveyed the seas about us and then shook his head. 'Where are they? Why haven't they responded to our signals?'

It was then I realised that I couldn't see any other ships' lanterns. We'd lost sight of the invasion fleet.

'Shouldn't we turn back?' I shouted.

The Dutchman nodded. 'Yes, before we lose too many ships. But it is up to the prince. He must give the order. No doubt he will take advice from his captain on board the *Leiden*. If he decides to make for shelter back in Amsterdam he'll signal the fleet with three blasts of cannon in quick succession.'

'And if he doesn't?'

'I fear a good many men will perish.'

'Ship ahoy! Ship ahoy! Forward to starboard.'

The cry had come from the crow's-nest. We all squinted to try to make out what the lookout's keen eye had spotted. At first I couldn't see anything through the darkness and rain except the charcoal grey mass of sea and cloud that formed a single smudge. But then, as the ship rode the crest of a wave, lifting and then pitching forward, a faint distant light briefly came into view. Just as quickly it was gone again, swallowed by another wave. Had our eyes been deceived? We all held our gaze in its direction, De Veer struggling to steady his spyglass. And then we saw it again. 'Can you tell which of our ships it is?' I shouted.

De Veer shook his head.

'That's odd. We should have remained ahead of the fleet. I'm surprised to see a ship so far ahead of us,' said the Dutchman.

'She's getting nearer too,' De Veer added. 'I think she's heading towards us.'

'I agree,' the Dutchman replied. 'Sound the alarm.'

Chapter Twenty-three

THE ship's bell rang out.

'Tell Mr Jacobsen to prepare our upper gun deck for action,' the Dutchman shouted to me as I headed below. 'We dare not use cannon closer to the waterline, as in this swell no sooner we'd open the lower gun ports than the ship would be inundated with water. I'll not have us sink through error.'

'Right, upper gun deck only.'

As I hurried down the companionway I spotted Jacobsen emerging from his cabin and relayed the Dutchman's message.

'Come with me, Master Daniel. You can make yourself useful.'

Below decks, men ran to and fro, responding to orders bellowed by McLeish. The upper gun deck, one of three, was being stripped of the hundreds of hammocks that just minutes earlier had been weighed down by men, and mess tables were being hoisted towards the ceiling. Quickly the deck was cleared of everything except the rows of guns. Gun crews, each numbering half a dozen, took up their well-drilled positions and awaited further orders.

'Mr McLeish, are you a man short at any of your stations?' shouted Jacobsen.

'Aye, sir, number sixteen.'

'Master Loodvelt, show Master Daniel what to do. He can deliver the powder cartridges.'

Peter nodded. 'This way, Danny. I'll show you.' He led me to a series of companionways. 'We have to run down these steps to reach the powder magazine deep in the ship. There we have to pick up a cartridge and carry it carefully to our gun station. Don't go dropping it or else one of two things will happen.'

'What things?'

'Either you'll blow us to hell, or you'll make Mr McLeish so angry he'll have you flogged. And another thing, it's best to carry the cartridge under your shirt. That way, if there are sparks flying about, and there always are once we get busy, there's less chance you'll blow yourself up.'

Fearful, I grabbed hold of Peter's arm. 'You mean I'm going to be a powder monkey?'

'Uh-huh. It's an important job. They can't fire the guns without us.'

'Yes, but . . .'

'But what?'

'That's how Cornelius . . . you know . . . lost his sight. His ship got blown up.'

'Then pray it doesn't happen to us. Now, once you've carried your cartridge back to your gun station, you place it carefully into one of the cartridge boxes. Then you stand back and let the gun crew do their work. Best cover your ears when they fire or you'll go deaf. And don't go fetching another cartridge until they've fired the gun, as that's too risky. Ready?'

'I think so,' I lied.

Everyone was in position and the gun deck fell silent. The ship rolled through the swell and we all held onto whatever we could to steady ourselves. Then I felt the ship turning to starboard.

Orders from the Dutchman and De Veer on the quarter-deck were relayed down to Jacobsen by men repeating them at the tops of their voices.

'Aim to disable . . . shoot on the rise . . .'

'. . . mix of shot to be used.'

'Enemy within range in three minutes.'

'Two minutes.'

Jacobsen straightened his tunic. 'Right, Mr McLeish, time to find out how well you've drilled your crews. And let's pray for a swift demise of our enemies.'

McLeish nodded, turned and snarled, 'You all know what's expected of you. No man shall abandon his station unless I give the order, no matter how bloody this gets. There'll be double rations of grog for all once we're done, and a Spanish gold doubloon from the ship's strongroom to each man upon our victory.' He stiffened up and took a deep breath as everyone cheered. 'Powder monkeys!' he yelled. 'Fetch your first cartridges!'

With Peter and a crowd of other boys, I ran along the gun deck, down the companionways and to the magazine. There, each of us in turn received our powder cartridge through a small hatch. I tucked mine beneath my shirt just as Peter did, and then headed back the way we came. Our return was more measured, taking great care not to drop our explosives, especially when climbing the steps. Once back on the gun deck I saw the impatience of my cannon's crew. I wanted to hurry, to impress them, but thought better of it. Gently I placed the charge in the cartridge box and backed away.

McLeish issued more orders. 'Cast loose and run out your guns.'

The crews burst into action, unfastening their cannons,

raising the gun ports, and then, using all their weight and muscle, they pushed their cannons forward.

'Gun captains, prepare to fire,' McLeish shouted.

Each crew had its own man in charge. My cannon crew was led by a bearded old man who looked like he been at sea for a hundred years. 'Elevate and load! . . . Prime! . . . Make ready!' he roared.

McLeish raised a hand. 'Wait for it! Rapid fire on the port side from stern to bow on my command.'

There was absolute quiet on deck. My heart was pounding. I glanced along the row and saw Peter. He'd clasped his hands over his ears so I quickly did the same. The ship lifted and pitched in the storm's swell. Up and down we rocked, rolling heavily to port and then to starboard. I could see McLeish was waiting for just the right moment. He wanted the port side to be well on the rise, the angle perfect for our shot to pepper the upper decks, masts and sails of our enemy. The order had been to disable them, and there was no better way than wreaking havoc with her masts. I held my breath.

'Fire!'

McLeish's command echoed down the gun deck as each gun crew captain repeated the order for his team: 'Fire! . . . Fire! . . . Fire! . . .'

Nothing could have prepared me for the deafening blasts. One after the other the cannons exploded, each thrown back under the force of its charge. They flashed, spewing their shot with bright orange flames and billowing smoke, smoke that was quickly driven back into the ship by the wind. Despite my hands about my ears, my ears rang as if I'd stuck my head inside a church bell. And the *Endeavour* shook too, her timbers shuddering under the mighty roar of our guns.

'Come on, Danny,' Peter shouted. 'Hurry! They need the next cartridge.'

Running as fast as we could and then scrambling down the companionways, we tore towards the magazine. I heard distant crumps of cannon.

'Hear that, Danny? They're returning fire. If it's an English warship we'll have a real tussle on our hands. They're well-drilled. They can fire every hundred seconds, almost as quick as us. And they won't run, Danny. The English never run.'

Clutching my next cartridge I was close to Peter's shoulder as we headed back. As soon as we reached the top of the companionway we were greeted by a mighty explosion and bloodcurdling screams. The enemy's shot had blasted through one of our gun ports, striking down two of its crew and forcing another off his feet. He flew past us in the air, struck the other side of the hull and dropped limply to the deck. Hot metal tore into wood, setting it alight and sending splinters about us like a thousand arrows. Straight ahead of me, another man fell, screaming as blood pulsed from a shattered leg. I froze in horror.

'Hurry up, Master Daniel,' bellowed McLeish. 'Don't just stand there.'

Peter shook me to my senses. I delivered my cartridge and then pressed back against a bulkhead. The gun deck's air was thick with smoke and the smell of gunpowder. My knees were quaking.

'Fire! . . . Fire! . . . Fire! . . .' And the *Endeavour* shuddered as our port-side cannon blasted in turn a second time. More flames. More smoke. And then I was running again to fetch yet another cartridge. I heard our ship being pelted with what sounded like stones, only they weren't stones but red-hot chunks of metal and chain.

When I reached the gun deck once more I could see we'd taken another hit. More men lay dead, others screaming as they bled freely from hideous open wounds. The deck grew slippery underfoot from all the spilled blood, and there were boys with buckets, some chucking sand beneath our feet, others water to dowse the flames. The glowing hot metal shrapnel hissed, adding steam to air already thick with the heat of battle. Gun crews, their skin glistening with blood and sweat, cheered as each of their cannon blasts returned death and destruction towards the enemy.

'Well done, Master Daniel,' McLeish bellowed. 'Keep going. We're not done yet.'

Back and forth I ran. I was trembling with terror at the horror of it all, the deafening blasts, the foul smell of gunpowder and death, and the screams of agony. We took another hit, just as the cannon next to mine was being reloaded, a great ball of flame tearing through the hull. It seemed to hang in the air, glowing orange and red, and from it spat scorching metal that fizzed and pinged as it cut down the entire gun crew – six men dead in the blink of an eye. The blast knocked me to the deck and momentarily stunned me. With McLeish yelling my name, I quickly gathered my wits and tried to get up, but my hands and feet slipped and slithered uncontrollably on a deck now turned into a river of blood.

'Cease fire! . . . Cease fire! . . . Cease fire!'

The ship's cannon fell silent. Smoke hung in the air and I could barely make out the far end of the deck. From this ghostly haze lit by lanterns came the cries and whimpering of wounded men. For a moment nothing seemed to move.

Men stood at their stations, their chests heaving for breath. They were all gazing out through their open gun ports.

I slithered over to where I could see through mine. It was then I saw what damage we had delivered to the enemy. The English warship had lost all three masts and her fallen sails were ablaze along with a good section of her hull. Men were abandoning ship, diving overboard, dropping like stones into the deadly cold swell, some men burning like embers. Still no one on board the *Endeavour*'s gun deck moved. We just stared. And then, without warning, the English ship blew, a fire having reached her powder magazine. The explosion was louder, brighter and more horrifying than I could ever have imagined. And when the blast was done, we could see she had broken into three sections, each heading to the bottom of the sea. It was at that moment everyone around me began cheering at the top of their voices.

'Fasten and secure your guns,' McLeish shouted. 'Well done. Now let's clear up this mess. Master Daniel, help carry the wounded to Mr Anstey's surgeon's station. He's going to be busy with that saw of his.'

Anstey's job was a horrid business. I diverted my eyes each time he announced that a damaged limb was beyond stitching or repair and so had to come off. Strong men held the wounded down, the patients told to swallow a good measure of rum and then bite hard on a piece of whalebone while Anstey wielded his saw. Their screams echoed through the ship, and the horror of it was enough to dampen the crew's celebrations.

Exhausted, I eventually ventured back onto the quarterdeck. The Dutchman was receiving a damage report from Jacobsen.

'Twenty dead, sixteen badly wounded. Our masts thankfully remain intact but two sails are beyond repair. We were lucky.'

The Dutchman nodded grimly. 'My orders to you were merely to disable that English warship, not sink her with the loss of all hands. Still, in these conditions, it can't be helped. We'll do a sweep of the area in case there are any survivors to pick up. Well done, Mr Jacobsen. Issue double grog rations, and pray we don't encounter further trouble.'

'Aye, sir.'

The Dutchman turned to face me. 'Unlike the crew, I do not rejoice in their demise, Master Daniel. They were brave souls, each to a man. The English navy is the finest in the world and I have no doubt that should they have encountered any ship other than the *Endeavour* they would have prevailed.'

The storm continued to batter us throughout the night. From time to time the lookouts shouted that they'd spotted lanterns of other ships, and each time they did so I feared a repeat of the horror I'd been part of. Thankfully they were our ships, and not the English navy.

'Signal about turn, damn you,' De Veer cursed, hammering a fist against the rail in frustration. He'd spotted the prince's ship, the *Leiden*. He issued instructions for her to be signalled with lanterns, demanding to know why the order to return to port hadn't been given. The lack of a response merely redoubled his fury. 'I'm minded to abandon this folly here and now.'

'Stand fast, Mr De Veer. We are under orders and shall not break them,' shouted the Dutchman.

About to head below and get some much needed sleep,

I heard a faint pop quickly followed by two others.

'At last!' roared De Veer.

'Thank God,' said the Dutchman. 'Finally the prince has seen fit to end this madness. Bring her about, Mr De Veer, and let us hope we all make it safely back to Holland.'

Initially I shared their relief, but it was quickly replaced by a growing sense of unease. As I settled down and cursed my aching body, I wondered what it all meant for the timing of the invasion. Would we try again as soon as the storm broke? Would ships be damaged and need repair? If we were delayed, would it destroy any chance I had of reaching England in time to rescue Mother?

Chapter Twenty-four

THE fleet limped back into Amsterdam. Daylight revealed a great deal of storm damage to many ships, especially the smaller supply vessels, and the prince ordered that repairs be undertaken without delay. His flagship, the *Leiden*, was damaged too. It would take almost two weeks to get the fleet shipshape and ready to sail again.

I returned to the Herengracht with Miss Lucy, and judging by the expression on Mr Deveraux's face he wasn't exactly pleased to see me. Ever since the evening of the prince's visit and my ill-judged words about the house one day being in my family's name once more, he had eyed me with a mix of distrust and loathing. He said nothing to me and seemed keen to avoid me at every turn.

Once again I found myself walking the streets at night, and often this took me past the warehouse Father once owned. One evening I saw the clerk, Karl van Keup, emerging from the entrance.

'Working late?' I called out.

Startled, he turned and peered through the dark. 'Who's there?'

'It's me, Daniel Drake. Remember? I came to ask about Father owning this place.'

He relaxed. 'Ah yes, I recall.'

'I saw Benjamin recently,' I said without thinking, quickly fearing that I'd been unwise. Given the clandestine and dangerous nature of his work, Father's whereabouts had to remain secret, just as the prince had told me. I kicked myself for being so indiscreet.

'Hope you found him in good health.'

'Yes. We didn't have much of a chance to talk as he was rather busy.'

'What's his line of business these days? I've not heard his name mentioned among Amsterdam's merchants.'

I bit my tongue, thought a moment, and then replied vaguely, 'Oh, this and that. Not really sure. Mostly he's abroad.' Then I had an idea. 'I want to be a successful merchant one day, just like Father used to be. Only I know little of commerce, and he hasn't the time to teach me. If you could ever spare a few hours, could you tell me a little about what is involved?' It had occurred to me that Karl might be a rich source of information about Father's life, a life about which I knew very little other than what the Dutchman had told me.

'I see. Well, it is a vast subject and I'm not sure I'd know where to begin. Anyway, you need to be able to read and write to even make a start.'

'I can do both,' I said proudly, realising all those hours spent with Miss Lucy and musty old books might bring a reward after all.

'Indeed. I'm impressed.' He caught sight of my face in light emerging from a window and frowned. 'You look as though you've been in a rough fight and one that you appear to have lost.'

'Not exactly. It's a long story.'

'Listen, I'm heading for a nearby alehouse where I eat supper most evenings. If you wish, you can accompany me.'

I seized the chance.

In a busy tavern we found a small table and bench in a corner and, as Karl drank beer and ate bread and soup, he spoke at length about the fluctuating price of sugar and cotton, of the need to strike hard bargains and avoid contracts with clauses that could lead to ruination should a harvest fail. It was so complicated it made my head spin.

I tried to steer the conversation towards Father's companies and what had happened to his great wealth. 'So I suppose Father returning to Amsterdam on a ship without cargo and having lost his sugar plantation's harvest must've led to desperate times. You said you worked for him back then.'

Karl nodded. 'It was amazing how quickly it all changed. Overnight, many men your father respected turned on him. Goodwill vanished. Instead of giving him time to get back on his feet and sort out his problems, many sought to invoke penalty clauses in their contracts with him, knowing that he had no way of fulfilling them.'

'And that led to the seizure of his ship and warehouses?'

'Yes, and all they contained. He had to sell his fine house too.'

'Where does Mr Deveraux fit into all this?'

'Ah! Now that's an interesting story, Daniel. They were great competitors until it all unfolded so badly. Despite their endless commercial battles they always remained on good personal terms. Friendly competitors, you might say. And yet . . .'

'What?'

'Well, there were rumours floating around at the time, rumours that I personally didn't believe. At least, not back then.' He leaned forward and whispered. 'Some said that Mr Deveraux was looking to purchase a sugar plantation

165

in the Caribbean, just like your father had, and his enquiries revealed the growing discontent among the other plantation owners. Benjamin's kindness towards his slaves was frowned upon, you see.'

'So?'

Karl leaned even closer. 'Some say Mr Deveraux was behind the uprising, and that he'd struck a deal with the other plantation owners.'

'What sort of deal?'

Karl shrugged. 'Like I say, I didn't believe any of it. But if it were true, then I suppose the attack on the Oyster Bay plantation was just part of it. With Benjamin ruined, the plantation was sold for a bargain price and to none other than Mr Deveraux. This only served to fuel the rumours, of course.'

I detected a little hesitancy in Karl's voice. 'But what about now? Do you believe those rumours now?'

'I do not wish to, Daniel, but there are matters I confess trouble me somewhat. You see, as well as importing sugar from Oyster Bay, Mr Deveraux trades sugar from many other plantations in the Caribbean and he has done so on terms most generous and profitable for the owners, much more so than any other merchant would offer.'

'So, are you trying to say that what the other plantation owners got in return for raiding Oyster Bay was a favourable trading partner and bigger profits?'

'Yes. And, of course, Oyster Bay returning to being run in a way they approved of, with slaves being treated like, well, slaves! No more treating them kindly or allowing them to rest on the Sabbath. And that avoided trouble and discontent spreading to the other plantations.'

I slumped back against the bench and shook my head. I

thought of the story the Dutchman had told me, of how he'd witnessed his friends and family slaughtered, of how he'd had to wield an axe to save Father from certain death, all the while the cane fields and plantation buildings ablaze. It was a night of unparalleled horror and brutality. Could that rather dull Mr Deveraux, a man whose head was full of figures and contracts, the father of Miss Lucy, have had a hand in such terror?

'Are you alright, Master Daniel? You've gone rather pale.'

'I'm fine. Father was rescued by a man called John Garret. Most know him as the Dutchman. Have you heard of him?'

'Who hasn't? The most feared pirate sailing the world's oceans. Although he's much more than a pirate, of course, and I'm sure our beloved Dutch prince is happy to have him on his side if he is to take on France – and England, of course. Everyone's seen his ship anchored in Amsterdam's harbour. It's been the talk of the city. Such is the Dutchman's reputation, many have begun to believe that Prince William might actually succeed.'

'And do you approve?'

'Most certainly I do. Our livelihoods and freedom depend on it, none more so than Mr Deveraux's, in fact. Two years ago he branched out into trading wine and invested a great deal of his fortune in the venture. It could end up ruining him as King Louis of France recently ordered the seizure of our wine fleet. Many believe Louis has his heart set on invading Holland as well. These are dangerous times for all of us. If the Dutch prince can put an end to our worst fears, then I'll be among the first to drink a toast to him.'

Walking back to the Herengracht, I felt troubled. Something inside me was screaming that the rumours Karl had spoken of were true, and it made me want to hate Mr Deveraux every bit as much as I hated Lieutenant Thackery. And yet, several things didn't add up. Mr Deveraux was looked on kindly not just by the Dutch prince but also the Dutchman, and when Father had instructed Jules to return me to the house his words had contained no hint of malice. Had they dismissed the rumours too? Were they mistaken? Or did they know something I didn't?

I was juggling all these thoughts in my head when I reached the front door. It swung open in front of me and Miss Lucy appeared and called out excitedly, 'There you are, Master Daniel. Come quick, you have visitors.'

She ushered me into the living room and I almost fainted the second I set eyes on his familiar face.

'Cornelius!'

Chapter Twenty-five

MY best friend had not shown up alone. His brother, Edmund, sat warming his hands by the fire. As I gave Cornelius a hug and repeatedly asked what on earth he was doing here, and how did he manage to reach Amsterdam, Edmund interrupted me.

'Cornelius insisted. Making my life a misery, he was. Kept saying to me that you had to know, that you had to be warned. He said that you were his best friend and that being best friends meant nothing unless you are willing to do anything to help each other. My God, we've had a difficult and dangerous journey too. And it's cost me dear. I'm virtually bankrupt. All my shop's profits have gone towards paying for our passage here.'

I let go of Cornelius. 'Warn me of what?'

'Danny, Lord Blackfoot has been arrested by Lieutenant Thackery,' Cornelius began. 'King James even sent extra soldiers to Dartmouth to make sure the arrest warrant was served, and in case Lord Blackfoot mustered his local militia. Lord Blackfoot's in gaol with your ma, Danny. They're both going to the Exeter assizes. A date's been set. The seventh of November. Unless we do something, both will hang.'

'Hell, that's only just over a week away.'

'I know. That's why I came. We heard rumours that the invasion fleet had set sail, and so I thought I'd see you at Edmund's shop in Kingsbridge just as you promised. But then people were saying that the Dutch fleet got scattered in the storm and had to abandon the journey. And I reckoned it was all going to end in you being too late and your ma hanging from a gibbet on Crowbeak Hill. I had no way of getting a message to you other than bringing it myself. I remembered you saying you were staying with Miss Lucy. With the Deverauxs being such an important family here in Amsterdam you were easy to find.'

'Thank you, Cornelius. Thank you for coming here. I had no idea. The Dutchman feared something like this might've happened though, because messages from Lord Blackfoot suddenly stopped reaching Prince William.'

'So, what do we do now, Danny? And have you dreamed up your perfect plan to deal with Thackery?'

Ignoring his question, I looked to Miss Lucy. 'Do you know when the fleet is setting sail again?'

She nodded. 'All being well in three days from now.'

'And do we know whereabouts in England we'll go ashore?'

'No.'

I paced the room. There was so little time. And my rescue plan was little more than a vague idea, wishful thinking even. It was easy to imagine an ambush on the road to Exeter, but actually organising one was a whole different matter. Be positive, I said to myself. Believe, just like Miss Lucy had said, believe that it can happen, as without such hope I had nothing to hold onto.

'We must speak with the Dutchman as soon as possible,' I declared, trying to sound positive and in control. 'There are men among the crew who have said that they will help us. We're planning an ambush. We—'

'Don't forget about me, Master Daniel,' Miss Lucy

interrupted. 'I can be relied upon too, you know. Unless, that is, you think a mere girl will get in your way.'

'No, I'll be glad of your help. Thank you.'

Edmund stared at her, puzzled at her offer.

I explained, 'I too doubted what use Miss Lucy would be in a fight, but then I saw her spar with Mr Delaney, a skilled swordsman, and was astonished to witness her prevail. She hadn't let on that she'd been taught by the finest swordsman in all of Holland. Believe me, there are few who could defeat her.'

Miss Lucy glared at me at the mention of Delaney's name.

Edmund shook his head and sighed. 'I'm just a simple shopkeeper, Danny, you know that. All I want to do is wish you well and get back to my shop.'

'And you shall, Edmund. You'll sail with us on the *Endeavour*. I'm sure the Dutchman won't mind.'

'T . . . t . . . that pirate ship?' Edmund looked terrified.

'Yes, but don't worry, you'll be among friends.' I suddenly had a thought and reached deep into my pocket. 'And I'll not see you go bankrupt simply because you risked everything in doing a good deed. Here, take this.' I removed my gold Spanish doubloon, my reward for fighting on board the *Endeavour*, and pressed it into his hand. It shone in the firelight.

Edmund's eyes widened. 'Is this real gold?'

'Indeed it is. If it isn't sufficient compensation, I'm sure I can persuade the Dutchman to make up the difference.'

Cornelius and I spoke together well into the night, and for most of the following day too. I took him and Edmund around the city I'd grown to know well. I spoke of all that had happened, of Delaney's treachery, of my rescuing the fleet, the demise of Catchpole and Weeks, of me being a powder monkey, and of seeing Father for the first time in so many years. It was good to have Cornelius at my side again. I felt all the stronger for it. In a world where trusting those around you could prove fateful, I knew there was at least one person who could be utterly relied upon.

It came as a huge relief that the fleet set sail on schedule. The wait had tested my patience to the limits and even Cornelius was beginning to tire of my constant worrying. As the *Endeavour* weighed anchor, the prince's ship hoisted colourful flags and fired a volley of shots. He'd abandoned the damaged *Leiden* in favour of another ship, the smaller twenty-eight gun *Brill*. The weather seemed set fair and spirits among the crew were running high.

I was sitting on deck talking with Cornelius, Peter and Edmund when McLeish stuck his head out of a hatchway and shouted, 'Master Daniel, the Dutchman wants to see us both without delay.'

In the Dutchman's cabin stood one of the crew. I'd never spoken to him but I recognised his face from our battle with the English warship. He'd been a gun crew captain at the opposite end of the ship's upper gun deck.

The Dutchman introduced us. 'This is Mr Trelawney, Master Daniel, and prior to a promising career as a pirate on board this ship he made a more than adequate living relieving rich men of their money and valuables by holding up stagecoaches on various highways and byways in the counties of Cornwall and Devonshire.'

'Sounds like just the man we need,' I replied.

Trelawney grinned. 'Aye, Master Daniel, it seems I might be able to offer you some assistance. You want to know if there are any good places between Dartmouth and Exeter to launch an ambush. Well, there are several I know of, and I can point them all out on a map to you. One in particular would serve you well, depending on what resistance you anticipate encountering.'

'I see. Some soldiers, I guess. Can't say how many.'

'Hmmm.'

The Dutchman leaned forward over his desk. 'We must assume from the latest information brought to us by Master Daniel's good friend, Cornelius, that as both Mary and Lord Blackfoot will be transported together, and because King James has sent reinforcements to Dartmouth, we shall face significant opposition on the road. I'd estimate twenty or so experienced soldiers.'

'I see.' Trelawney scratched his stubbly chin. 'In that case the place I had in mind would be perfect. It's not too far from the coast, and offers various escape routes in case you have to beat a hasty retreat. It affords plenty of opportunities for concealment and lies at a point in the road where it twists and turns so you can maximise the element of surprise.'

'Sounds ideal,' replied the Dutchman.

'Thank you, sir. In fact, I was only telling my crewmates about it the other day. It's not far from the market town of Totnes either. It's a road I can guarantee they'll use as there is no alternative. It follows the banks of a river before turning into a wooded area with steep slopes. Pretty much perfect, I'd say, especially as it's the right side of Totnes.'

'What do you mean the right side?' I asked.

'That's easy to reason, lad. They'll change the gaol wagon's horses there just as the stagecoaches do. If you were to ambush them after Totnes, they'd have fresh horses and might outrun you. But get them just before Totnes, when their horses are worn out, they'll not be able to make a dash for it.'

'Quite so. Thank you, Mr Trelawney. Most helpful,' said the Dutchman. 'You're dismissed.' As Trelawney turned to go, the Dutchman added, 'Don't suppose you'd care to join us on this little adventure, would you? Your assistance on the ground would be much appreciated.'

'Thought you'd never ask, sir. Be delighted to. Don't suppose I can bring along one or two others, could I, sir? There's been much talk below deck about a rescue and I know at least three dozen men who have old scores to settle with the English.'

'Put together a list of names, Mr Trelawney, and we'll see.'

Once Trelawney had left, the Dutchman addressed McLeish. 'Totnes is further inland than I'd like, but we'll be guided by Mr Trelawney's advice. Can I leave you to organise those keen to participate and make sure they are suitable for our mission? We don't want any complications from men acting on their own agendas.'

'Aye, sir, leave it to me. I'll sort out some explosives too. A few kegs of powder might assist us.'

'Yes, and we'll need sufficient horses. Find out from Mr Edmund Trotter the precise whereabouts of livery stables located in Kingsbridge. And talk to Miss Lucy, as I know she has family contacts in the area. We need somewhere safe to gather and await the right moment to make our move.'

'Right you are, sir. I'll get onto it straight away.'

'Thank you,' I said to the Dutchman no sooner than McLeish had closed the cabin door behind him. 'But I'm worried. We've so little time.'

The Dutchman nodded in agreement. He held up a piece of paper. 'Until I received this message an hour ago from the prince's ship, I would have judged any notion of an attempted rescue as ill-conceived, foolhardy and downright impossible.'

'Why? I don't understand.'

'You see, Master Daniel, the prince was intending to land on the Norfolk coast two days from now. Even if we encountered little resistance along the way, it would be impossible to get to Devonshire and organise our ambush in time. To have pursued such a mission would have been folly.'

I took the piece of paper he was holding and read it. 'It says here simply that the wind has changed from the south west to an easterly blow.'

'Yes, and do you see its significance?'

I shook my head.

'A south-westerly wind, Master Daniel, was ideal for the prince's initial plan for heading for the Norfolk coast. An easterly will impede our progress, however, causing further delays. Along with the captain of the *Brill* I have persuaded the prince to change his plans. An easterly wind can be used to sail us to the west at a good rate of knots, and the coast of Devonshire offers as good a landing place as any. We'll go ashore at Tor Bay.'

'I see. For once the weather's actually working in our favour.' I felt a warm glow inside. I was starting to believe we really could save Mother. 'Will Father be able to join up with us?'

'I shall make the prince aware of our plans before we go ashore. I'm sure word will reach Benjamin.'

'Good. So now all I have to figure out is a way to get to Lieutenant Thackery.'

The Dutchman's expression darkened. 'Remember what I told you? Be content with our mission to save Mary and leave Thackery to receive justice from the prince once the invasion has succeeded. Do not risk everything, your life even, for personal revenge.'

I swallowed hard and avoided the Dutchman's glare. I turned to leave.

'Wait, I'm not finished with you.' He leaned down and began searching through a small drawer in his desk. Producing an ornate brass key, he then knelt beside his grand wooden chest, the one I'd marvelled at on my first day aboard the ship. 'Let me see your pistols,' he said while fiddling with the lock.

Pulling them from my belt I held them at arm's length so they could be inspected.

'Put them on my desk,' he added, heaving open the lid.

I did as asked.

He cast an eye over them. 'Ah, as I suspected. Those pistols have seen much use and abuse and are like mules, sturdy but of poor breeding. Beyond ten paces, they will have the accuracy of drunken blind men peeing in the wind.' Having opened the chest and reached inside, he stood up clutching a rectangular box fashioned from glowing cherry wood. 'Tell me, what do you think of these?' He carefully lifted the lid to reveal a fabulous pair of pistols.

The light from the cabin's windows glinted off polished metal bearing ornately carved scrolls and depictions of coiled serpents. The black ebony of their grips shone as though few men had ever held them for more than a few seconds. 'They are the finest pistols I've ever seen.'

'Aye, you speak the truth. At fifty paces and with a

steady arm, it would be possible to split an apple with every shot. Here, test their feel and weight.' He lifted them from the box and handed them to me.

Though heavier than the pistols I'd been carrying, they possessed perfect balance and, peering along the barrels, I realised he was right. I'd never seen barrels so straight and true. I offered them back.

'No, they are yours now,' he declared, closing the box firmly. 'Treat them kindly and they shall defend you well.'

I gulped. 'Mine? But these are your pistols. I can't take them.' I placed them carefully onto his desk and took a step back.

He picked one up and held it tightly. 'Aye, these are mine. They were given to me on the day I no longer had to bear chains and no longer had to cower before other men. And it was the man who gave me my freedom who gave me these great pistols.'

Father! I reached out and picked one up again.

'Trust me, Master Daniel, I am certain Benjamin would approve of my gifting them to you. After all, he would not forgive me should I stand by and let you meet with your destiny without the proper tools to succeed. Take them. Think of it as a reward for saving the *Endeavour* in Amsterdam's harbour.' He placed the box back into the chest and set about securing the lock.

'Are you sure?'

'Yes. First they were Benjamin's, then they were mine, and now they are yours. Use them for what Benjamin intended, to defend those you love.'

Tucking the pistols proudly into my belt, I suddenly felt six inches taller.

Chapter Twenty-six

PASSING Dover on the English coast caused great excitement on board. We gathered on deck to witness the spectacle, hundreds of vessels cramming the sea and all with their sails set. Cannon boomed and then cheers and whoops of delight rang out.

'What's happening? Has the battle started?' Cornelius shouted in alarm.

'No, it is merely a celebration,' De Veer replied. 'We are entering the English Channel and are at its narrowest point. To port you can make out Calais, to starboard Dover. Our armada's so great that some ships lay barely one league from the chalk cliffs of England, while others are but one league from the sandy beaches of the continent. The Dutch prince issued the order to greet both the English and French coastal fortresses simultaneously with ceremonial shots.'

'Why?' asked Edmund.

'Just letting them know that we mean business!'

We sailed west. Lookouts maintained a keen eye on the horizon for any sign of the English fleet but saw nothing.

When it came to Peter's turn in the crow's-nest, Cornelius leaped at the chance to accompany him. I still reckoned he was mad as he couldn't see anything once he got there, and he risked his life climbing the rigging. Edmund looked on in terror, and cursed that his younger brother failed to heed his warnings. I spotted Miss Lucy alone near to the ship's bow. A question had been nagging away at me ever since

I'd spoken with the clerk, Karl van Keup. It was an awkward question and I wasn't quite sure how to ask it. She was gazing out to sea and looked deep in thought.

'I can't get over how wrong I was about Mr Delaney,' she said, without turning to greet me. 'I always thought myself a good judge of character. Now I feel I don't understand anything anymore.'

'Can I ask you something?'

'Yes, as long as it's not about that swine.'

'No, it's not about him. It's about your father, or rather both our fathers.'

She cast me a glance and nodded.

'When I was in Amsterdam I got talking to a clerk at that warehouse Father used to own, and which now belongs to your father. He told me a bit about what happened when my father returned from the Caribbean a ruined man.' I hesitated as I was getting to the really tricky bit. 'He said there were rumours at the time that your father might have had something to do with the attack on Oyster Bay.'

'What? How ridiculous. Although I was much younger back then, I know of those rumours and they were put about by men who'd see my father ruined too, just like yours, Master Daniel. Who was this clerk you spoke to?'

Not wishing to get Karl into trouble, I ignored her. Instead I pursued my questioning. 'But your father did acquire Oyster Bay at a knock-down price afterwards, didn't he?'

'That was just good business. Anyway, Father was here in Amsterdam at the time. No way could he have been responsible.'

'Oh, I see. It was just that—'

'Just what?' Miss Lucy snapped irritably.

'Well, this clerk didn't believe the rumours either, not back then. Now, though, he's less certain.'

'Why?'

'Because the other plantation owners have contracts with Mr Deveraux for transporting and trading their sugar on terms that greatly increase their profits, terms that the clerk says they wouldn't get from anyone else.'

'I don't understand. What are you saying?'

'That such good terms were part of some sort of bargain. In return for enabling Mr Deveraux to obtain Oyster Bay cheaply, the other plantations owners were guaranteed both good profits and an end to the favourable treatment of slaves that they feared would spread unrest to their properties.'

'Dear God,' Miss Lucy hissed, 'why do some men have such evil tongues? This is all nonsense. I'll hear no more about it. Understand? I'll not have anyone speak badly of Father.'

I heard a whistle blow and looked up. From the crow's-nest Cornelius yelled down, 'I kept your whistle for you, Danny. I kept it safe.' He blew it again.

'Thanks, but you keep it for now,' I called back.

'Mr McLeish spoke to me about the plan to rescue your mother,' Miss Lucy said, changing the subject. 'I have an uncle who owns a fine manor house at a place called Buckland not far from Kingsbridge. So, once ashore, we can return Mr Edmund Trotter to his shop in Kingsbridge and then make for my uncle's home. Mr McLeish reckons it is better that Cornelius stays with his brother than accompany us on our mission. He fears the boy will get in the way or hurt in crossfire.'

McLeish was right, of course, but my best friend

wouldn't see it that way. Cornelius was determined to be at my side, and I figured that if he could make it all the way to Amsterdam to deliver a message to me, then he'd earned the right to be included in our scheme. I'd look out for him, just as he looked out for me.

The following morning I caught my first glimpse of Tor Bay through my spyglass.

De Veer ordered more colourful flags to be hoisted, and all the other ships in the invasion fleet did likewise. I stood with Peter and Edmund and described the incredible spectacle to Cornelius. 'Hundreds of flags, Cornelius. All different colours. It looks more like a regatta or pageant than an invasion.'

Peter pointed towards the cliffs. 'Look over there. What are all those people doing?'

I swung my spyglass round and focused it on the jagged rocks of Berry Head. 'There are hundreds of them. Some are even waving to us. Don't they realise we've come to invade England?'

Instinctively we all waved back.

'A most incredible scene,' said the Dutchman, climbing onto the quarterdeck. 'Prince William has waited so long for this day to arrive. And it appears he isn't the only one.'

'Why aren't they afraid?' I asked.

'Some probably are. Many, though, will know that we come in peace, to save England from King James's perilous notion of stronger ties with France's King Louis.'

'I've been thinking about that,' I said, 'and I reckon it's a lie.'

The Dutchman frowned. 'What on earth makes you say that?'

'I've never heard the Dutch prince say anything about

saving England or its Parliament. All I've heard from his lips is his desire to possess the English army and navy, and using it to defend Holland against the French.'

'There is much truth to what you say. Defending Holland is indeed the prince's main objective. But it is not the only one. And don't forget the "Seven", those Englishmen of great influence who have helped bring today about. For them, the protection of their country's Parliament and church is indeed what this invasion is for, and nothing more.'

Peter was listening intently. 'It's like killing two birds with one stone, isn't it?'

The Dutchman smiled. 'Indeed it is, Master Loodvelt. Ah! I see the *Brill* has raised the prince's flag.' He pointed.

Squinting, I tried to make out the wording but realised it wasn't in English. I tried to read it aloud.

The Dutchman interrupted me. 'It says, more or less: "I will uphold liberty and religion". And the white flag flying above it indicates he's come in peace, although the red one below warns that he'll go to war with any who opposes him. So, you see, Master Daniel, the prince has more than simply defending Holland on his mind. He wants every Englishman and woman to know of his good intentions.'

'What happens now?'

'He'll go ashore. It'll be interesting to see what kind of welcome he receives.' The Dutchman signalled to De Veer. 'The fleet will be heading much closer to the coast. We'll hold off and patrol the perimeter. Once we're certain that the prince has landed and secured the beach, we'll head west.'

'Aye, sir.'

The prince's ship made for inshore waters while surrounded by dozens of smaller boats, each containing soldiers readying their weapons. The boats seemed to swarm and jostle to maintain a protective cloak about him. Frequently they moved so close to one another that I reckoned you could jump from ship to ship. Through my spyglass I saw a mix of different uniforms, and I saw men of pale skin, of olive skin, and even black men. 'There are slaves in our army,' I shouted in astonishment. I looked to the Dutchman, anticipating his anger, but he remained calm.

'The prince has mustered an army of men from many lands,' he replied, pointing to a gaff-rigged boat some hundred yards to port. 'There are mercenaries aboard that one. At a guess, I'd say Swiss, Swedes and maybe a few Poles. And see those men in bearskins?' He pointed to another ship. 'They're Finlanders. Always up for a good brawl. And yes, I expect there are indeed slaves among them. A few may even have been promised their freedom if they fight with loyal courage.'

Jacobsen spotted the *Brill* signalling the fleet. 'They're landing at Brixham on schedule. He'll go ashore once the advance party has secured the area.'

'Excellent,' the Dutchman shouted. 'Mr McLeish, sound the bell and have all gun decks put on standby. I do not expect trouble, but you never can tell.'

Climbing a few feet up the rigging, I watched the final preparations with Cornelius and Peter. Soldiers headed ashore in a stream of rowing boats. With bated breath we waited for the first shots to ring out, for men to fall, for the battle to begin.

'Can't hear a thing, Danny. What's happening?' asked Cornelius.

'Nothing. Our rowing boats have reached the beach and men are climbing out and mustering. Nobody's fired a single shot.'

'Maybe Thackery's running scared, Danny. Maybe he's run to his castle in Dartmouth, shut the door and bolted it. Probably hiding under a table by now.'

'Aye. Probably seeing us here made them scarper like rabbits down their burrows,' Peter added. 'No man in his right mind would dare to raise his musket if he knew the *Endeavour*'s cannon were pointing straight at them.'

I was puzzled. 'I can't see any English soldiers anywhere. It can't be this easy, surely?'

'Ah, but they didn't expect us to land here, did they?' said Peter. 'Right at this very minute there are probably hundreds of English soldiers standing on the beaches of Norfolk, scratching their heads and thinking, where the hell are they?'

'Hang on a minute,' I said. 'Something's happening.' I raised my spyglass to my eye again. 'Prince William's climbing down into a barge. He's going ashore.'

Stood proudly if a little unsteadily on his barge while men heaved on oars, the prince made for the beach.

'Ha!'

'What, Danny?' Cornelius grabbed my arm. 'What's happening?'

'The tide's out. The prince's boat has run aground.'

Cornelius sniggered.

'Wait! Now he's waving his arms. He wants all those people on shore to come down to the water's edge.'

'What for, Danny?'

'Don't know. This is amazing. He's addressing the crowd. He's making a speech. Wish we could hear him. What on earth can he be saying?'

Peter roared with laughter. 'Probably something like: "Ahoy, there. I'm rather keen on invading your country but I'd rather not get my feet wet."'

Now we all roared with laughter.

'My God, Peter, I think you're right. A fisherman's wading out towards the prince's barge . . . Now he's shaking his hand . . . And now the prince is climbing onto his back . . . The man's carrying the prince ashore.'

'This has to be the strangest invasion ever,' said Cornelius. 'Or are you making all this up just to tease me, Danny?'

'No, Cornelius. I'm not making any of it up. The Dutchman once told me that he hoped it would be peaceful like this. I reckoned he was mad. But . . .'

'It's early days, Danny,' said Peter. 'He's got to make it all the way to London. I doubt his journey will be all plain sailing. I reckon as soon as word reaches King James, every soldier and militia will be on the alert.'

As the sun set I ran below to get ready to go ashore. Not looking where I was going I bumped into the massive belly of McLeish.

'What's the hurry? Not being chased by a pretty girl, are you?'

'No, I'm going to fetch my old pistols. I left them in the Dutchman's cabin. I told Peter he could have them. He needs something to fight with.'

'Did you now? And has Mr De Veer given young Master Loodvelt permission to go ashore?'

'I don't know. Does he need it?'

'Aye. Leave it to me. I'll have a word. I'll say I need someone to help me carry the powder kegs and that one of the ship's powder monkeys has volunteered.'

'Thank you. How many men have we got?'

'Mr Trelawney came up with forty names of men keen to go ashore but a good many may cause us more trouble than they're worth. Many have their own scores to settle, you see. I've narrowed it down to twenty, including Mr Trelawney. Then there's the Dutchman and Mr Jacobsen, Miss Lucy, Master Loodvelt and your good self.'

'And Cornelius.'

'Is that really wise? Better we drop him off at Kingsbridge with his brother, Edmund.'

'No. I insist. If it wasn't for Cornelius coming to Amsterdam to warn me, we'd probably have arrived too late.'

'Well, let us hope the Dutchman agrees. I just pray we have enough men.'

'You forgot to include yourself in your reckoning.'

'Aye, suppose I did.'

'And you're worth a dozen men.'

McLeish grinned. 'Maybe two dozen with my powder kegs.'

Chapter Twenty-seven

THE *Endeavour* dropped anchor between Prawle Point and Bolt Head, as close as we dared to the craggy shore. Three of the ship's largest rowing boats were readied for our trip to Kingsbridge, each having four sets of oars. Jacobsen mustered everyone involved in our mission on the main deck and we waited for the Dutchman.

A pot of dark grease was passed around and we were all instructed to blacken our faces and hands. Our boats would need to be rowed as silently as possible and without lanterns lit or voices raised. To get to Kingsbridge we had to pass the fishing village of Salcombe and we needed to do so without being seen.

The Dutchman emerged from below and spoke to De Veer. 'The *Endeavour* is under your command now. Keep her well offshore and return here on tomorrow evening's tide. If we do not make it back, sail along the coast and return again the following evening. If there's still no sign of us, say a prayer for our souls and re-join the rest of the invasion fleet in Tor Bay.'

'Aye, sir.'

Armfuls of muskets were lowered into the boats, followed by McLeish's small kegs of gunpowder and a sack of fuses. Then we climbed down the rope ladders, settled into our boats, set our oars and made for the coast. I rowed with McLeish, Jacobsen and Peter, our boat also carrying the Dutchman, Cornelius, Edmund and Miss Lucy.

A favourable tide drew us in and within the hour we could see lights from the huddle of fishermen's cottages that made up Salcombe to our left. We altered course and rowed to the other side, towards land that possessed fewer buildings and hopefully fewer prying eyes. Our oars made barely a sound.

When a tavern door opened and laughter spilled out, we froze mid stroke. The laughter carried across the water, sounding much nearer than it actually was. Anxiously we stared at the commotion. Someone came out, shouted something to those inside and then staggered off along the street. My heart was racing. If he saw us, he'd raise the alarm. But the man seemed drunk and unsteady. He vanished round a corner. I breathed a sigh of relief.

For an hour we rowed on until the Dutchman ordered us to ease off. We lifted and rested our oars. Not a moment too soon either as my hands had grown sore again beneath the bandages. He surveyed our surroundings and then pointed. 'It isn't safe to go any further. We'll go ashore there and conceal our boats as best we can. Mr Trotter, am I right in thinking that from here it is just a short walk into town?'

'Yes,' Edmund replied. 'There's a disused boathouse over there. You can conceal your boats inside it. No one will ever know.'

'Excellent.' The Dutchman signalled to the other boats and we made for the shore.

With our boats well hidden, the muskets were distributed among the crew. Despite the late hour, in the distance we could hear a church bell ringing and it put everyone even more on edge. We all knew what it meant. The law of the land demanded that bells be rung in the event of an invasion to warn everyone to be on their guard.

The Dutchman took Edmund to one side. 'We must part company now. You cannot be seen with us. Wait here with Cornelius and give us about ten minutes' head start before you return home to your shop. We shall skirt around the edge of town and pray our presence goes unnoticed. Here, take this.' The Dutchman pressed a small purse into Edmund's hand. 'There is enough gold to reimburse you for your trip to Holland and a little extra to express the Dutch prince's gratitude. Had you not made the trip, Mary Drake and Lord Blackfoot would almost certainly have perished. It is down to me and my men now to see if we can save them from the gallows.'

Cornelius had overheard and protested, 'I'm not going with Edmund. I'm staying with Danny.'

The Dutchman's mind was made up, and even my pleas fell on deaf ears.

'You all go on ahead,' I suggested. 'I'll walk home with Edmund and Cornelius and then catch you up.'

Once beyond the Dutchman's earshot I intended speaking to Cornelius of our oath to exact revenge against Lieutenant Thackery. I reckoned he'd be satisfied with that.

'Very well, Master Daniel. The livery stables lie at the very top of the High Street. Meet us there. And do not loiter at Mr Trotter's shop because we must not remain in town a minute longer than necessary.'

Kingsbridge High Street rose steeply from the riverbank. Candlelight glowed from the windows of the church. I suspected a good proportion of the townsfolk had turned out to pray, but were they rejoicing or were they fearful? I couldn't tell. What also struck me as we made for Edmund's shop, Trotter's Emporium, was that the streets were deserted.

'Ah, home at last,' Edmund declared as we reached a small side door.

Cornelius had barely said a word during our walk. 'It's not fair, Danny. I want to help you save your ma,' he complained. 'Anyway, why should I take orders from the Dutchman?'

'I know,' I replied. 'It does seem unfair. But tomorrow we're anticipating that Mother and Lord Blackfoot will be accompanied by a lot of soldiers, and it may prove quite a battle to free them. We'll have our work cut out and you'd be in great danger. I might not be able to protect you.'

'I don't need protecting, Danny.'

'Listen, I'll return within a day or so to collect you. Don't forget, we have to deal with Thackery. The Dutchman won't help us with that as he doesn't approve. So it'll be up to you and me.'

'Shush!' Edmund whispered. He'd spotted two soldiers heading up the street. 'Quickly, come inside.'

Edmund lived above his shop. We climbed a steep narrow staircase to reach another door. It opened just as Edmund reached it and his wife, Anna, flung her arms about him and sobbed loudly.

At first I thought her outburst was simply her relief at seeing Edmund's safe return, but that thought was quickly shattered.

'They came two days ago. Soldiers from Dartmouth's garrison. Thackery's men. They wanted to know where Cornelius was. They said he wasn't in any trouble, but that they were after a friend of his. When I said Cornelius wasn't here and I didn't know any of Cornelius's friends, they turned nasty and searched everywhere. They threatened me. They said if I didn't tell them where you were, they'd come back another time, arrest me and confiscate everything in the shop. They said we were all guilty of treason and would hang. But I told them nothing.'

'It's me they're after,' I said. 'Thackery must have finally found out that my best friend from Cotton Lane had a brother in Kingsbridge. I'm sorry. It's my fault.'

Edmund was distraught. 'I knew getting involved was too dangerous. I have a young family.' He began pacing the room, tearing at his hair. 'They're bound to return. What then?'

'Is there anywhere you can go? Somewhere Thackery would never think of looking. Just until it's all over.'

Edmund shook his head.

'In that case it's too dangerous for Cornelius to remain here. He'll have to come with me,' I said.

Neither Edmund nor Anna protested and Cornelius was delighted. I, however, felt only trepidation. Thackery was closing in on us. Fearing the shop was being watched I moved to a small window and glanced furtively up and down the street.

And then I was struck by an awful thought. When Cornelius arrived in Amsterdam with the news that a date had been set for Mother's move to Exeter, he'd also talked of rumours about the invasion fleet, and of how it had been forced back to Holland because of bad weather. What worried me was that if ordinary folk like him knew about it, then so must King James, Thackery and just about everyone else in England. Had King James panicked and brought forward Mother's trial date? Were we too late after all? I turned to Anna and asked if she knew.

Wiping away her tears, she shook her head. 'They're taking her to Exeter tomorrow, just as Cornelius told you.

Soldiers have even put up posters here in Kingsbridge, inviting folk to come and watch Lord Blackfoot and your mother being paraded through the streets of Dartmouth when they depart. And they speak of a great day of celebration to be held at Crowbeak Hill should Judge Jeffreys sentence them both to hang. And he surely will.'

Edmund shook his head. 'Turning it all into such a spectacle is enough to make my stomach turn. It's incomprehensible.'

'Unless . . .'

We all turned to Cornelius. 'Unless what?' I asked.

'Unless they're hoping we'll try to rescue them. They know Lord Blackfoot and your ma are important, Danny. They know the Dutch prince and the Dutchman won't stand by and do nothing. Maybe it's a trap!'

Chapter Twenty-eight

'I thought I said—'

Despite the Dutchman's wild-eyed anger, I wasted no time in explaining why I'd brought Cornelius with me to the livery stables and that my friend reckoned we might be heading into a hornet's nest of trouble.

'He might be right,' Jacobsen offered. 'Given that we foiled their attempt to scupper the fleet in Amsterdam and that a number of King James's spies have been killed, including Catchpole and Weeks, I wouldn't put it past that scheming Lieutenant Thackery to dream up such an audacious plan. And maybe King James figures that seizing the Dutchman and key members of the *Endeavour's* crew, and possibly Master Daniel's father into the bargain, is well worth chancing.'

The Dutchman shook his head. 'It all seems too far-fetched to me.'

Miss Lucy wasn't convinced by our talk either. 'If I were King James I wouldn't place responsibility for such an important mission in the hands of an oaf like Lieutenant Thackery. I'd want one of my most experienced and reliable men.'

'I agree,' said the Dutchman. 'Still, even if it were true, it changes nothing. We proceed as planned.'

We rode through the night across country, Miss Lucy guiding us towards the manor house at Buckland. It proved to be remote and surrounded by woodland, the perfect place to hold up for the night. Better still, her uncle, the lord of the manor, was sympathetic to the Dutch prince's cause and even more so to our determined efforts to rescue Lord Blackfoot. We received a warm welcome.

'See that the horses are properly tended to,' Jacobsen instructed one of our men. 'We need them to be well rested and in good shape by dawn.'

'Aye, sir.'

'Mr Trelawney, I need you to brief us on our place of ambush so that we might be fully prepared,' said the Dutchman.

In the manor house's great dining hall, we assembled and listened to Trelawney describe his chosen spot in great detail. I marvelled how he did so from memory, even down to the positions of trees and their distance from the winding road. When some began to question this he took great delight in reminding us all that a highwayman's life depended on knowing every inch of his place of work.

With a vivid picture painted in our heads, the Dutchman went about assigning tasks. There'd be advance lookouts along the road. Groups of us would be hidden, positioned among bushes, behind rocky outcrops, and up on the hillside. McLeish would place gunpowder at the base of two large beech trees. Setting the charges off would fell the trees so that they blocked the road in front of and behind the gaol wagon. Our target would have no escape.

'We can't fail,' Peter whispered to me. 'It's the perfect plan.'

The Dutchman instructed us all to get some rest. We'd be leaving at the crack of dawn.

Trelawney settled among the group of volunteers from the *Endeavour* and seemed to relish being centre stage, recounting many of his escapades as a highwayman in tales that I had little doubt were exaggerated for the benefit of his audience. Peter and Cornelius joined them. I noticed that the Dutchman and Miss Lucy had retired to another room with Lucy's uncle, so I sought out Jacobsen and McLeish, who'd ventured outside. They stood talking in the cool night air. They heard me approaching and by the way their conversation broke off I had the distinct feeling I'd interrupted a private discussion.

'You should get some sleep,' Jacobsen remarked.

'Can't, my head's buzzing about tomorrow. Am I interrupting? Tell me to go away if I am.'

'No, lad, it's fine,' said McLeish. 'We were just talking about what Master Cornelius said to you. You know, about the possibility of a trap awaiting us.'

'It's probably nothing,' I replied. 'Cornelius always worries too much about everything. Always has. Anyway, like the Dutchman said, it changes nothing. And I was thinking about it just now. I suppose that although it's possible, it is one hell of a long shot for King James or Lieutenant Thackery to take. I mean, they didn't even know that we'd come ashore in Devonshire, let alone near enough to mount a rescue in time. The more I think about it, the more I think the whole idea is far-fetched, like the Dutchman said. Don't you agree?'

McLeish shifted uncomfortably. 'Actually, we don't.'

'Why?'

Jacobsen explained. 'There was much talk below decks on the *Endeavour* about mounting a rescue attempt. And Mr Trelawney, although being a trustworthy fellow, does rather like to speak loudly and often about his previous business. I believe over many an evening's grog ration he has told anyone who'd listen that he's the man to consult over the ideal place to mount an ambush anywhere in the south-west of England.'

'So? I don't understand.'

'Well, lad, think about it,' said McLeish. 'Setting a trap would make perfect sense if the English knew that we were planning an ambush.'

'How could they? We were at sea.' Then I thought of Catchpole and Weeks and shuddered. I spoke their names. 'Do you think it was their doing? Once they'd been flogged and sent ashore by the Dutchman?'

'Possibly. They had the opportunity. But we were thinking of someone else.'

They both stared at me, expecting me to figure it out.

I realised who they meant. 'Of course! Mr Delaney.' I swallowed hard. 'Oh no, it was Delaney who suggested an ambush to me in the first place!'

'Well, well, well. You have to give the man credit where credit's due. I've never had the misfortune to meet anyone more devious.'

'Aye,' said McLeish. 'Or dangerous. After his escape in Amsterdam, we must assume he's either managed to get a message to someone over here in England or, God forbid, he's actually here too. And if he is here, the danger is all the more real. We must speak with the Dutchman right away.'

Chapter Twenty-nine

WITH a fresh horse provided by Miss Lucy's uncle, one of the crew was immediately sent on an errand. The Dutchman's orders were simple. He had to ride to Dartmouth. There he was to mingle with the crowds in the morning and observe Mother and Lord Blackfoot being paraded through the town. He was to count the number of soldiers escorting the gaol wagon and then ride like the wind to furnish us with the information.

Just before dawn two further men were dispatched. I saw them ride off at breakneck speed. They would scout the road ahead and be on the lookout for any signs of an ambush being set against us.

Miss Lucy placed a foot in the stirrup of her mount. She lifted herself into the saddle and gathered the reins, her expression a mix of anger and determination. I reckoned she was hoping that we'd encounter trouble, and that such trouble included a certain Mr Delaney – she had the look of the huntress about her. 'Are you ready, Master Daniel?'

Reaching down, I gave Cornelius a hand. He clambered up and settled behind me on my horse. 'As ready as we'll ever be,' I replied. 'Hang on tight, Cornelius.'

We rode steadily through the morning, sometimes on the road, sometimes across country. Approaching a crossroads where we joined the main road to Totnes a rider hidden among some trees burst out and blocked our way.

He called out a greeting. It was the man the Dutchman had sent to Dartmouth to witness Mother and Lord Blackfoot being paraded through the streets.

'What news?' shouted Jacobsen.

'Hundreds of townsfolk turned out this morning. They behaved as you might expect, jeering and pelting the gaol wagon with rotten fruit. Although it must be said the soldiers received their fair share. It almost got out of hand at one point. The gaol wagon was accompanied by a dozen mounted soldiers led by Lieutenant Thackery.'

The Dutchman frowned. 'I'd expected a larger escort.'

'I've more to report, sir. Thackery led the wagon up the hill out of Dartmouth. But then they stopped and I was able to see the full extent of their dastardly scheme.'

'Go on.'

'Waiting for them was a substantial force. I counted ninety mounted soldiers, and I reckon they are battle-hardened troops sent from the garrison at Exeter.'

That made over a hundred men in total, I realised. We were vastly outnumbered. My heart sank.

'I didn't hang around. I reckon they'll ride a short distance behind the gaol wagon and its escort. Just out of sight. They'll probably make their move at the first sign of trouble.' He glanced up at the sun. 'I'd estimate we are about half an hour ahead of them.'

'Was Mr Delaney among them?' Miss Lucy asked.

'Didn't see him, miss.'

She looked disappointed.

The Dutchman turned in his saddle. 'Mr Trelawney, did you catch all of that?'

'Aye, sir.'

'Any suggestions?'

Trelawney shrugged. 'The odds are stacked against us, Captain. I had not anticipated so many.'

'Do we turn back?' asked McLeish. 'We've come this far.'

I felt fearful. If we gave up now, we'd not be able to stop Mother reaching Exeter. And not knowing how long it would take Prince William to secure a complete victory, seize power and be in a position to order Mother's release, I was beginning to realise that maybe saving her from the hangman's noose might not be possible, after all. But I refused to give in so easily. 'I don't care how many of them there are. Let Thackery bring a thousand soldiers. I'm not giving up now. Even if I have to stand in their way alone armed only with Father's pistols, I shall do so.'

'Brave words, lad,' muttered McLeish, 'but foolhardy ones.'

'Don't worry, Master Daniel,' said the Dutchman. 'You'll not have to stand alone.' He called out to our messenger, 'You know what to do.'

The messenger nodded, swung his horse round and set off at the gallop.

The Dutchman turned to address me. 'They aren't the only ones capable of devising dastardly schemes, Master Daniel.' He stiffened in his saddle. 'We ride on.'

'What do you think he meant?' asked Peter as he rode alongside Cornelius and me.

I had no idea.

'Maybe he'll use Mr McLeish's gunpowder to blow them all to hell,' Cornelius suggested.

Peter grinned.

'And you heard what our messenger said, Danny,' Cornelius added excitedly. 'Thackery's with them. The time to seek our revenge has come.'

'Yes, Cornelius. Today is the day we fulfil our oath spoken on Tobias's grave.' I tightened my grip on the reins and dug my heels into my mount.

Chapter Thirty

NEARING our planned ambush site the road descended into a deep valley and followed the meanderings of a shallow but fast flowing river. Our two scouts returned and said they had nothing untoward to report.

We crossed a stone bridge and quickly left the river behind. The road snaked into steeply sloping woodland, the leafless branches of great beech trees and ancient oaks leaning and reaching out above our heads. Trelawney galloped to the front and called out to the Dutchman, 'The spot lies just beyond the next bend.'

We drew our horses to a stop and dismounted. Everyone spent a few moments studying our surroundings. Trelawney's memory of the place had been almost perfect. The road narrowed and there were two huge beech trees that once felled would render the road impassable.

The Dutchman issued orders. 'Mr Galbraith, retrace our steps to the bridge and act as lookout. Return as soon as you spot the gaol wagon. The rest of you, get our horses out of sight and then check each of your weapons. When the time comes every shot must count. Mr McLeish and Mr Jacobsen, a word in private, if you please.'

Sensing my nervousness Miss Lucy placed a hand on my shoulder. 'Don't worry, Master Daniel, I'm sure it will all turn out alright. We'll soon set Mary free.'

Cornelius suddenly froze. I knew he was listening out

and had heard something the rest of us hadn't. 'What is it? Can you hear them coming?'

'Not sure.' He lowered his head slightly and then shook it. 'No, a hundred horses would sound different. But there's definitely someone out there. We're not alone, Danny. I'm certain of it.'

Startled, Miss Lucy and I shot glances left and right, up to the top of the steep slopes to either side of us, and then along the road in each direction. We couldn't see anyone.

'You're imagining it,' Miss Lucy declared.

Cornelius shook his head again. 'I ain't.'

'I believe you, Cornelius, but if there are people watching us, there's not much we can do about it until they show themselves,' I said.

McLeish ambled towards us. 'Right lads, you can give me a hand setting the charges. You've both carried powder at one time or another, so I figure you're the least likely to make a mistake and blow us all to hell. Miss Lucy, the Dutchman wants a word in your ear.'

Carefully carrying the small kegs of gunpowder, we watched as McLeish placed one among the roots of each of the two beech trees that would block the road. 'We'll use long fuses for these,' he declared. 'Men hidden behind those rocks and in those bushes will light the fuses on the Dutchman's signal.' The Scotsman straightened up, rubbed the ache from his back, and muttered, 'Perfect.'

Gathering beside the Dutchman I noticed that Miss Lucy wasn't among us. I looked around but couldn't see her anywhere.

'It is almost time,' the Dutchman began. 'The enemy is stronger in number than we'd hoped. Fearing that this might indeed turn out to be the case, I took the liberty of planning ahead for just such an eventuality. Our number and force shall be more than a match for Thackery's men as we have reinforcements available to us.'

Miss Lucy came scrambling down a slope, almost tripping over a branch. At the bottom she regained her composure and nodded to the Dutchman. 'They're in position.'

'Who are?' I asked.

'As you know, Master Daniel, I said I'd make the prince aware of our plan. He kindly offered some men from his personal guard, an offer I think I was wise to accept. They stationed themselves overnight the other side of Totnes, awaiting my instructions. Once we knew what we were up against I sent a rider to bring them here. Thackery's men might believe they have outwitted us, but with luck it'll be the other way round. The prince's men are one surprise our enemy will have not bargained for.'

Our lookout, Galbraith, suddenly appeared, waving frantically as he ran back from the bridge as fast as he could.

'Everyone into position and await my command!' the Dutchman shouted.

My heart raced. I drew my two pistols and headed into the trees and bushes. There I settled down with Peter, Cornelius, Miss Lucy and Jacobsen. The Dutchman climbed a little way up a great oak and, straddling a branch, settled his back against the trunk. He raised a hand in readiness for signalling the lighting of the fuses to fell the trees to block the road. Jacobsen and Miss Lucy gently pressed the barrels of their muskets through the bushes. Peter gripped my old pistols in trembling hands. 'Here, Cornelius,' I said, reaching for my powder and bag of shot. 'Take these. You can help us reload.'

'Aye, Danny. I can hear them coming. Make sure you save a bullet for Thackery.'

We waited. We heard the distant clop of hooves and the clatter of wagon wheels as they negotiated a dirt road full of ruts. The clattering grew louder. Eventually they came into view, advancing at little more than walking pace. There were two riders in front of the gaol wagon. A driver and soldier sat on top of the wagon and eight more riders followed behind.

'Can you see him, Danny? Can you see Thackery?'

'Not yet, Cornelius. Be patient. They're still some distance away.'

As they drew nearer I sensed the enemy's anxiety. Their eyes darted everywhere and several clutched their muskets in a manner that would quickly enable them to be raised and fired. Others held pistols beneath their capes. I could tell they knew this was the place they were likely to be ambushed.

The gaol wagon possessed tiny, barred windows, but I couldn't make out anyone inside. I switched my gaze to the faces of the soldiers. Where was Thackery? I still couldn't see him. I'd reserved my first bullet for the scoundrel. My second too, if needed. 'Damn it, Cornelius. It looks like Thackery has retreated and joined the main force bringing up the rear.'

'Then we'll get him later,' Cornelius spat.

The wagon continued trundling slowly towards us. The Dutchman dropped his hand and carefully slid out of the tree and out of view. The fuses were lit and we braced ourselves for the blasts.

McLeish knew his business well. The explosions were loud and sent dirt and stones high into the air. Both beech trees shuddered and then slowly toppled.

Startled, the two horses in front of the wagon reared up

and threw their riders to the ground. The other cavalry horses leaped and spun wildly, their riders fighting to regain control. The gaol wagon slewed abruptly to one side, almost tipping over as one of its wheels crashed into a deep rut. The driver leaned back and pulled on the reins with all his might, fighting to bring it to a halt. We opened fire from both sides of the road. Riders who had regained control of their mounts turned and fled. Others less fortunate fell to the ground, struck by our hail of bullets. Within seconds, only the driver of the gaol wagon remained. He let go of his reins and raised his hands into the air.

Two of our men broke cover while others hastily reloaded their guns. They ran down the slope, shouting cries of victory.

'Get back, you idiots!' Jacobsen bellowed. 'That's an order. It's not over yet.'

They ignored him and made for the gaol wagon. In one swift movement, the driver lowered his hands, deftly drew pistols from his belt and fired. His aim proved true and our men fell. Crouching next to me, Peter stood up, pushed his way through the bushes and charged down to the road, pointing his weapons. The wagon driver saw him and grabbed a musket from the dead soldier slumped beside him. Peter raised his pistols and pulled the triggers. They sparked and cracked. He missed. The driver swung his musket round and Peter froze and shrieked in fright.

A deafening bang right next to my head made my ears ring. The musket slipped from the driver's grasp and he fell forward in his seat. I turned and saw a smoking flintlock pistol in Jacobsen's outstretched hand.

By now we could all hear the thunder of hooves. Soldiers at the gallop came into view. Ninety cavalrymen were bearing down on us. Peter scrambled back up the hillside towards us and dived into the bushes.

There was no time to break open the gaol wagon. Rescuing Mother and Lord Blackfoot would have to wait.

Smoke from our pistols and muskets betrayed our positions. Although we had the advantage of higher ground, we were so few in number that I realised we were pinned down in positions that would eventually be overrun. I looked towards the gaol wagon and wondered why Mother or Lord Blackfoot weren't screaming at us to come and release them. Were they bound and gagged? Were they too weak from torture to be able to raise their voices, or hands to the bars? I felt an extra wave of desperation surge inside. I had to get them to safety while there was still time. Despite the danger, I lunged forward, intent on dashing to the wagon.

'No, Master Daniel.' The Dutchman grabbed my arm. 'Wait!'

The enemy was upon us. Some dismounted and took cover behind the fallen beech tree behind the gaol wagon. The air was full of pops and cracks as we exchanged musket and pistol fire. Lead fizzed through the undergrowth, pinging and ricocheting among the branches and trunks of trees, gouging out chunks of wood and showering us with splinters.

'They're coming,' Cornelius shouted. 'I can hear them.' He pointed along the road in the direction of Totnes.

Seconds later Dutch soldiers burst into view riding at full gallop, some with swords drawn, others leaning forward, pistols sparking. And they kept on coming, yelling their battle cry. They numbered more than I could count.

With surprise on our side, the English soldiers beat a hasty retreat. They knew when they'd been outwitted. Each grabbed the nearest horse, swung into its saddle and rode off amid a storm of lead shot. Many fell before they reached a bend in the road and could vanish safely out of sight.

The road was quickly crammed full of horses ridden by Prince William's men. The Dutchman hurried down the slope and greeted their commander.

'Come on, Cornelius,' I shouted. 'Let's get that gaol wagon open. Let's get my mother out of there.' I grabbed his arm and we ran.

I reached the door to the gaol wagon at the same moment as McLeish. 'It's got a pretty grand lock on the door,' he shouted.

'Stand back.' I aimed one of my pistols and blasted the lock. The force made the door swing open. 'Mother? Lord Blackfoot?'

The inside of the gaol wagon was dark and dingy, the floor covered with fetid straw. I could see two figures slumped at the back. They looked like little more than sacks of cloth.

'Mother?' I screamed in horror.

McLeish shoved me out of the way and clambered inside. He reappeared moments later clutching a heavy bundle of rags. 'They're not here!'

Chapter Thirty-one

I locked eyes with first the Dutchman and then Jacobsen. 'I don't understand,' I shouted. 'What does this mean?'

The Dutchman's lips curled in fury. 'It means we've been conned.'

'Then where's Mother?'

'Mr Jacobsen, see if there's a wounded man among the enemy still with enough breath to speak. I want answers.'

'Aye, sir.'

Korporaal Jules van Elber appeared at my side. 'Daniel, are you alright? When I learned of this mission I volunteered.'

'Jules, is my father among you?'

'No. I haven't seen him since we set foot in England. But he sailed with us on the *Brill*. I think he had urgent business to see to on behalf of the prince. Otherwise, no doubt, he'd have joined us.'

A prisoner tightly restrained by Jacobsen and McLeish soon spilled answers to all the Dutchman's questions.

We learned that Thackery had ridden out of town with the gaol wagon and then, having met up with the main force, returned across country to Dartmouth castle, taking Mother and Lord Blackfoot with him, both bound and gagged and tied to the saddles of horses. Thackery was going to wait in town for news of our death or capture. He had indeed known about our planned ambush, just as McLeish and Jacobsen feared. But it was learning of his next move that made me feel so unsteady that I had to sit down on the ground. Thackery had received new orders from King James: *'Execute both prisoners tomorrow at dawn and hang their bodies in iron cages on Crowbeak Hill.'*

'Who's that?' Jules pointed to a lone horseman silhouetted against the sky on the crest of the hill above us. The horseman was stationary and appeared to be observing us.

Jacobsen snapped open his spyglass. 'Now there's a familiar face I didn't ever expect to see again. We were right, Mr McLeish – Mr Delaney has had a hand in all this.'

'Delaney?' Miss Lucy pointed her pistol towards the figure. Without hesitating she pulled the trigger. Delaney didn't even flinch; he must've known he was out of range. He gathered his reins, slowly turned his horse and disappeared from view behind the ridge.

'Want us to go after him?' asked the Dutch commander.

The Dutchman shook his head. 'You won't catch him. He's got too great a head start. Still, mark my words, his day of reckoning shall come soon enough.'

'Then I should like to return to Brixham without delay. The prince intends heading for London shortly and requires us to escort him. I'll give him my report. He shall be most disappointed at today's outcome.'

'Is there no hope?' asked Jules. 'Can't we find some way of getting them out of the gaol at Dartmouth castle?'

'Our orders do not include such a venture,' the commander replied. 'In any event, without cannon we do not have enough men to take the castle. Our artillery was brought ashore at Brixham. It would take days to deliver them here. Knowing the prince, he will not spare valuable guns on such a mission.'

I'd never felt so helpless. I stared at the bodies of men

and horses littering the road, the empty wagon and fallen trees and realised it had all been for nothing. McLeish stood in front of me, scratching his beard.

'Master Daniel, suppose of an evening I wanted to find Lieutenant Thackery. Where might I look?'

'What? Oh, I don't know,' I replied angrily.

'Didn't you tell me that he forced Elsbeth Hawks to sign over the deeds to the Shipwreck tavern to him?'

'Yes. So?'

'Then that's where he'd most likely be, isn't it?'

I looked up. 'Suppose so, along with his mob. Why? Do you suggest we burst in there and shoot him? Because if that's what you have in mind I'll be first through the door.'

'No, lad, I was thinking that it would be better if the lieutenant led us into the castle and showed us where he was keeping your ma and Lord Blackfoot.'

'Ha! And I suppose he'll give us the keys to their cells too, if we ask nicely,' I snapped sarcastically.

'What exactly do you have in mind, Mr McLeish?' asked Jacobsen.

'Well, sir, we have a gaol wagon and a few passable English uniforms from those men lying in the road. All we need is a volunteer prisoner.'

'Let me get this straight,' said the Dutchman. 'You're suggesting we turn up in Dartmouth dressed as English soldiers and with a prisoner in our wagon, and use the deception to get inside the castle.'

'Aye, sir.'

'I see. But do we need Thackery to be part of it? The castle guards would see we are delivering a prisoner and let us in, wouldn't they?'

'Aye, sir, they might. But if Thackery is with us, the

guards won't be suspicious or ask awkward questions. He's in charge, after all.'

The Dutchman nodded thoughtfully. 'I suppose it could work. But to do so, our prisoner would have to be of sufficient interest to Thackery to make him interrupt an evening's drinking and gambling.'

McLeish grinned. 'My thoughts exactly, sir.'

'No!' Jacobsen shouted. 'That would be madness. It's too dangerous.' He grabbed the Dutchman's arm. 'Don't do it, Captain. Let me be the prisoner.'

The Dutchman shrugged off Jacobsen's offer. 'I shall be the prize to entice Thackery away from his tavern. After all, I would not pass as an English cavalryman, not with the colour of my skin. But if we are to undertake such an audacious scheme, we must do so this very evening if we are to prevent their execution at dawn.'

Jules mounted his horse. 'Daniel, if I see your father I shall tell him what's happening. Good luck!'

'And tell him to come and find me as soon as he can,' I shouted, as Jules rode off

Jules raised a hand to indicate he'd heard me.

'Right,' said McLeish. 'We'd better get busy. We'll start by moving that tree and then we'll sort out those uniforms. We'll have to wash and scrub them free of blood if they are to be any use to us.'

Jacobsen shook his head repeatedly. 'I don't like this at all. It's madness.'

Chapter Thirty-two

WE waited until after nightfall before trooping down the hill into Dartmouth, the Dutchman inside the gaol wagon and cursing every rut in the road as it jarred his ride. Cornelius, being unable to control a horse by himself, had been given a stark choice. He could either be left at the side of the road or be a prisoner too. He chose to ride inside the wagon. It was too risky letting him travel alongside the wagon's driver, Trelawney, as Cornelius's face was too well known in town, and would be a giveaway the moment Thackery set eyes upon him.

Our uniforms remained bood-stained, despite our attempts to wash them in the river. Had we rode into town during daylight our deception would have been quickly spotted. And with only a handful of serviceable uniforms between us, the majority of the crew, including Peter, were instead ordered to return to Kingsbridge and row out to meet the *Endeavour* on the evening tide. They had orders to give to De Veer. He was to sail to Dartmouth and, all being well, we would signal the ship to pick us up.

The fine details of our plan had been hastily put together and, worryingly, left much to chance, not least whether Thackery would even be at the Shipwreck tavern that night. This was our last chance to save Mother and Lord Black-foot, and I could tell from the silence as we rode that many thought it was no real chance at all.

'So, Cornelius, we're heading back to where it all began,'

I called out. His face appeared at the bars of the wagon. 'That night when I was working at the tavern and Tobias came crashing through the door covered in blood seems like a lifetime ago now.'

'Aye, and you've changed, Danny.'

'What do you mean?'

'I can hear it in your voice. You don't sound so scared.'

'Really?'

'Uh-huh. You always scared easily. Just catching sight of Thackery was enough to make your voice tremble.'

I stiffened. 'Well, not anymore.'

Jacobsen and McLeish rode at the front of the convoy, Trelawney held the reins to the gaol wagon and Miss Lucy and I rode behind.

On the edge of town, Jacobsen raised a hand and we all drew to a stop. He turned in his saddle. 'I still think this is folly and that we will live to regret Mr McLeish's bright idea. However, we have made it this far and so I shall do my best to maintain our deception. For God's sake try to look and act like soldiers as we ride through the streets. We'll make for the quay and stop as close to the tavern as we dare. You will remain mounted, and if challenged simply state that you are on the king's business. I shall go inside the tavern and determine if Thackery's present. If he is, I'll inform him of our prisoner's identity and ask him to join us on the final leg of our journey to the castle. I have no doubt he'll relish setting eyes on the Dutchman.'

'And if he's not at the tavern?'

'Then, Master Daniel, we simply head for the castle and pray that nothing we do makes the guards suspicious.'

We rode on, down to the banks of the river and then, turning right, we made for the centre of town, its narrow streets leading us to the quayside. It was tempting to ride stiffly in our borrowed uniforms, pretending to be crack cavalrymen on the most important of missions. But I'd seen many English soldiers from the garrison in the past, and the experienced among them rode in a relaxed manner, confident and not scared to show their weariness after a long day's ride. And I recalled how the soldiers never gave way to others on the streets, however old, frail or infirm, instead belligerently shooing them aside and cursing them if they did not move out of the way quickly enough. Determined to be as convincing as possible I followed their example. I had a growing sense of power high up on my fine horse, looking down at folk ever fearful at the sight of a uniform. For the wrong sort of soldier it could lead him to abuse his authority for his own amusement and gain.

Thackery was just such a soldier. I was looking forward to seeing him again. And I suspected that Cornelius had in mind the same thoughts as me. If we were successful and got to the castle and released Mother and Lord Blackfoot, our final act would be to avenge Tobias's death.

The quay was busy, a small coastal vessel unloading its cargo not far from the Customs House. Men were offloading barrels by rolling them down planks. Officials were studying paperwork, no doubt making sure taxes and duties were paid in full. I thought of the tunnels and wondered how much smuggled cargo evaded their watchful eyes. With word of the Dutch prince's landing further along the coast it was clear that the town was on alert. Soldiers bearing muskets were posted at intervals, others patrolling in pairs. Our arrival did not go unnoticed. All eyes fell on the sight of a gaol wagon trundling towards the Shipwreck tavern.

Jacobsen signalled for us to stop. 'You there,' he bellowed to a small gathering of soldiers huddled around an open fire in an iron basket. 'I have been led to believe that Lieutenant Thackery might be found at this tavern.' He gestured towards the door to the Shipwreck. 'Is this correct?'

'Aye, he's in there.' The soldiers switched their attention to the wagon. 'You got a prisoner in there, or have you come to make arrests?'

Jacobsen rode up to them. 'Never you mind. We are here on the king's business. So kindly do not interfere.' He dismounted. 'Here,' he said to the man closest to him, 'you can make yourself useful. Hold my reins.'

Before the soldier could protest, Jacobsen had placed the reins of his horse into the soldier's hand, signalled a nod to McLeish, and briskly headed off for the entrance to the tavern. He entered, closing the door behind him.

We waited.

I'd anticipated that within barely a minute we'd see a jubilant Thackery bursting out of his tavern, demanding to see our prisoners with his own eyes. It didn't happen. In fact, nothing happened. We just sat on our horses and waited. And very quickly the soldier holding Jacobsen's horse's reins grew tired of the task.

'Come on, you can tell me. Is there anyone in that wagon? Or are our enemies inside that tavern? Are there Dutch spies among us? We've heard lots of rumours. People are saying the country's awash with them, that you can hardly tell them apart from Englishmen.'

By now the soldier's comrades' curiosity was growing too. They approached us and several rose on their heels, trying to glimpse into the barred windows of the wagon. 'You heard the major,' bellowed McLeish. 'We are on the king's business and it is of the utmost importance and secrecy. Back away!'

Only two reacted to the might of McLeish's bulk and voice and retreated, a third persisting in his quest to get a good look inside the wagon. Miss Lucy drew and cocked one of her pistols and thrust it in an outstretched arm, aiming at the man's head. Shocked by her action, he raised his hands and stepped back. To onlookers they'd just seen one English soldier draw their weapon against another, and I thought Miss Lucy's action would cause our deception to unravel. But as soon as the man retreated, she returned her pistol to her belt.

It had been five minutes since Jacobsen went inside the tavern and still no sign of him or Thackery. My nerve was failing. It was meant to be a quick in-and-out, irrespective of whether Thackery was there or not. Standing around, drawing ever more attention to ourselves from soldiers, sailors and customs men was not part of our plan. Something was wrong. It had to be. I rode forward, past the gaol wagon, and stopped next to McLeish. In a low voice I said, 'We can't remain here. Whatever is going on inside the Shipwreck was not part of our plan.'

McLeish nodded grimly. 'I was just thinking the same. Any ideas?'

'Yes. There's a narrow street behind the tavern. It's little wider than an alleyway but I reckon the wagon can negotiate it. Turn us round and we'll make for there. There's a rear entrance. I suggest we use it to find out what's going on inside.'

McLeish nodded. 'Agreed.' He raised a hand. 'Follow me, Mr Trelawney.'

We moved off, the wagon turning a half circle before

heading back the way we came. I guided McLeish and the others towards the narrow back street but then had an idea. 'You carry on. I'll see you inside.'

Before McLeish could reply I dug my heels into my mount and set off at a canter parallel to the quay, heading for the granary. There I dismounted and tethered my horse to a railing. Crouching, I edged forward to see if soldiers were patrolling here too, and they were. Just two of them, back and forth, back and forth they marched, muskets slung over their shoulders.

I'd need to be quick. If I ran swiftly and made little noise I could pass between them before they turned, and I could reach the jetty without being spotted. From there I could slip into the water and swim to the entrance to the tunnels. I hurriedly wrapped my pistols up inside my cape, saying a quick prayer that they'd stay dry during my swim.

My dash was light-footed. In a flash I'd sped between the two soldiers, leaped a rail and run halfway along the jetty. I quickly lay flat and then rolled over the edge, lowering myself gently into the water, being careful to make barely a ripple. Clutching the bundle containing my pistols, I swam as fast as I dared, making for the entrance to the tunnels, an entrance most ordinary townsfolk thought to be nothing more than a storm drain. Only the top was visible because the tide was high. The twenty yards didn't take long to cover. As I swam I remembered the last time I'd done so, a bullet lodged in my arm, the Dutchman at my side.

Reaching the tunnel I swam a little way in and then realised I could stand up, the water lapping about my chest. The tunnel was pitch-black inside and, as I waded on, I reached out and felt for the walls covered in slime. They guided me and kept me from stumbling. With each step the level of the water receded, and once it was below my waist I hurried along.

Soaked through, I began to shiver. My wet uniform felt as heavy as a coat made of lead. I stopped, unbuttoned my cavalry tunic and tore it off. Removing my pistols from my cape, I wedged them into my belt, wrapped the cape about my shoulders, and drew its hood over my head.

The tunnels were reached from the Shipwreck by an entrance concealed by a large oak cask in the tavern's cellar. If my memory was correct, the hole in the wall behind the barrel was roughly hewn. I ought to be able to feel the uneven edges in the dark. Ignoring the squealing rats squabbling about my feet and the dank fetid air filling my nostrils, I almost cried with relief when the tips of my fingers no longer felt slime but a gap. Yes. This was it. I dipped down and stepped into the hole, my shoulder pressing up against the smooth wood of a large cask. I pushed. It barely moved. I pushed harder. Still it barely moved. I pushed harder still. It shifted an inch.

I took a deep breath, planted my feet firmly and then threw myself against it, driving forward with all my weight. I felt it give and topple forward. Rocking wildly, the cask rolled across the cellar floor and clattered into a wall. I fell heavily. Lying on the floor, gasping for breath, I feared I'd made so much noise that I was bound to have given myself away. On my back, I drew both my pistols and aimed them up the stone steps towards the door leading into the back of the tavern. I waited, expecting the door to burst open, expecting someone to come to investigate the noise, anticipating that person to be armed and ready for trouble.

No one came.

I scrambled onto my knees and stood up. Slowly I climbed the steps. There were voices and laughter beyond the door and the nearer I got to it, the more I was certain that the loudest of those voices belonged to Thackery. And he sounded mighty pleased about something.

Carefully, gently, I lifted the door's latch and opened it a tiny fraction. The light of lanterns and candles seemed blindingly bright and made me blink furiously. I couldn't make out a great deal, but what I could see confirmed my worst fears.

Jacobsen was there, seated and bound tightly with ropes to his chair. Thackery held a knife to his throat.

Chapter Thirty-three

'I'VE not had the pleasure of your acquaintance, Mr Jacobsen. When you marched in here just now I must say I was fully taken in by that uniform of yours. If it wasn't for Mr Delaney here, pointing you out to me and revealing the truth of who lay behind the disguise, I might even have offered you a tankard of ale.'

Delaney! I felt a shiver of fright.

Jacobsen cursed and spat at the floor. 'You may have the upper hand right now, Lieutenant, but not for long.'

I craned my neck to catch a glimpse of Delaney. And there he was, leaning against a wall. I had the overwhelming urge to wipe the grin off his face. I had two pistols, two bullets, one for Thackery and one for him. I was sorely tempted. But I held back, praying that at any moment the others would burst in through the back door and the tables would be fully turned.

A handful of Thackery's men stood with their backs to me, their attention focused on the lieutenant and his prisoner. Without making a sound, and keeping low, I slipped inside and scurried behind a bench. There I could see more of the room. I readied myself for action.

'Your victory is a hollow one,' said Jacobsen. 'With Prince William riding to London, within days England shall be his, and when that day arrives it shall be you who'll be heading to the gallows on Crowbeak Hill.'

'Perhaps. Who knows what tomorrow shall bring. But

right now, I'd say I have the upper hand. Isn't that right, men?'

A chorus of *Ayes* rang out.

The back door to the tavern opened and I saw the Dutchman and McLeish. About to reveal myself in our moment of triumph I suddenly realised something was terribly wrong. Neither held pistols and their hands were raised above their heads. Musket barrels were pressed into their backs. Trelawney and Miss Lucy followed, both also disarmed and helpless.

'Ah, welcome,' Thackery beamed. 'How very kind of you all to join us. I assumed Mr Jacobsen would not dare venture here alone, and so I sent some of my best men outside to round you up the moment you showed your faces. Please, take a seat. All of you.'

The Dutchman and the others were forced to sit on chairs. Men with ropes set about binding their hands behind their backs.

Where was Cornelius? I waited for him to appear too, expecting to see him being dragged in through the door kicking and screaming, as I knew he wouldn't submit without a fight. But there was no sign of him.

Miss Lucy proved their most troublesome prisoner, wriggling like mad as they struggled to bind her wrists. She hissed and spat a volley of curses in Delaney's direction.

Delaney drew his rapier and pressed the tip against Lucy's neck. 'So pretty and so full of spark. It'll be a shame to see you die, but die you shall before tomorrow's dawn.'

The Dutchman gazed up at him. 'Why, for God's sake, man? At least tell us that.'

'It is not so difficult to understand,' Delaney replied, returning his rapier to its scabbard. 'We are the same, you and I, Dutchman. We just happen to be on opposite sides, that's all. I have no doubt you were promised great rewards by the Dutch prince for your loyal service, and I was offered the same but from a different employer – King Louis of France. I was happy to take up his offer to try and thwart the Dutch prince's plans. And I shall be paid handsomely for my work into the bargain. I shall rejoice on the day Louis conquers the Low Countries and sets his sights on England.'

'What about loyalty and friendship? What about honour?' He glared fearsomely at Delaney. 'I wish no money or riches for my part in all this. My bargain with the prince was simple. In return for my help I only asked that those who murdered my family and all the other slaves at Oyster Bay receive justice. He promised that those responsible would be arrested and would stand trial for their crimes. No, Mr Delaney, you and I are not the same at all.'

'Grand words, but you're a fool,' Delaney replied.

Thackery hammered a fist onto a table. 'Enough idle chatter. Now that you're all sitting uncomfortably, Mr Delaney and I have some questions. We want to know all about the Dutch prince's plans. We want to know everything about his army and ships.'

Slowly I stood up and edged my way to the back door of the tavern. With everyone's attention drawn towards the prisoners I slipped outside. The gaol wagon had been left a few yards up the narrow street.

'Cornelius?' I whispered. 'Are you in there?' In the dark I couldn't make out anyone inside.

'Psst, up here, Danny.'

I looked up and saw Cornelius's face peering down at me. 'What are you doing up there?'

'Hiding, Danny. When they caught us they didn't see me in the back of the wagon under those rags. Once they'd gone, I reckoned it was safer outside. But I had no idea where I was, and so figured up here was the best place. What's happened, Danny? Where have they taken them?'

'Thackery has them all tied up inside the tavern and is about to interrogate them about the Dutch prince's plans.'

'Can't you go in and shoot him?'

'No. That's a daft idea. I'd never get near him. His mob would either grab me or stand between us. What I need is some sort of diversion, and a pretty convincing one too. I need to get close enough to take Thackery by surprise. I reckon if he's faced with either releasing his prisoners or getting a bullet in the back, he'll choose wisely.'

'How many men are there inside?'

'Thackery's lot plus Mr Delaney.'

We sat in silence, both desperately trying to think of something. My mind was blank. Suddenly Cornelius scrambled along the top of the wagon, grabbed a sack and held it out towards me. 'There's always this, Danny.'

It was McLeish's sack and it still contained a couple of fuses. 'Great! What do we do with those?'

'Use one with this.' Cornelius picked something up and held it out towards me. 'Mr McLeish had one small keg of powder left over from our ambush today.'

'Well, we can't go blowing the place up. We'd kill everyone, including ourselves.'

'I've got an idea, Danny.' He reached into his pocket and took out my whistle. 'See! I kept it safe for you. And now you're going to take it back. You'll need it to give me the signal. Let me tell you what I have in mind . . .'

Cornelius's idea was as mad as it was brilliant. It took us

just a couple of minutes to prepare ourselves. Leaving my best friend in position outside the tavern's back door, I slipped inside and stood at the back of the crowd.

To my relief, Thackery was still intent on questioning his prisoners and stood before them barking questions, each of which failed to get a reply. The Dutchman spotted me but thankfully did not react. Instead he held their attention by hurling a string of abuse at them.

'I grow weary at your stupidity,' snapped Thackery. 'Talk, damn you, or one by one I'll slit your throats.'

I had to act fast. Moving as close to Thackery as I dared, I raised my whistle to my mouth and blew a short, high-pitched pip.

Men turned to look at me but were instantly distracted by the back door crashing open.

'Penny for a blind boy? Anyone got a penny for a blind boy?' Cornelius called out. He walked in clutching the keg of gunpowder, the fuse lit and fizzing.

'Dear God, the lad's carrying a bomb!'

Chapter Thirty-four

THACKERY'S mob scattered, diving for cover.

Drawing a pistol I ran forward and shoved the barrel into Thackery's back. 'Stand still, Lieutenant. Call your men to order and tell them to lay down their weapons.'

'What on earth?'

'Tell them to lay down their weapons. Now! Or do you want to be blown to hell?'

Cornelius stood alone in the centre of the tavern, the majority of Thackery's men pressed hard up against the walls and shielding their faces. A few crouched fearfully behind tables. One or two dared to watch the fuse burn. There was a moment of silence as the fuse fizzed and sparked. The Dutchman and the others looked on in horror.

'Someone grab that bomb and snuff out the fuse!' Thackery shouted.

'Stand fast,' I responded, sensing a few might just try. 'If any of you move the lieutenant gets my first bullet, and he who tries anything gets the second. Now, give the order, Lieutenant. Tell your men to place down their weapons. Quickly now, if you want to live.'

Reluctantly Thackery nodded to his men and they flung their pistols and swords to the floor. 'Daniel Drake. I should have had you hanged years ago.'

'But you didn't and now here I am and you are going to help us set free my mother and Lord Blackfoot.'

'Like hell I am. You're just a boy, and you'd not dare to

shoot a lieutenant in King James's army, because you know full well that if you did, you'd be heading for Crowbeak Hill.'

'Shoot him, Danny,' Cornelius spat.

'Not yet.' Peering round the tavern, I sought out the smallest and weakest of Thackery's men. 'You! Untie the prisoners. Quickly, before the bomb goes off.'

The man sought the nod from Thackery before hurrying to untie the Dutchman. Even as he did so, all eyes remained on the shortening fuse.

'Put it out,' someone cried, 'before it's too late.'

Amid cries of anguish, the fuse feebly burnt itself out, leaving just a waft of smoke hanging in the air. Cornelius grinned. 'Well, you didn't think it was a real bomb, did you?'

Before Thackery's mob could regain their wits, the Dutchman and the others had seized weapons and offered me much needed reinforcements.

'Well done, Master Daniel, you appeared in the nick of time. But you had us all fearing for our lives when we saw that fuse,' said the Dutchman.

'It was Cornelius's idea. The perfect plan. We emptied the powder keg outside.'

Retrieving her rapier, Miss Lucy made strides towards Delaney. 'How dare you make a fool out of me.'

'No!' commanded the Dutchman. 'This is not the time to settle old scores. Lower your weapon.'

'I shan't, not until it drips with that rat's blood.'

'But I am unarmed,' pleaded Delaney. His stare towards her hardened. 'Now if you would care to furnish me with my blade and offer a fair fight, I'd gladly take you on.'

'I said, lower your weapon, Miss Lucy. We have work to

do. Mr Delaney shall be detained alongside the others and the prince shall determine his fate.'

Letting out a shriek of frustration, she lowered her sword. 'I will restrain myself until the moment Mary Drake and Lord Blackfoot are freed. After that I promise nothing.'

'Mr Jacobsen, Mr Trelawney and Mr McLeish, we must secure this place. Make sure all the lieutenant's men are fully disarmed, bound and gagged. Also, secure the front entrance. When we leave we shall extinguish all candles and lanterns. This place must look closed for business. We do not want people wandering in and discovering our plans.'

'Aye, sir.'

The Dutchman approached Thackery. 'This is how it is going to work, Lieutenant. From here we ride to the castle. There you shall lead us safely inside and take us to the place where you are holding Lord Blackfoot and Mary Drake. You shall order their immediate release into your custody. And then you will see us safely out. We shall have pistols aimed at you at all times. One false move or slip of the tongue and it shall be your last.' He grabbed the lieutenant by the throat. 'Have I made myself understood?'

Thackery's face twitched with fury.

The Dutchman tightened his grip. 'Have I made myself understood?' he roared.

Thackery nodded.

'Good.' The Dutchman turned and glared at Delaney. 'Mr McLeish, throw that traitor into the gaol wagon.'

'It'd be a pleasure, sir.'

Extinguishing the last of the tavern's lanterns we slipped quietly out of the back door. Trelawney climbed up and grabbed the wagon's reins. 'Master Cornelius, put on this cape and draw the hood down over your face. You might as well ride alongside me. After all, I dare not let you ride inside with Mr Delaney. You might do something horrible to him.'

Cornelius grinned. 'Aye, I might.'

The Dutchman swung into his saddle. 'Mr Jacobsen, lend me your cape. I shall need to conceal the colour of my skin until we are past the castle's guards.' He turned to Thackery. 'Remember, one false move and it will be your last.'

We moved off at a walk, the wheels of the gaol wagon rattling against the cobbles. Miss Lucy and I rode behind again. I kept hold of one pistol in my belt beneath my cloak, just in case Thackery made a run for it, and in case the others failed to stop him.

Slowly we trundled through the dark, narrow streets. We had to head beyond the town's centre and towards the mouth of the estuary. There, high up on a promontory, lay Dartmouth castle, its cannon pointing out to sea in defence of England's coast.

'This has been quite some adventure, hasn't it?' Miss Lucy remarked to me. 'You and Cornelius have demonstrated great courage and resourcefulness. If it hadn't been for you, we'd not be here now.'

Cornelius overheard. He turned and grinned.

'Yes, but it's not over yet,' I replied. 'I shan't be happy until Mother is safe. No, actually that's a lie. I shan't be happy until Mother's safe and the two of us are reunited with Father.'

'That reminds me, Master Daniel. You recall what you asked me about my father's activities in the Caribbean?'

'Yes.'

'I've been giving it a great deal of thought. Maybe I was

too quick to dismiss the fears of that clerk you mentioned. I have witnessed the way my father has reacted towards you ever since you enquired about your family's business in Amsterdam, and I have come to the conclusion that if he had nothing to hide then he would not have been so discourteous. When I am next home in Amsterdam I shall conduct my own enquiries and, if necessary, confront him about it.'

'Thank you.'

'I shall have the truth laid bare and if there has been any wrongdoing on his part I shall make certain your father is compensated.'

Although Miss Lucy's offer was well intended and gratefully received, I couldn't help thinking that she was misguided. Compensation could only be given in the form of money, property or goods. What about all those men, women and children who'd worked at Oyster Bay as slaves, and who'd been brutally slaughtered that hot summer's night so long ago? I looked at the Dutchman. What sort of compensation would he demand from Mr Deveraux if all the rumours proved true?

On the edge of town we turned a corner. A steep climb lay ahead and I could see the castle silhouetted in the distance against the night sky. Just a few hundred yards more and we'd be at the gates. I felt the urge to shout out, to let Mother know I was coming to rescue her. Of course, to do so would be foolish, so I bit my lip.

Cornelius suddenly turned to face me. He looked worried. 'Danny, I think I can hear —'

They struck without warning.

Chapter Thirty-five

SOLDIERS appeared from everywhere. In seconds we were surrounded. 'Halt and place your hands in the air where I can see them,' yelled one.

'What's happening, Danny?' Cornelius cried out.

Recognising the soldier who spoke as being among those we'd encountered by the quayside, I cursed. 'Think we're done for,' I replied, slowly raising my hands.

'No, Danny! Not now. Not when we've come so close.'

I glanced at Miss Lucy and then McLeish. Both looked in shock from the suddenness of the ambush and our drastic turn in fortune.

'Well, don't just stand there. Untie me,' Thackery bellowed. 'At once.'

A soldier hurried to him and began undoing the knots.

'Do something, Danny,' Cornelius fretted.

I thought about snatching my pistols from my belt and aiming them at Thackery, but I knew I didn't stand a chance, not with all those loaded muskets pointing at me.

Thackery dismounted and turned to face us. I could see the bloodlust written all over his face. The soldier I recognised from the quayside delivered his report.

'I deduced mischief was afoot when that gaol wagon turned up and then promptly left without sign of any arrests being made at your tavern, sir. And the men accompanying it were acting most secretively. Too secretively for my liking, so I decided to investigate. I lay in wait, observing you leave the tavern by the back entrance. Seeing you were in difficulty, sir, I rounded up some men and set up an ambush.'

'You've done well,' Thackery replied. 'Now drag them from their horses, remove their weapons and throw them into the wagon.'

As soon as the door to the wagon was opened Delaney emerged, brushing fetid straw from his tunic. He glared at each of us in turn, reserving his most hateful gaze for Miss Lucy, who returned his stare with one equally vengeful.

'You,' Lieutenant Thackery bellowed, pointing at the Dutchman. 'You shall suffer every instrument of diabolical torture I possess in the castle's dungeons. And believe me, I possess many. I'll have you begging to tell me everything I wish to know about the Dutch prince's plans.'

The Dutchman said nothing.

Two soldiers manhandled me off my horse. I fell to the ground. One seized my arm and dragged me to my feet. 'This one's just a boy,' he called out.

Thackery marched up to me and cuffed me hard about my head until my ears rang. 'Well, well, well, Master Drake, thought you'd got the better of me, did you? Dared to threaten me, eh? Threatening a lieutenant in King James's army carries a heavy price.' He briefly looked up as more soldiers dragged a screaming and kicking Cornelius from on top of the wagon. 'You and your friend shall pay dearly for all your mischief. You said you wanted to be reunited with your mother and you shall, Daniel Drake. You shall watch her hang. And as soon as she's stopped twitching at the end of a rope, it'll be your turn to greet the hangman's noose.'

Despite being unarmed and feeling a little dizzy, no way

was I going to cower before him. Instead, I spat in his face.

'Why, you little—'

He knocked me out with a single punch.

I regained consciousness inside the crowded gaol wagon. I was lying on the stinking layer of straw. Cornelius was beside me, quietly sobbing. The road beneath us was rough and we rocked and bounced wildly as we headed up the hill to the castle.

I pushed myself up and leaned against the side. I felt my sore jaw and groaned. No one spoke. I knew that this was it. We'd done all we could. We'd tried, failed and then tried and failed again. Our luck had finally deserted us. Each and every one of us knew it, and we knew the end was drawing near. I felt most sorry for my best friend. Cornelius should've had no part in it all. He should have stayed with his brother, Edmund, in Kingsbridge. The Dutchman had been right about that. It would have been safer. I reached out and tried to comfort him. 'I'm sorry,' I whispered.

'It's alright, Danny. I'm not scared of dying.'

'Gah!' McLeish cursed. 'I'm not going to meet my Maker in the uniform of my enemy.' He tore off his cavalry tunic and cast it angrily to the floor.

I could see the Dutchman was staring straight ahead, his eyes like pearls reflecting the moonlight filtering in through the barred window.

'Thank you,' I said.

He turned his head and frowned. 'For what?'

'For looking after me. For trying to save Mother.'

He forced a weak smile. 'I must admit I had not expected it to end this way. Still, I'm certain the Dutch prince shall succeed. England shall have a new king and the country's Parliament shall be safe, at least for now.'

The wagon drew to a stop. I got to my feet and craned my neck to peer out of the window. The castle's entrance lay before us. I slumped back down. 'Guess this is it.'

The Dutchman took a deep breath. 'Aye. Well, lady and gentlemen, the hour is upon us. Although we are unarmed and cannot possibly prevail, personally I'd rather die fighting alongside friends than stood beside the hangman. As our hands and feet have not been bound we can at least put up a decent fight.'

I looked to McLeish. He nodded.

'Agreed,' said Jacobsen.

'Aye,' murmured Trelawney.

'May God have mercy on us,' Miss Lucy muttered under her breath.

The wagon remained stationary for several minutes. Calls for the castle's heavy wooden gates to be opened fell on deaf ears, even when Thackery pounded the butt of a musket against the iron-braced timbers.

The Dutchman rose to his feet and peered through the barred window.

'What's going on?' asked Miss Lucy.

'I'm not sure,' he replied. 'For some reason the castle gates have remained closed.'

Our curiosity pricked, we all got up and tried to peek through the bars.

'If I'm not mistaken, I can't see any sentries posted outside,' Jacobsen observed. 'That's odd.'

'Maybe they fear an attack,' said Miss Lucy.

'Perhaps,' said McLeish. 'But that doesn't explain why they're not responding to Thackery's orders to be allowed in.'

A face appeared high up on the battlements. He called down to Thackery. An argument ensued.

Listening intently, the Dutchman frowned. 'As best I can make out it appears that while Thackery was entertaining his friends at the Shipwreck tavern this evening, troops from the garrison at Exeter arrived with orders to take over control of the castle and defend it against a possible attack by Prince William's men. Since they do not know the lieutenant personally, they can't be certain that all this isn't some sort of trap. They can't be sure Thackery and his men aren't Dutch soldiers in disguise.'

'So what happens now?' asked Miss Lucy.

The Dutchman raised a hand, gesturing her to be quiet. A second soldier appeared on the battlements and offered a solution. His voice was loud enough for all of us to hear.

'The wagon will not be allowed in. Those prisoners you speak of must be brought out where we can see them. You must also lay down your weapons. When you have done so, the castle's guards will be sent out to escort you inside.'

Lieutenant Thackery realised that he had no alternative but to comply. He turned to his men and gestured for them to place down their arms. 'You two,' he snapped. 'Open the wagon. The rest of you form a circle about it. We don't want the prisoners escaping.'

'I sense a moment of opportunity approaching,' muttered Jacobsen. 'There's a fair chance some of us might be able to grab a weapon or two.'

'Agreed,' replied the Dutchman.

The door to the wagon swung open. 'Out!'

We emerged and quickly assessed the opposition, a circle of men, all expecting we would cause them trouble. McLeish took a deep breath and cracked his knuckles. I clenched my fists while turning circles on the spot.

Cornelius reached out and managed to seize my arm. 'What should I do, Danny? How many of them are there?'

'Get ready to run, Cornelius,' I whispered. I'd spotted a weakness in their circle to my left, two elderly soldiers standing about a yard apart. If Cornelius ran like the wind he might just evade their outstretched arms. I knew he was quick on his feet as many a time we'd evaded arrest for all our filching on market day by running away from the scenes of our crimes.

I grabbed hold of him and turned him to face where I thought he might break through. 'Stand perfectly still. When I tell you to, run like hell. Try to get away. There is woodland straight ahead of you. About twenty strides away. Once you're among the trees the soldiers won't be able to make you out in the dark.'

'But I don't want to abandon you, Danny.'

I could see the others were readying themselves to strike. My heart was pounding in my chest and I was shaking. 'I know, Cornelius. But it is better that someone lives to tell our story to others in days to come. And, if you get away, ask Edmund to help you find my father. Give him a message from me.'

'What message?'

'Just that I am glad I finally had the chance to meet him. And that I tried to save Mother . . . that I tried my best.'

'Now!' yelled the Dutchman.

'G . . . g . goodbye, Danny.'

'Goodbye, Cornelius. Run! Run like the wind.'

My friend wasted no time in charging for the cover of the trees. The two elderly soldiers tried to grab him as he sped past but their attempt proved feeble, their attention drawn to the bulk of McLeish who was also thundering towards them.

Turning on my heel, I spotted Miss Lucy heading after Delaney. He'd broken rank and was making for where he'd dropped his trusted rapier. Retrieving it, he turned to face her. Miss Lucy seized another sword.

I ran. I'd spotted my pistols lying among a pile of weapons. If I could get to them, I intended to use them against Thackery. As I dodged and dipped I saw that several of Thackery's men were reclaiming their muskets. I had so little time. I saw Thackery out of the corner of my eye – he was hurrying back towards the castle's entrance, its heavy oak doors slowly opening.

A musket shot rang out, Trelawney let out a cry and fell.

Reaching the pile of weapons I threw myself to the ground and grabbed the handles of my pistols. Lying flat, I aimed one at Thackery, desperately trying to calm my breath to steady my aim. I had him in my sights. I squeezed the trigger.

A boot sank into my ribs and I felt a sharp pain. My pistol fired as it slipped from my grasp, my shot wayward of its target. I twisted round, looked up and saw the glint of a sword. Instinctively I rolled and scrambled hurriedly to my right, but the soldier was intent on running me through. Desperately I rolled and rolled until giddy. Lying on my back, I saw the figure bearing down on me, his blade arcing through the air. Pointing my second pistol at him I pulled the trigger. He let out a scream, fell forward and landed on top of me.

I felt crushed under his weight. Pushing and shoving, I tried to shift him off me but couldn't, no matter how hard I tried. The kick to my ribs had weakened me. And just yards to my left Miss Lucy and Delaney were embroiled in a ferocious battle. All I could do was watch.

'I shall have my pound of flesh,' Miss Lucy screamed breathlessly.

Spinning, lunging, and leaping back and forth, they each launched attacks so fast and furious their blades were a blur. The clash of steel against steel filled the night, the metal glinting in the moonlight. Miss Lucy suddenly sped forward at lightning speed, forcing Delaney to retreat a good ten paces.

I held my breath, expecting her to prevail, but Delaney was not out of tricks. He spun and dashed her rapier to one side, counter-attacking with a lunge that caught her arm and drew blood. He backed away and laughed. 'You may do well enough in light sparring, but in a real fight your inexperience shows itself all too clearly.'

'Aaargh!' Miss Lucy ran at him, her sword swishing with renewed speed and urgency.

I tried again to shift the body on top of me. Straining every sinew, I finally managed to shove it aside and I leaped to my feet.

'If Mr van der Stolten could see you now, my dear, he would be so disappointed at the feeble efforts of his star pupil. Have you had enough?'

Heaving for breath, Miss Lucy regained her composure and took up a new stance, sideways on. She raised a hand and beckoned Delaney forward. 'Don't you "my dear" me. We're not done yet.'

With no time to reload my pistols, I ran and grabbed a sword.

Delaney edged forwards. The second he was in range, Miss Lucy spun round and swung her blade in a wide, sweeping arc. Delaney blocked it. Miss Lucy altered her grip and twisted her blade free and then lunged at him. He managed to fend her off but she'd almost succeeded. The near miss changed Delaney's expression to one far more earnest. Taking to a two-handed grip he battered her with strokes, advancing as she retreated. And each stroke grew faster and more brutal.

'No!' I shouted, fearing he was about to succeed.

Miss Lucy stepped back out of range and also switched to a two-handed grip. Then she raced forward, forcing Delaney to leap back. Losing his footing, he staggered and tripped, falling heavily. This was Miss Lucy's chance. At least, I thought it was until Delaney grabbed a handful of dirt and flung it into her face. Momentarily blinded, she screamed. Delaney scrambled back to his feet. Now he had the upper hand.

With Miss Lucy disorientated and unsure where her enemy stood, all she could do was swing her blade wildly and hope for the best. Delaney raised his sword for the final blow.

I threw myself at him, bundling him to the ground. There we wrestled, rolling in the dirt until somehow we untangled ourselves and both managed to stand up, swords in hand.

His blade moved fast, fizzing as it sliced the night air. I dodged and dipped and stepped first one way then the other, fending off his blade as best I could.

'Ready for your final lesson?' he hissed.

'So sorry you won't live to give me another,' I spat back.

He laughed, lunged – and cut my arm.

Ignoring the stinging pain, I swung my blade as ferociously as I could, advancing one step at a time. He backed away, fending off my blows as if they were nothing more dangerous than a child waving a twig.

'Daniel! Back away, Daniel. Or he'll kill you.'

I was conscious of a commotion around me, and I could hear someone calling to me, but I didn't dare take my eyes off Delaney for one second, as I knew it would be my last.

'Daniel!' My name was being shouted with breathless urgency.

I tried to remember all Delaney had taught me, all those hours of practice. Ignoring everything around me, I steadied my stance, locked eyes with my opponent and advanced with the slashing strokes I'd perfected in the house on the Herengracht.

'Not bad,' he called out. 'For a beginner . . . Tell me, did I ever show you this move?'

He knocked my blade aside and lunged. I felt the tip of his rapier pierce my shoulder and I let out a cry of agony. He withdrew his sword. The energy drained from me in an instant. I slumped to my knees. My sword fell from my grasp. Kneeling, giddy and gasping for breath, I was defenceless. Delaney lifted his blade. This was it. I was going to die.

A shot rang out.

Delaney hesitated. His expression changed and I saw blood on his tunic. His rapier slipped out of his hand and he slumped to the ground.

'Daniel!' The loud voice was just behind me and I felt a hand grasp me. The Dutchman held me. 'Here, press this cloth against the wound. It's deep but you'll live. Mr Anstey will have some stitching to do once we get you back aboard the *Endeavour*.'

'Did you shoot him?' I asked.

'No. Gather your wits, Master Daniel, and look towards the castle.'

I turned and saw dozens of Dutch soldiers, their muskets poised. They had Thackery and his men surrounded. From among them I spotted Jules van Elber hurrying towards me. Smoke wafted from the barrel of his musket. He had fired the shot. He had saved my life.

'Jules? What are you doing here?'

'After our ambush this afternoon failed, I rode like the wind and sought out your father. Hearing the news that your mother was to hang at dawn, he convinced Prince William to allow him to make one last-ditch attempt at saving her. We were given sufficient troops to seize control of the castle. My commander quite enjoyed that little act just now, pretending to be soldiers from the garrison at Exeter. It certainly got the better of Thackery. Are you alright?'

I nodded. 'Think so. Thank you. I owe you my life.'

'You saved me from drowning. I think we're even now.'

Together he and the Dutchman helped me to my feet. I felt confused. 'But I thought your commander said you'd need cannon to take the castle.'

'True enough,' Jules replied. 'We managed to signal the Dutchman's ship. She's lying offshore and has all her port-side cannon aimed at the castle's defences. Her guns are larger and with greater range and power than many of those here. We gave the garrison a simple choice. Surrender or we'd blow them all to hell. When they saw the ship, they knew we'd prevail. We have them all safely locked up.'

'Daniel!'

I looked up and saw Father standing in the castle's entrance. He was carrying Mother in his arms. Was I dreaming? Was I delirious from my wounds? Were they real?

Mother's clothes were rags. She struck me as being older than I remembered, her face gaunt and her body feeble. But she was alive. I ran to them.

'I'm so sorry, Daniel. For everything,' she said. Then she saw the blood seeping through the cloth I held pressed against my shoulder. 'Dear God, you're hurt.'

'The Dutchman says I'll live. Needs a bit of stitching, that's all. You should have told me. I would have kept your secrets.'

'I know. But I didn't want to place you in danger.'

'Well, danger is exactly what came knocking at our door. Promise me, Mother. No more secrets.'

She nodded. 'No more secrets, Daniel.'

I let go of her and wiped the tears from my cheeks.

Father rested a hand on my shoulder. 'I think we have a lifetime's catching up to do, lad.'

'Aye, sir.'

'Danny? What's happening, Danny? Are you dead, Danny?'

Father frowned and peered into the darkness towards the woods. 'Who's that?'

'Come, there's someone I'd like you to meet. Cornelius Trotter's my best friend. He made it all the way to Amsterdam to warn me of Mother's fate. Without his help we'd never have been able to rescue her in time. We all owe him a great deal.'

Chapter Thirty-six

OVER the following weeks and months, and as Mother and I recovered from our ordeals, the revolution unfolded. Prince William advanced towards London. Staring at defeat, James II fled to France with his new-born son, and in time Prince William was crowned King of England. He finally had control over the English fleet.

Thackery was escorted to Exeter under armed guard where he would eventually stand trial for his various crimes. It wasn't quite the outcome Cornelius and I had dreamed of, as it would be left to others to decide his fate. Father and the Dutchman, however, insisted that Tobias would have approved.

The deeds to the Shipwreck tavern were returned to Elsbeth, but with Tobias dead she had firmly made up her mind to sell up and move to St Ives, closer to her niece.

Father and I talked day and night, filling in all the missing years and making plans for the future. My most burning questions finally got answers, including why my parents had become embroiled in the revolution.

For Father, his bargain struck with the Dutch prince was more than just a promise of freedom from Amsterdam's debtors' prison and regaining his fortune. Father was driven by the hope that one day he would see justice served on the plantation owners in the Caribbean, all those men who'd delivered death and destruction to Oyster Bay that night so long ago. The prince vowed to make it so.

It was the same demand the Dutchman had made to the prince. I learned that on their long and arduous journey back to Holland, together with Tobias, Father and the Dutchman had spoken of little else, swearing an oath that somehow they'd find a way. It was this same desire for justice that had led Mother to willingly risk everything – it had been nothing to do with religion, Parliament, or to help the Dutch prince defend Holland against France's King Louis.

The clerk in Amsterdam, Karl van Keup, hadn't known the full story regarding Oyster Bay. Saddled with debt, Father had sold his house on the Herengracht and the plantation to Mr Deveraux on the understanding that one day he could buy them back should his fortunes take a turn for the better. Mr Deveraux and Father had always remained on good terms and Mr Deveraux kept to his side of the bargain, so the house on the Herengracht was to become our home once more. Father, however, let Mr Deveraux keep Oyster Bay as it had cast such a shadow over his life – and Father vowed that he would never again purchase a sugar plantation, having made it clear to all who'd listen that he had lost any appetite for owning slaves.

It was because Father and the Dutchman had unfinished business in the Caribbean that two summers later I was once more riding high in the crow's-nest of the *Endeavour*, Cornelius and Peter at my side. It was warm with just a light southerly wind. After a lengthy voyage west I'd spotted land through my spyglass and was excitedly relaying what I'd seen to my friends.

'It's just as Father and the Dutchman described it. There's a sweeping bay of golden sand and palm trees almost down to the water's edge.' I looked down to the quarterdeck where Father stood between the Dutchman and Mr De Veer. 'Land ahoy!' I shouted.

Father cupped his hands about his mouth and called out, 'Oyster Bay, Daniel. That's Oyster Bay.'

'So, justice will finally be served,' said Cornelius.

'Aye, we're here at last.'

The *Endeavour* had not set sail for the Caribbean alone, but with two naval warships, each with a hundred soldiers aboard, their commander armed with arrest warrants signed by King William for those Father and the Dutchman recalled as having been responsible for the massacre at Oyster Bay. These men were to be transported back to England in chains and tried for their murderous acts.

As McLeish and I rowed us ashore, my father and the Dutchman clasped one another's hands tightly.

'We've waited a long time for this day, John,' said Father.

'Aye, Benjamin, we have so. Justice will be served. And I shall be content with that.'

I knew that was only partly true. As men were rounded up and the list of charges read out, I saw that bitterness remained deep within the Dutchman's eyes. The charges referred to the white men slain that summer night and to the damage caused to the plantation by fire; the only reference to the slaves who had been slaughtered was in the list of Father's 'property' lost during that night's bloodshed.

I understood the Dutchman. Revolution and the Dutch prince's victory had already resulted in many changes, but it had not heralded an end to slavery and bondage. I think the Dutchman knew the truth too – he'd not see such a change during his lifetime.

After much pleading with Father, he'd finally agreed to

let me stay on board the *Endeavour*, where I'd learn the ropes and receive instruction in navigation under the watchful eyes of the Dutchman, Jacobsen, and De Veer. One day I would become a master mariner too. I'd tried to give Father back his spyglass and sextant, but he could see my attachment to them and so entrusted them into my safe keeping. The *Endeavour* was to continue its work as a privateer with John Garret, alias the Dutchman, as captain, and we had orders from King William to seek out his enemies' ships and seize their cargoes.

I reckoned it all might turn out to be quite an adventure.

And I let Cornelius keep my whistle. I had no need of it anymore, as I had a pair of the finest pistols lodged in my belt. They would keep me safe.

Notes from the author

The Glorious Revolution

AT the time of Daniel Drake's adventure, Europe had already witnessed centuries of deep divide between the Protestant and Catholic churches, a divide that often led to war. In the decades leading up to England's Glorious Revolution, kings had come and gone, there'd been civil war and rebellion, and yet men still remained divided. Parliament too was fragile and often at odds with the monarchy to such an extent that its very existence was threatened.

The 'Seven' to whom Mary Drake addressed her letter in this story really existed. They became known as the 'Immortal Seven'. If you do a little research of your own you will discover who the 'Immortal Seven' were and why they did what they did. Fearful of King James II's alliance with the French king they 'invited' Prince William of the Dutch Republic (William of Orange) to invade England.

After a false start, during which the Dutch fleet was driven back to Holland by bad weather, the invasion eventually unfolded in the winter months of 1688, the prince landing at Brixham in Devon in early November – the fleet was driven westwards by strong easterlies that became known as the 'Protestant wind'. Stories abound that when the prince's landing craft ran aground a fisherman waded out and carried him onto dry land. Whatever the truth of those first few moments, it did turn out to be a largely bloodless start to the revolution.